# HEIR OF MAGIC

## THE KINGDOM WAR I

J. D. RUFFIN

Join me every step of the way at **www.jdruffin.com/ newsletter**. I'll never share your email and will send you updates, discounts, etc. for future books. You might even get free sneak peeks now and then!

# FROM THE AUTHOR . . .

There couldn't be any magic without the help of an army of amazing people.

**Tori**. How do I even describe the impact you've had on this book and my passion for writing? You have been accountability partner, coach, mentor, counselor, Sherpa, and therapist. This dream would have never come to life without your constant positivity and encouragement. I'm sorry I killed your favorites—pretty much every time. But you love me for it, right?

**Kaitlin Dunford**, editor extraordinaire. From day one, you were a partner more than an editor. You made this series better—and helped me become a stronger wordsmith.

**Nadia** and the amazing design and art team at **MIBLart.com** who reached into my brain and pulled out amazing art for covers and interiors. I will never understand how you make scribbles come to life, but you're brilliant.

**Kara**. Psychology/people/character-relater-in-chief. You helped me better understand motivations and impacts that ultimately helped our beloved characters feel more real. Thank you for *always* being there for my family.

Referring to these folks as Betas is a gross understatement (and makes them sound like those strange fish you see swimming alone and angry in the pet store). They helped edit, re-write, re-work, re-everything. They poked and prodded and made my unsufferable author ego deflate to normal human proportions. Thank you for your time, feedback, patience and support. **Ria**, **Kat**, **Jeremiah**, **Rachel**, **Sally**, and **Maria**.

Finally, **Christopher**, thank you for believing in this crazy journey and putting up with endless hours of brainstorming and reading. You told me to sit down and write—and yes, you were right. Thank you.

# 1

## A THOUSAND YEARS AGO
### IRINA

I rina's heart raced as she surveyed the battle from her mountainside perch. Her eyes were wild, and the flesh of her arms pimpled as power coursed through her veins. Magical fire raged from her silver staff, scorching men and earth alike, leaving blood and madness where stout enemies stood moments before.

The war seemed almost too easy, one crushing victory after another. She'd spent the last year hunting every Mage she could find and repaying them for her stolen youth. Of the original ten, she'd already killed six. The remaining four scurried and hid like rats somewhere across the border in Melucia. She'd never dreamed of ruling or power or war, not before they'd ripped her future from her grip. First, they stole her childhood dream of Healing, turning her magic from something good into a pool of angry, raging anger. Then, they destroyed her home, slaughtering her parents as she watched in horror, then burning everything to the ground with their unholy flames. They killed anyone she cared about, stole anything she valued.

Now it was her turn. It didn't matter how many innocents would die in the wake of her wrath. Innocence died when her mother fell. She would destroy each of them and take everything they held dear.

She threw her head back and laughed as she poured the last of her energy into the enemy line. Her magical endurance far outpaced anyone alive but still had its limits. She would need to eat, rest, and recover before casting again.

*Time to watch the men battle it out.*

As the enemy lines buckled, something in the distant sky flashed. She looked away and shielded her eyes. A brilliant … something … flew toward her.

She stepped to the edge of the cliff and raised her spyglass. Far to the east, a massive shimmering blue-white glow streaked across the sky, leaving a trail of light in its wake that twinkled and faded. Her breath caught as the form sharpened in her lens. Its outstretched wings dripped iridescent flames as it soared. She instinctively stepped back as it lifted its head and uttered a screeching, otherworldly cry that stilled the raging battle below. Men on both sides cowered and stared in disbelief.

"That's impossible!" Her hand trembled and the spyglass bounced off the ledge before shattering a thousand hands below.

Irina turned and sprinted toward the assembled Mages, her sycophantic band always waiting to please their mistress. "GET ME THE ORB—NOW!"

The men jolted, then scattered in all directions, desperate to avoid her wrath. A moment later, a man clad in all black and carefully cradling a maroon velvet sack approached. When she was within reach, he dropped to one knee and raised the pouch, arms outstretched, avoiding her eyes.

"The Orb, Your Majesty."

She snatched the sack out of his hands and removed a perfect sphere of deep scarlet that pulsed as though a heart thrummed inside. The man gained his feet and retreated a step, eyes wide.

"Listen to me," she snapped. "I have to cast the Spell of Return. When the Orb draws my essence, its magic will send you far from here. The spell will also create a monolith with golden text revealing the path for my return."

She looked back at the fast-approaching Phoenix, then turned and clutched the man's arm. "I command you to bring me back!"

"Your Majesty?" The man's voice quavered, his brow knitted in confusion.

"The Phoenix has risen, you fool. Even fully recovered, my power could not stand against her!" She locked him in place with her iron grip. "Now, open yourself. My strength is spent, and yours will have to do."

Irina closed her eyes and screamed toward the sky in the language of Mages. With every phrase, the pulsing glow of the Orb grew until its brilliance forced those around her to look away.

The man peered past Irina as the Phoenix belched fire in streams the size of city blocks, destroying thousands of soldiers in seconds. The mighty bird snapped its head, looked directly at Irina, then launched itself toward the ledge.

She spoke the final words of her incantation seconds before the Phoenix slammed into the mountainside. The beast's feathery body flared a brilliant crimson and dissolved into liquid smoke that poured itself into the Orb. The terrified man vanished as the Phoenix dove headlong into the ledge, obliterating everything in its path. Blue-white flames billowed in every direction, filling the sky with rippling waves of energy. The world trembled, and the sound of earth rending could be heard across the continent. Mountains rose, replacing the battlefield below and forming a range—a barrier between aggressor and foe.

Far to the west, at the edge of the Kingdom's capital, a glassy black stone rose from the cold earth. The man in black pulled his coat tight against the chill and gawked as lettering flared into existence. Brilliant blue faded to gold, searing deep into the ebony surface. Line after line appeared, giving him purpose and direction, a path to restore what was lost. In that moment of chaos and fear and loss, he raised the pulsing Orb above his head and pledged his life to her cause. To her Return.

# PRESENT DAY

Tiana

Tiana looked around her little infirmary and smiled. The military-style building was basically a log cabin that had been outfitted for medical use. But it was *her* log cabin.

The walls of the building mirrored those throughout Melucia's municipal quarter, bare and displaying little more than shaved logs. There was a sitting room in the front for patients to wait their turn, and two exam rooms in the middle that kept Tiana busy as she rotated patients through as quickly as their injuries would allow. She broke protocol by hanging her father's tapestry in the little foyer to comfort and distract patients while they waited for care. In the back, she stored bandages, herbs, and a wide variety of potions and creams to treat patients who didn't need a magical cure. If Healing magic didn't make her so tired, she would prefer to use hers on every patient who walked through the door. She supposed every Healer had to learn when not to use their Gift at some point.

The days in her youth, working with her father, were often long and exhausting. Today she felt like she had worked three of those days in one. She scrubbed her hands, but her healer's smock, her "Blues," were streaked with a combination of dirt and blood that would take more effort to clean. She sucked in a deep breath, sitting for the first time in hours, and rested her head against the wall, visualizing the steam wafting off the hot bath to come.

Her eyes had almost closed when a familiar shout from the front door shook her from her daydream. "Miss T, don't pack up yet. One more for ya."

She sighed, straightened her smock, and stood to see who had hurt themselves now. Healing was her calling, and she loved it more than life itself, but some days just wouldn't end when they were supposed to.

She entered the little foyer and was greeted by two men in uniform, one holding the other upright. She couldn't help but chuckle when she saw her patient. At twenty-two, Constable Ridley Doa stood nearly nineteen hands tall and had the beginnings of broad shoulders. After nearly three years of Guard training, Ridley's once boyish features now held the beginnings of a hardened edge.

Ridley normally carried himself with the athletic grace of a sportsman, but today his left leg looked as though it would barely support any weight, and he needed help just to get through the infirmary entrance. He was supported by a large muscled man who wore a Lieutenant's chevron on one shoulder and the golden collar of the Gifted around the nape of his uniform. A small sack dangled off one side, its strap stretch tightly across his broad chest and shoulder. The man was enormous, standing over twenty hands tall. His piercing blue eyes offset a scruff-covered square jawline.

She grinned as they entered. "What have you dragged in today, Keelan? Our 'Constable in the Making' fall out of his bunk again?"

She gave Ridley a playful mock salute.

"T, our young Guardsman actually hurt himself today sparring against a cadet twice his size and ten times his talent. I guess the Guard uniform makes some folks think they're invincible, even if it doesn't really fit yet," Keelan returned Tiana's grin.

"Third visit this week, Ridley? One might think you just want me to see your legs again," Tiana took his other shoulder and helped Keelan walk him back to her exam room. Ridley blushed furiously but didn't say a word. Sparring with Tiana was a losing battle, and he'd already lost enough dignity for one day. When they reached the exam table, Keelan set his sack on the floor and helped her settle the injured Guardsman into place.

"Let's see what we've got today." Tiana cut away the lower leg of his uniform trouser and began gently prodding below his knee. Ridley finally found his courage and his deep brown eyes sparkled with mischief, "Easy there, Miss T. Touch me like that again and I might question your motives."

She took her thumb and applied a bit of pressure. "Hey now," Ridley said, wincing.

"Just making sure the Lieutenant knows you're actually hurt and not just paying me a visit," Tiana said as innocently as she could.

Keelan had to turn his back to hide his laugh.

She couldn't help herself. Like most Guardsmen, Ridley was a little full of himself, but he had a good heart and made her smile. It didn't hurt that her stomach fluttered a bit when he looked directly at her with those wintery eyes. So much for the Healer's professionalism her father lectured her about all the time.

As the familiar warm glow started in her palm, Keelan and Ridley stared with wide eyes. They both carried a Gift, but to see a Healer in action inspired awe unlike most other magic. Tiana closed her eyes, focused, and willed the Light to brighten, causing Ridley's leg to glow softly. He failed to hide his gritted teeth as the magic mended muscle, tissue, and bone.

Moments later, Tiana's eyes opened, and the glow faded. "That should do it, Ridley. Please try to pick on someone your own size next time."

"Spirits, you're amazing."

"Oh, I'm well aware," she smirked.

He stood carefully, putting a little weight on his leg. Without warning, he shot forward and wrapped Tiana in a tight hug, planting a kiss on her cheek. A wave of heat rushed through her body before she gathered her wits and gently pushed him back. She tried to think of something pithy to say, but her head was spinning and Ridley spun toward the door. He grinned back over his shoulder, eyes glittering with mischief, "Next time I'll try to get hit a little higher up the leg. You really have quite the touch!"

He disappeared through the door, leaving Tiana speechless and Keelan laughing through tears.

An awkward silence settled over the room as Keelan's laughter abated and he stood gazing at the exam table while Tiana eyed him. "Need something else, Lieutenant Rea?" she asked.

He ran a hand over his rusty hair and looked down at his boots. He finally summoned his courage and picked up the sack and set it on the exam table. "Well, Miss T— Tiana." Keelan never called her by her name. The corner of her mouth quirked into a curious grin.

"I thought maybe, um, you might like a glass of wine at the end of a long day." He set a bottle, two glasses, and a bowl on the table, then looked up at her with sheepish eyes. He'd wanted to ask Tiana out for dinner for weeks but only worked up the courage when Ridley's injury happened earlier in the day. The wine was actually the young Guardsman's idea. *I'll either thank him or demote him for this tomorrow.*

"Lieutenant, are you asking me on a date? In my infirmary?" Her grin turned wolfish, eyes glittering.

"Well, uh, when you put it like that—"

She laughed. Not a girlish giggle, a full-throated, from-the-gut bellow. One hand went to her stomach while the other braced her against the table. Keelan chuckled nervously, unsure how to take the outburst. A little boy inside cringed.

"I wondered how long it would take you to ask. I mean, this isn't exactly the romantic setting I had pictured in my mind, but it is very Keelan-esque." She smiled warmly.

The goofy grin that split his face made her laugh again. When he fumbled the bottle, nearly dropping it onto the hard floor, she stepped to his side. "Please, let a professional," she said with a wink.

She pulled the cloth off the bowl, and her smile turned from teasing to pleasant surprise.

"Hope you like strawberries," Keelan said.

"They're one of my favorites. Thank you, Keelan." She took one and rolled her eyes with the first bite. Keelan took a long sip of wine and blew out a deep breath.

They spent the next half hour talking of little things. The Guard. Keelan's rise to fame as the country's most successful investigator. She grilled him on cases she'd read about in the papers, asking detailed question about how he connected the dots. He couldn't believe she was actually interested in what he did. In him.

He never liked talking about himself much and turned the conversation. "Enough about me. I want to know about you. Are you from Saltstone? Did you grow up here? What's it like dealing with sick people all day?"

She laughed at his litany and refilled her glass, giving him time to reach the end. "So, yes. Yes. And some days I wonder why I chose this path." Her eyes drifted a moment. "But I love being a Healer. It's all I ever wanted, and I can't imagine doing anything else with my life."

"Even with patients like Ridley?"

"Especially with patients like him. After all, without

Ridley's unfortunate fall, we wouldn't be having this elegant exam room soirée." She waved around the room with her wine glass, clearly enjoying teasing him about the setting for their first date.

He smiled. "Promise I'll do better next time."

She reached across the table and placed her hand on his, meeting his eyes. "You did great this time." The blush ran down his face into his neck, disappearing at his collar. She grinned again.

"When did you start Healing? I mean—you're young to be a full Healer, aren't you?"

She nodded. "It all started with my father. He was a pretty famous healer."

"I've seen the statue of him over at the Triad's building. You're *that* Healer's daughter?" his eyes widened.

"That's my dad. He was amazing. When I was a little girl, I idolized him, followed him everywhere. I even made my own Healer's smock from one of his old ones, knitting it together with ratty brown yarn. I wouldn't let him take it off me, even to sleep. I miss him …"

Keelan watched as she searched her memories, a swath of emotions crossing her face.

"When I was seven or eight, I had this scruffy dog, Ollie. He'd terrorize our horses, chasing them all over. I think they actually liked it, even when they'd kick and bray. One afternoon, I heard Ollie wailing out back. He'd gotten his paw caught in the joints of the picket fence. He pulled and tugged, but the fence wouldn't budge. By the time I squatted by his side, the paw was full of splinters, bleeding and raw. He looked up at me and nearly broke my heart.

"It felt like forever, but I managed to free his paw. The howling ceased, but then he started to whimper, and his breathing turned shallow and quick. I knew he'd hurt more than just a paw."

"What did you do? Was your dad able to help?" Keelan asked.

"No, I don't think he was home at the time." She took a sip and shook her head. "I had to help him myself, so I spread him out on the ground, forcing him onto his back so I could inspect the rest of his body. I didn't really know what I was doing, but I had to do something. The unexpected glow that flared from my hand startled me so badly that I nearly fell over backwards. I'd had only seen my father use the Light, but now it was flowing out of me. Without thinking, I placed my hand over his leg and watched as the glow brightened and the pup's leg mended.

"Ollie's bloody leg was my first Healing."

Keelan raised his glass. "To the finest paw-Healer in the land."

She giggled and clinked her glass against his, finished the last of her wine, then set the glass down. "Alright, Lieutenant, I need to clean this place up and get home. Tomorrow comes way too early."

Keelan smiled and packed up the empty bottle, bowl, and glasses. She followed him to the door. When he turned to say good night, she reached up and placed a hand on his chest.

"Thank you for a wonderful time. I really do look forward to our next … date." Her eyes grinned.

He didn't know what to do as he stared down into her

deep brown eyes. *Should I kiss her? I really want to kiss her. No, that's too forward. Wait, she might think I don't like her if I don't. But I really like her. Why is this so confusing?*

Her woman's intuition heard the whole debate. She stood on her tiptoes and gave him a peck on the cheek. "Good night, Lieutenant." Then she shooed him out the door with both hands. She leaned back against the closed door and smiled, thinking of strawberries and wine—and clear blue eyes.

---

KEELAN LAUGHED TO HIMSELF AS THE DOOR CLOSED BEHIND him. Tiana could snap him out of the worst of moods with her quick wit and irresistible smile. He struggled to wipe the boyish grin from his face as he walked back to the Guard compound.

---

TIANA HUMMED TO HERSELF. SHE *NEVER* HUMMED. EITHER of those men could make her blush, but together they were too distracting to get any work done. Ridley was lucky she didn't accidentally grow him an extra finger the way he flustered her. The mental image made her laugh out loud. And then Keelan pulled wine and strawberries out of nowhere. How did he know she loved strawberries?

She locked the door and began her nightly ritual of returning her medical practice to order after a day of heavy patient traffic. She wiped down the exam rooms, then put away the small bottles of herbs and balm she had used throughout the day, careful to align them perfectly with their neatly printed labels facing outward. Her father's habit. A wistful smile curled her lips.

She fastened her small overstuffed Healers' bag. Carrying the light-blue satchel was another habit her father instilled at an early age. She'd lost count how many times they would happen into someone needing medical aid. It didn't matter whether they were running errands, shopping in the market, or simply out for a walk, they always seemed to run into someone sick or hurt. She had to be ready for anything.

As she hummed softly, Keelan's face popped back into her mind. A goofy, girlish grin bloomed and sparked life into the sterile room. *"C'mon, T, knock it off,"* she chided herself with a chuckle.

The sound of the front door rattling snapped her out of the daydream.

A Healer never turned away those in need, but her back ached, and her stomach was dancing for dinner. A very stomp-heavy dance. Sometimes, you just have to draw a line.

"I'm sorry. I've closed for the night. Unless it's an emergency, please come back in the morning," she called through the door.

The rattling stopped.

She waited a few moments, hoping the would-be patient would take the hint. After a couple minutes of silence, she walked back to the storage room to grab one last bottle for her bag. A loud thud startled her, and the vial in her hand fell, shattering across the floor.

"Who's there?" Her voice trembled.

Slow, heavy boots slapping against the hard wooden floor were the only reply. They came closer … and closer.

Tiana dared a peek around the corner. She had to remind herself to breathe.

A tall man in a long brown robe stood in the center of the exam room, his head swiveling as he inspected the space. When he turned toward her, cold eyes stared back through tiny holes in a nightmarish mask depicting the snarling face of a bobcat with tusks that curved forward and upward from the lower jowls. Tusks? She stopped her rational brain from wasting time on the odd combination. There was a sinister yet dead look in the eyes that bored through her.

When Bobcat locked eyes with his prey, a raspy voice hissed, "Come, Mistress. It is time to take your rightful place."

Mistress? *Spirits, is this man touched?* Her mind instinctively raced through treatments she might apply to a mentally ill patient, professional compulsion overriding a far healthier fight or flight response.

Until the man's hand reached out and grabbed her shoulder.

Tiana yanked her shoulder away, grabbed the nearest bottle from the shelf, and hurled it at her attacker. The bottle shattered and a hazy, noxious cloud billowed. The man sneezed.

She darted past, ramming him with her shoulder as hard

as she could. He stumbled backward a step, then fell into the exam table, stumbling to the floor. The front door flew open without protest, its lock dangling uselessly from the wooden doorframe.

Two more masked figures stood ten strides from the now open front door. She didn't get a good look at their masks, but thought one resembled some hideous bird. They were blocking her path to the Guard Compound, so she darted around the infirmary, the same route she would normally take to go home. The figures lurched forward in pursuit.

She passed the little pond where resident ducks called to her for their nightly feeding. Her pursuers gained ground as her feet hit the rusty surface of Brick Road.

A tug at the Healer's Bag dangling off her shoulder made her turn. She screamed as one of the figures pulled, nearly forcing her to a dead stop. The attacker fell backwards when the bag came free, scattering its precious contents across the road. The second man danced over the bottles and wraps, joining his partner on the hard ground.

Thank the Spirits, the moon was hidden behind a thick haze, shrouding the night in cool, near-complete darkness. Tiana crept into one of the inlets that allowed one carriage to pass another along the narrow lane, ducking behind the thick hedgerow. Her heart continued its sprint long after her legs had stopped theirs. She fought to calm her breathing, to remain still and quiet. A chorus of crickets and the occasional chirp of a night-friendly bird obscured her labored huffs.

Then she heard the boots again. Men running toward her.

Getting closer.

She closed her eyes, afraid her gaze might draw the eerie eye of the bird or his twisted companion.

And then … they ran past.

She sucked in a deep breath and held it, listening intently to the receding patter of footfalls. What a beautiful sound.

She waited ten minutes to make sure the blessed silence continued before poking her head above the shrubbery and surveying the darkness around her. Nothing stirred. After a short internal debate, she decided to head back north toward the safety of the Guard Compound. The men were headed toward her home, and she couldn't think of anything safter than the police headquarters—and Keelan.

Something snapped sharply and she jumped. Her head wheeled around, but there was nothing behind her. She stood in the middle of the road for a few seconds hoping to see some animal tromping through the hedges. Nothing stirred.

*Breathe, T.*

She turned back to resume her route and ran headlong into Bobcat. His strong hands gripped her shoulders. She kicked his shins, earning a loud grunt and doubling him to the ground. She tried to sprint away, but a loose brick gripped her toe, sprawling her onto the cold potter's road. A sharp elbow pressed into her back while a dripping cloth was slapped over her mouth and nose. She squirmed and tried to kick or punch, but Bobcat's weight won. Somewhere in the back of her mind, a tiny voice asked, "When did the world start spinning?"

The sound of more boots smacking brick drained the fight from her rebellious consciousness. The last thing she remembered before blacking out was moist rag across her face and the pungent, strangely sweet smell of the infirmary after a good cleaning.

# 3

## KEELAN

I n the nine years since he joined the Guard, now
twenty-six years old, Keelan had risen from lowly
Cadet-Recruit to one of four Lieutenants who ran the entire
field operation for the Capital's police force. The childhood
years he spent studying and sparring with his Guard family
in the Mages' Guild had prepared him for his new service
beyond anyone's wildest expectations, and Keelan's
responsibilities now included oversight of the training for
each year's class of new Cadet-Recruits.

His only superior—aside from the Triad that ruled
Melucia—was Captain-Commander Dev Albius of the
Guard, a stern, incomprehensibly muscular man who
somehow even towered over Keelan's twenty-hand height.
Albius had been a Guardsman for nearly thirty years and
was the longest serving Captain-Commander in Saltstone's
thousand-year history, running his force with a strength,
efficiency, and expectation of unquestionable honor that

marked him as a great man of the Melucian Empire, not just Saltstone.

Keelan remembered trying to swallow the lump in his throat as the weight of his new responsibility sank in under the scrutiny of more than a thousand eyes. When Albius personally placed the Lieutenant's chevron on his shoulder in front of the fully assembled Guard corps in the massive yard of the compound, he told Keelan he now had a unique opportunity to help shape the future of the peacekeeping force in his city. To help shape Saltstone itself.

Since that day, he carried himself with self-assurance, but there was always that little voice in his head, the one that started whispering to him when he was a child and second guessed his decisions at every turn. He tried desperately to silence that voice—hating it, yet somehow knowing he needed it. He grew stronger because it said he was weak, and he studied harder because it told him he was stupid. Someone on the outside might say that his internal companion was his best ally, driving him to be a better version of himself. To Keelan, it was a quiet reminder of how he would never be good enough.

He didn't bother hunting for food when he walked back into his house, just tossed his boots by the door and stripped down to his small clothes. The bed was calling and wouldn't take no for an answer.

After more than twenty minutes, his eyes fluttered open. He was exhausted but unable to quiet the voices in his head. For some reason, Atikus's wispy beard and fatherly smile captured his mind's eye. It had been too long since he'd seen the old Mage. He grinned as he thought about the many times he'd had to rescue the man from his precocious little brother. Before he knew it, Declan, his younger brother, streaked through his waking dream. Wild, unkempt hair waved like medusa's snakes as men in blue robes surrendered their chase, doubling over with hands on knees and labored breaths, failing to wrangle the toddler.

Keelan staggered into the kitchen and sat at the round wooden table and allowed his eyes to wander aimlessly around the room. They settled on a tiny roughly carved wooden owl staring back at him from a shelf on the opposite wall. It was the last thing Declan had given him before he'd left the safety of the Mages' Guild to join the Guard. He'd forgotten it was even there. Something in the little creature sparked long-forgotten memories.

---

18 Years Ago

EIGHT-YEAR-OLD KEELAN AND HIS TWO-YEAR-OLD brother stood in front of an elderly snow-topped Mage whose hands were clasped firmly behind his back. A little over eighteen hands tall, he towered over the two boys. The deep creases around the Mage's eyes and throughout his forehead, and his scholarly nobility and warmth, calmed the nervous boys. His deep-blue robes stretched all the way to the floor and were lined with two rows of glittering gold trim.

They stood in the Mage's private study on floors of deep polished wood inlaid with intricate designs of lighter shades. Keelan thought these beautiful images looked like symbols or letters he had seen on the cuffs of some Mages throughout the Guild. He had no idea what they meant but knew they had to be important. Mages didn't do anything without a purpose or secret meaning. Dusty, leather-bound tomes filled most of the shelves that towered from floor to ceiling, each made of the same dark wood of the floors, leaving little room for the occasional vial or bottle filled with brightly colored liquids that churned and swirled when Keelan looked closely. At one end of the room, there were five oversized chairs covered in rich patterns of maroon and gold cloth, resting on ornate legs carved with inter-woven vines and leaves. Any one of the chairs could have easily held both boys comfortably. On the other end of the room, completely at odds with the grandeur all around, sat a rickety-looking wooden chair covered in puffy, faded yellow cushions. The chair was partially hidden behind a simple table the Mage used as a desk. Keelan couldn't wrap his mind around why he would keep such simple furniture when the rest of his study was so elegant, but something about this simplicity made him like the man a little more.

After a few silent moments, Mage Atikus Dani cleared his throat and looked down at them with fatherly affection. His eyes creased and his voice tremored slightly when he spoke. "Boys, they're gone. I'm so sorry, but there was nothing we could do."

Tears welled in Keelan's eyes. He balled his hands into fists, wrestling the storm of emotions as understanding gripped his mind. His parents were dead, but that wasn't why he cried. He couldn't remember the last time he had seen them and, as he closed his eyes, couldn't even summon the image of his mother in his mind. No, he didn't cry for the loss of unknown parents, but deep in his heart he knew what the Mage's pronouncement really meant.

He and Declan were alone.

Keelan grabbed his little brother and held him as he shook through the tears. Declan was too young to understand what was going on but was swept away in the emotions of the grownups and began sobbing in unison with his brother. The Mage watched with misty eyes of his own.

Some time passed before Keelan gathered himself, dried his tears, and looked up at the Mage to learn what would come next.

Then something strange happened.

The small space between Keelan's shoulder blades just below his neck tingled and grew slightly warm. As he focused on the sensation, the tingling grew stronger. It wasn't painful, but it refused to be ignored. He looked up at Atikus, startled. As he opened his mouth to ask one of the million questions racing through his mind, the look of excitement on the Mage's face froze him in place.

"Keelan, what are you feeling right now?" Atikus asked, his tone turning from sympathetic to serious, even urgent.

"Mage Atikus, I don't know. It's … well … it's like my back is warm and itchy. I promise I didn't do anything. It just started on its own. Can you make it stop?" Keelan grabbed onto little Declan again, holding him tight.

Declan started squirming to pull away but, feeling the tension now consuming his big brother's body, relented and wrapped both arms around Keelan's waist, burying his face in the older boy's side.

Atikus's brow furrowed.

With some effort, he knelt to eye-level with Keelan, placed his weathered hand on the boy's shoulder, and stared directly into his eyes. In a measured, calm voice he said, "Keelan, listen to me. Don't be scared. You're not in trouble. I need you to tell me everything about what you're feeling—from the moment it started. The details are important, so please leave nothing out."

Keelan took a deep breath and looked down at Atikus's shoes as he mumbled, "It started when you told us our parents are gone."

His voice caught in his throat, and he squeezed his eyes shut to stop the tears from returning.

Atikus whispered, "It's ok, Keelan. Take a deep breath."

"It was like somebody put a warm cloth inside my body, and it kept getting warmer until I finally paid attention to it. Then the bees came."

"Bees?" The Mage's face scrunched, and Declan giggled.

Keelan ignored his brother. "Yessir. It felt like bees were crawling on my skin where it was warm. The feeling tickled at first but got stronger until … it was like they all stung me. It didn't hurt, just felt tingly."

"What were you thinking when the feelings started? Be as specific as you can," Atikus instructed.

"That you were wrong about our parents. No—that you were *lying*. It just popped into my head; I don't know why. I didn't mean to think that, but I can't shake the feeling that it's real. Why would you lie, sir?"

The old Mage slowly stood, joints expressing their dissatisfaction with his little adventure near the floor. He looked down at the boys from one to the other. His lips tightened as he searched for the right words.

He settled back on Keelan. "Son, I have never lied to you, and I never will. It breaks my heart to tell you about your parents, but they really are gone, and there is nothing the Mages or anyone can do to bring them back. I truly wish it were not so."

Atikus drew in a deep breath. He ran his hand through his fluffy beard, then placed it back on Keelan's shoulder.

"As for your bees, I think I understand what is happening there. You have a Gift, Keelan, and it has awakened. I know the news about your parents is terrible and sad, but *this* is exciting, wonderful news. It's time to change your collar to gold, young man."

Keelan let go of Declan, shrugging off the Mage's hand, and shuffled over to one of the big chairs. His heart wouldn't stop racing, and his mind ran even faster. He tried, but couldn't focus, so he turned to the last thing Atikus said.

"Me?" he asked with a timid, soft voice. "Why would a Gift want me?"

Atikus eased into the chair next to him, took Declan in

his lap, and leaned forward. "Keelan, a Gift doesn't choose us. We're either born with it, or we're not. Magic runs through family lines, meaning there's a better chance for you to have a Gift if your parents had one. Both of your parents were Gifted with extraordinarily powerful magic."

"But what does it mean? I still don't understand."

Atikus stood, set Declan back in the chair, and walked to a bookshelf. He skimmed a few titles, then selected a worn book with a faded brown leather cover embossed with silver script. He leafed through several pages before finding what he was looking for, turning it so Keelan could see the sketch on the page.

"Look at this, Keelan. What do you see?" He pointed to a hand-drawn image.

Keelan stared for a minute at the strange symbol. "It's the same weird bird I see on all the Mage buildings around the city. It looks like it's on fire."

"That's right. This is the Phoenix. It is the symbol used to represent magic throughout the entire world. Each part of this drawing represents something important about magic," Atikus explained. "Do you see at the bottom there are four flames under the Phoenix?"

Keelan looked closely and nodded.

"In the Academy, we teach that magical abilities present themselves in one of four areas: Mental, Physical, Elemental or Natural. The four flames represent these focus areas. Out of them rises the newly reborn Phoenix. What do you think the bird represents?"

"Well ..." Keelan ran a finger over the page. "A mage?"

"That's a good thought, and you're close. The Phoenix

represents magic itself. The symbology shows that with each new person born with one of the four pillars—or focus areas—*magic itself* is reborn anew. Keelan, by adding you and your new magical ability to the world, you help magic to be reborn into something new. Isn't that wonderful?" Atikus beamed.

He was so passionate about the story of magic's rebirth that Keelan thought he saw a small tear trying to escape one eye.

*Weird old man and his weird burning bird.*

"But I still don't understand. Does this mean I can talk to animals or something?"

Atikus chuckled. "Hmm … maybe. Probably not, though. Within the four pillars are many unique abilities. How can I explain this?" He looked toward the ceiling to order his thoughts. "Most people who have a Gift can do one specific thing that can be categorized using the four pillars. For example, a person with an ability that falls into the Natural area might be able to make plants grow faster or bigger, or they might be able to talk to animals. But not all three, just one of those. The Gift we receive is specific to one action—and only one action. I would say about eight in ten people in Melucia have a Gift. That's why you see so many people with gold collars or cuffs around the city."

"I just thought people wanted to look fancy. It never made much sense, and those collars look stiff and itchy."

Atikus barked a laugh that caught Declan off guard, making him giggle and squirm. "I can see why you'd say that. They can be itchy sometimes. But what they represent is an ability to do something special—something magical—

and that is cherished and respected throughout our Empire. In fact, we require all people who manifest a Gift to register with their city's Gift Registry and begin wearing the gold. It's not just a tradition, it's the Law."

Atikus walked to one of the side tables to pour a glass of water out of a heavy crystal pitcher. He took a long drink, set the glass down, and began pacing.

"Let's use the example I know best—my gift—which falls into the Mental area. I am Gifted with a powerful memory and can recall anything I see, hear, or read, even the smallest detail others might not notice. It isn't a flashy Gift that makes people's eyes pop, but it is powerful in its own way. It helps me be a better teacher and has led me to be the chief historian for the Guild."

Keelan pointed to the cuff on Atikus's sleeve, "Why do you have two lines of gold?"

Atikus grinned at Keelan's curiosity and attention to detail. "Sometimes, a small number of people are born with two abilities. Two Gifts. This only happens five or ten times in a generation—and may not even happen at all for some generations. I am one of those few for my time. It's why you see the two lines of gold on my collar rather than the single stripe or solid collar. When you meet him, you'll see that Arch Mage Quin also wears the double band. To my knowledge, we are the only two people in all Melucia with two abilities. Sadly, no one in the generations after us has displayed more than one.

"Now, there is one even rarer case—a person born with three Gifts. In the past two thousand years, there has only been one person like this. His name was Utu, and he lived on a small island off the eastern shore. There is a village there now that still bears his name."

"What about Empress Irina? I remember stories about her from when I was little. She could do anything with magic."

Atikus's laugh rumbled and Declan struggled to breathe between fits of tiny giggles. Irritated at the interruption of a good story, Keelan shot his brother a stern glance that froze the giggle fit. Atikus cocked a brow at the exchange.

"Those are just tales, Keelan. Empress Irina ruled The Spires, our western neighbor now called The Kingdom of Spires, over a thousand years ago during the Kingdom War. There's no doubt that she was a powerful Mage, and the histories even tell us she wore a golden robe, not one just trimmed in gold. Some think she did that to fool a supersti-tious people into believing she was all-powerful, a goddess even, but I've seen no evidence that she had more than two, *possibly* three abilities, like the island shaman Utu many years earlier."

Atikus realized Declan had escaped his chair and was straining on tippy toes to reach a bottle filled with swirling blue liquid. He hopped up to intercept the toddler before he could do any damage. "I think that's enough of a lesson for one day. Your mind is probably spinning while your heart is still heavy. Let's at least take the worry of 'what next?' off your plate. Our Mages will need to study your magic to understand what you're now capable of, but manifesting your Gift means you'll be admitted into the Guild and can live within the complex, likely even attend the Academy. I'm sure the Mages will also accept little

Declan into our home so you two can stay together. Would you like that?"

Keelan's head was reeling. He looked at Declan for a long minute before responding tentatively without making eye contact with Atikus.

"I guess so," he mumbled.

Atikus mussed Declan's dandelion-puff hair. "Excellent. I'll talk with the Guildmaster tonight."

Keelan stared into one of the stately old bookshelves, not really seeing anything. His heart was heavy, and his mind swirled at everything he'd learned. How could one person feel so many things? He wanted to *do* something, make things better for himself and Declan. But nothing made sense anymore. Their whole lives were changing so fast. He did the only thing he could think of in the moment; he buried his emotions deep down where they couldn't confuse or hurt him anymore. He thought that imaginary trunk might already be full, but today's passions vanished into it easily. He signed, relief washing over him at the pressure that lifted from his shoulders.

When he looked back at Atikus, the glimmer in the old Mage's eyes and broad smile parting his bushy beard gave Keelan a tiny spark of hope.

———

BEFORE THE BOYS KNEW WHAT WAS HAPPENING, SEVERAL members of the staff were ushering them to their new rooms and outfitting them with sets of blue robes. Keelan was a little intimidated when he saw the gold trim across the collar and sleeves of his. The matronly old staffer cupped his cheek and smiled warmly as she handed him the revered garment.

Declan looked up at his older brother sitting on the edge his bed, head in his hands. "Kee?"

Keelan peeked between his hands to find giant green saucers staring at him from a few inches away. A tiny slobbery hand went from his brother's mouth to grip his own, pulling it down from his face. The weight of the day couldn't stop Keelan's smile as he used his other hand to muss Declan's mass of untamed hair.

"It's you and me, Dec. And we're gonna be alright." Keelan's whisper trembled. "We're gonna live with the Mages from now on. You've gotta be good here, ok? It might be a little scary at first, but we'll figure it out and I'll protect you. I promise."

Arms and legs flailed as Declan climbed his way into Keelan's lap and sank his head deep into the comfort of his neck. "Big bubba."

Keelan chuckled and held him tight. "Yeah. I'm your big bubba."

———

LATER THAT EVENING, THEY HEARD A BELL TOLL THREE times, and the hallway outside their door came alive with activity. Keelan bolted upright at a sharp knock on their door.

"Boys, those three bells mean it's mealtime." The door crept open and Atikus walked in. "You don't want to miss dinner. Well, I know I don't! You'll get to meet some of the other students tonight."

Declan—fearless little Declan—hopped off his bed and raced to hug Atikus's leg. "Din din!"

The old Mage barked a laugh and tossed the little man into the air. "Yes, din din. We *love* din din here."

Keelan hadn't moved from his bed, so Atikus set Declan down and walked to sit by him.

"Son, it's going to be ok. You'll see."

"You said the new classes are all twelve years old. I'm just eight." He looked down at his feet as they dangled off the bed. "What if they don't want me hanging around?"

Atikus placed his arm around Keelan and drew him in. "For your first few years, you're going to have a very special teacher, one assigned just to you. Her job is to make sure you're ready to enter the Academy when you turn twelve. We'll find you some friends your age, so you don't feel alone here. But if you ever do feel alone, you come find me, ok?"

Keelan's eyes watered as he looked up.

"But right now, it's time for din din!" He stood and tossed Declan in the air again, earning a wild squeal and giggle for his effort.

"Again, Atti, again!"

Keelan stood and straightened his new robe, tracing a finger across the glittering golden line on his collar, then followed Atikus as they headed to the dining hall. The massive room opened to reveal tables crowded with students chatting and eating. Each class sat together at rectangular tables, with

the oldest seated near a raised stage at the far end of the hall.
Mages held court from a long table on the stage, enjoying their
meal together while keeping watchful eyes on their charges.

The table nearest the entrance held ten first-year
students, and all eyes snapped to the door to assess the
newcomer. Within seconds, children were huddled in twos
and threes, whispering, laughing, and peering back over
their shoulders at Keelan. He tried to hide behind Atikus's
bulk but quickly realized the old Mage was walking them
down the center aisle. There was nowhere to hide. With
each subsequent table, ten new pairs of eyes found their
way to him. Keelan wanted to turn and run, but Declan's
little voice kept him walking.

"Bubba! Look bubba!" He pointed around the room at
the tables filled with children.

He heard a snicker behind him.

He kept walking.

Atikus carried Declan onto the stage and took his seat
near the center of the long table. Keelan froze and had to be
prompted to climb and sit next to him, facing the seventy-
member jury that now stared in judgement. He had always
been large for his age, but that night he had never felt so
small.

Later, as Keelan stared into the darkness of his room,
images of the older boys and girls flashed through his
mind. He saw their laughter, their contempt. He didn't want
to cry, but the tears came anyway. Atikus might think this
was home, but he knew he didn't belong. At least not
among *them*. They were the smartest kids in the whole

country, and who was he? Some orphan. Some kid Atikus *felt sorry* for?

Then he scolded himself and guilt took over. He'd made a promise—a promise to protect his little brother. He couldn't do that if he was scared all the time. He couldn't do that if they were all enemies. He had to find a way to make them see that he *deserved* to be here.

———

THE NEXT MORNING, ATIKUS WOKE THE BOYS BEFORE THE sun had fully risen. Two women trailed behind as he entered their room. One lit their way with a ball of pearlescent flame that hovered above her palm. She wore the blue and gold of a Guild Mage. The other wore a simple brown uniform.

Atikus walked across the room and hefted Declan out of his bed. The child was still groggy and buried his head in Atikus's beard to hide from the light. Keelan sat up and stared openmouthed when he saw the ball of magical fire. The woman in blue smiled.

"Declan. Look up for me. I want you to meet someone." Atikus carried the boy to the woman in the brown uniform. "This is Zeedra. She lives and works here at the Guild. She's going to take care of you today while Keelan begins his studies. Is that ok?"

Declan peeked out from the bushy beard. A short pudgy woman sporting long dusty-gray hair that she wound into a tight bun stood before him. Her wide smile made her eyes twinkle. Zeedra had been a member of the Guild staff for over twenty years and couldn't have children of her own. When the call was raised for someone to help with a two-year-old, she jumped at the chance.

"Call me Mama Zee, little one. We're going to have *so* much fun today!" She held out her arms.

Declan giggled at her deep, booming laugh that rumbled from the depths of her large gurgly tummy. They bonded immediately. He leapt out of Atikus's arms into Mama Zee's, giggling louder as she bounced him and trotted out of the room, leaving Keelan to learn his fate by himself.

"Keelan, this is Mage Autumn. As you can see, her Gift involves magical fire, but her true calling has always been teaching. She was a schoolteacher before she came to study with the Mages, and I've asked her to be your tutor until you're old enough to enroll in the Academy."

Keelan nearly fell off his bed as Autumn sent a thin jet of flame across the room and lit the fat candle on the night-stand. She closed her palm, extinguishing the ball of fire, then squatted in front of Keelan's bed, locking eyes with the awed boy.

"Now, Master Keelan, let's talk about your studies without the distraction of that crazy fire." Her voice was kind but carried a tone that commanded attention.

"That was *so* cool!" Keelan grinned at her.

Atikus rose and walked to the door. "That's my cue. Mage Autumn will take good care of you, son. I'll check on you later, alright?"

"Mage Atikus?" Keelan's quiet voice caused the Mage

to pause and look back over his shoulder. "Umm … thank you, sir."

Atikus's smile lit the room brighter than Autumn's flame had. "Keelan, you're going to be just fine. You'll see."

---

DECLAN SPENT HIS YOUTH BEING PASSED BETWEEN MAMA Zee and a dozen Mages who delighted in the little boy's stories and antics. He was never alone and was, more times than not, the center of everyone's attention.

Magic was everything within the Guild Hall. Those not possessing a Gift were considered unremarkable, rarely noticed by the Gifted in the Mages' sanctuary, but Declan was an exception. There was no resisting the adorable, precocious little terror. He was a force of nature that transformed the Guild's halls from a quiet, stately place of study into a whirlwind of activity and laughter. Within, there were Mages proficient in all four of the primary lines of magic, but none could predict where the little towheaded toddler with the wild dandelion-puff hair and that bright, bubbly giggle might turn up next—or what he might've gotten into. Atikus often joked that little Declan had founded a new fifth line of magic—*High Mischief.*

Throughout it all, Keelan never wavered in his promise to protect his little brother. They were often seen tromping about the Guild complex together, laughing and chasing some imaginary villain.

———

Four Years Later

KEELAN AND NINE OTHER TWELVE-YEAR-OLDS STOOD IN A line in front of the Mage's table on the stage in the dining hall. Every member of the Mages' Guild stood behind them while all the Academy's students stared up at them from their tables. The Mage-Rector droned on about the importance of magic in society, and the children on stage were starting to squirm. All except for Keelan. He already stood a head taller than anyone in his new class, but it was his unshakable, stern demeanor that truly set him apart.

"… and magic is born anew with the addition of these fine young students. In the great traditions of the Mages' Guild and our illustrious Academy, I welcome and name each of you Mage-Apprentice."

The Rector took a breath but was cut off by thunderous applause that began behind him from his fellow Mages, who were obviously ready to move on with their day. The students in the hall took the hint and added their boisterous calls, ending any hope the Rector had of continuing his well-prepared speech. Mages and students scattered as a bell tolled, leaving the ten new students on stage with the befuddled Rector.

The students were then led to their first class. Mage Tinsley, a tall, oddly thin man, strolled into the classroom and had the children rearrange the desks into a wide circle facing each other.

"Now," Tinsley began, his lilting voice making a few of the children giggle. "Look around the room. This is your family for the next six years. The Mages are here to teach, but the classmates sitting around you are your brothers and sisters. We expect you to take care of your family. Do you understand?"

Ten heads bobbed.

"Good. Let's get to know each other." He turned to the student on his right. "Tell us your name, where you're from, and what you know about your Gift."

And so it began.

The first student's Gift was Water Control. The next Animal Communication. Then Fire, Telepathy, and Heightened Sight. Each student beamed at revealing his or her Gift. When the girl beside Keelan answered with the incredibly rare Gift of Healing, the room broke into uncontrolled chatter. Tinsley used his Telepathy, booming in each child's mind to *"Be quiet!"* to restore order.

Then it was Keelan's turn. He sat to Tinsley's left and was the last in the circle.

"I'm Keelan Rea. I guess I'm from here … and … well … Mage Atikus says I have a Gift … but we haven't been able to figure out what it is yet."

The children began glaring and whispering. Across the room, Keelan heard one boy whisper a little too loudly, "Mages felt sorry for him. Bet he's Mute!"

Other children giggled and bandied the word "Mute" around like some ball to be played with.

Keelan lowered his head. He wished he was anywhere else, that he'd never set foot in the stupid Guild Hall.

Later that night, when Declan came to visit, Keelan painted on a broad smile and described his first day of class in the Academy. He told his wide-eyed brother about his tall teacher in the robe that didn't quite cover his ankles, and how he'd actually *talked in the students' minds*! He described in detail all the incredible abilities of his class-mates, especially the meek Healer-to-be who'd sat beside him in class that day. Declan shared tales of his adventures with Autumn, Keelan's former teacher turned Declan's new tutor, and the boys laughed at how lucky they were to be in such a special place.

Six-year-old Declan would never learn of the looks and sneers, or the sleepless nights as tears fell quietly down his big brother's cheeks. He would grow up carefree, living the simple joys of the moment, believing the marble halls of the Guild to be the most magical place in the world.

---

FOR KEELAN, WHAT STARTED AS HOURS IN THE CLASSROOM grew into even longer days when, in his early teen years, they added strenuous exercise and martial lessons to his daily routine. He often resented what he thought was unfair extra work but learned to appreciate it in later years as his endurance strengthened and his body hardened well beyond his peers.

Sergeant Colton Sted, leader of the Guard unit assigned to protect the Mages' compound, took a personal interest in

Keelan when he was fourteen and would often stay with him long past dusk, practicing swordplay or some other martial art. Keelan excelled in anything athletic and quickly mastered every challenge Sted threw at him.

But lessons from the men of the Guard extended far beyond martial abilities. The "men in blue" spoke often of the honor and duty that compelled them in service to their city and its people. Doing the right thing, simply because it was the right thing, became an almost daily lesson. Through these long arduous days together, Sted and his demanding Guardsmen became more than just Keelan's trainers; they became older brothers and mentors, his ideals of everything honorable and good. He idolized those men and worked even harder to make them proud.

Keelan was fifteen when his own sense of honor faced its first test.

The older students, especially the boys, resented how he excelled in his training and grew stronger, taller, and faster than everyone else. His Gift hadn't reappeared since he'd first arrived years earlier, and it was a near-universal belief that Keelan was lying every day he wore the gold. Why hadn't the Mages taken the golden collar away from him? Why was he allowed to work out with the Guardsmen when he didn't even deserve to be in the Guild? Why was the Mute still there?

A small group decided that it was time to let him know his place in the Academy's pecking order.

Practice that day was intense and long, lasting past the dinner bells. Each of the students was filthy, tired, and hungry. The pack of sweaty boys staggered into the changing room to wipe down and switch from practice gear to robes before they missed getting something hot to eat. Leftovers were not very popular.

Each student was assigned a small footlocker in which they stored their clothes and gear while in class or on the practice fields. Keelan sat and opened his trunk. When he grabbed his robes and shoes, something metallic fell to the ground with a loud clinking sound, causing all the students in the room to turn.

One of the older boys was standing over his shoulder in an instant. He called out, "Hey! That's *my father's* medallion. What are you doing with that?"

The ornate pendant attached to a silver chain surprised Keelan. He had never seen the piece before, and the accusation in the boy's voice caught him off guard. Honor was expected—no, demanded—of every student. Any breach of a student's honor would be grounds for expulsion from the Academy and banishment from the Guild.

Keelan reached down to pick up the necklace, but the boy snatched it up before he could reach it, banging Keelan with his shoulder, knocking him to the floor as he returned to his pack of friends on the other side of the room.

"You're done, Rea. I'm getting the Sergeant right now," he sneered, leaving a stunned Keelan staring at the door.

Barely a minute later, Sergeant Sted entered the room accompanied by the boy-accuser and another Guardsman. The look of disappointment on Sted's face made Keelan's heart sink.

"Keelan, why was this necklace in your locker?"

"Sir, I don't know. I just opened my locker, and it fell

out of my robes," Keelan's voice was quiet, almost pleading.

A friend of the older boy who was accusing Keelan stepped forward and pointed at Keelan. "Liar. I saw you walking around earlier today, fiddling with that pendant. You're a thief!"

The Guardsmen marched the boys to the Rector's office, a procession of chattering students following in their wake. Keelan missed a step when he saw Atikus waiting. The old Mage's face gave away nothing of his thoughts, and Keelan harbored a small hope that his adopted father might believe him.

Sergeant Sted had each of the older boys recount their stories for the Mage-Rector and Atikus before holding the necklace out for one of the Mages to inspect.

"Keelan, what do you have to say? Can you explain why this was in your locker?" asked the Mage-Rector as he watched Atikus turning the medallion over in his weathered palm.

Before he could answer, Keelan's back began to crawl, and that warm sensation he hadn't felt in years flared between his shoulder blades, a sensation so strong and sudden that he wobbled a little on his feet. His already fragile emotional state in that moment kept him from mounting any defense against whatever his returning bees might have to say. Atikus snapped out of his thoughtful daze and swiveled toward Keelan faster than the boy had ever seen him move.

Then Keelan's eyes locked with his accusers', and he intuitively knew two things. First, the boys were lying. He already knew this, but now his magic was screaming inside his body that it was so. The second thing Keelan realized in that moment solved a long-obscured riddle—the power of his Gift.

"They're both lying," Keelan straightened to his full height, head high and shoulders back. He spoke calmly in a voice filled with confidence and command.

His sudden change in posture and tone caught everyone, even his accusers, by surprise.

His next statement, punctuated by its formality, turned the tables. "Mage Atikus Dani, test my Gift. My talent is to sense falsehood or untruth. *By the Magic of the Phoenix*, these two are lying."

Years later, Keelan still wondered how those words popped into his head. He had never heard them before, but learned the Arch Mage used them in proclamations and formal commands. Kings and Queens answered any call that began with those words. On that day, the Rector of the Mages' Guild Academy answered their call from the mouth of a fifteen-year-old boy.

---

As THE IMAGES OF KEELAN'S DAYDREAM FADED TO DISTANT memory, the swirl of emotions he felt on that first day with Atikus welled inside his chest. Sadness at the loss of his parents. Fear for his brother and their future. Wonder at the revelation of his new Gift. And the nagging, uneasy sense that the gentle old Mage who became a second father had never told him the whole truth.

## 4

### KEELAN

At the end of the fourth day following their visit to Tiana's infirmary, Ridley trotted up to Keelan on his walk home, "Lieutenant, have a minute?"

Keelan turned and crossed his arms. "Ridley, please tell me you're not hurt again."

Ridley's eyes glittered as he laughed. "You wish. I saw how you looked at Miss T. Doesn't take a world-class investigator to know what's going on there … uh … sir."

"Yeah, yeah. What was it you needed, Guardsman?" Keelan steered the conversation away from the blush streaking down his neck.

"Well, sir, it's actually about Miss T." Keelan's attention sharpened. "I went by the infirmary a couple days ago for a quick follow up, and to thank her for helping with my leg, but the place was empty. Tried again yesterday and this morning, and it didn't look like anybody had been there. I don't think Miss T's ever taken a day off, much less three in a row."

Keelan thought a moment. "You're right. She's always there. Did you talk to folks in the area? Has anyone seen her this week?"

"Yes, sir. I checked with every house and business in the area, and no one's seen her at all," Ridley said. "I walked around the infirmary and found a couple of packages in the post bin but couldn't tell how long they'd been there."

"Tiana makes rounds in the countryside every four or five weeks, and that's probably where she is, but I'll sleep better if we take a look. Why don't you get us a couple of horses and meet me at the south gate? I need to run up to my house for a minute. I'll meet you in ten."

"You got it, Lieutenant. Two horses coming right up." Ridley offered a quick salute, then turned and jogged toward the stables.

Thirty minutes later, the two constables made the short ride to Tiana's infirmary. As they reached the building, both men dismounted and tied their horses to the small railing on the side. Keelan walked to the front door and tried the handle. It didn't budge.

"Come, look at this." Keelan bent to inspect the bottom of the door.

"Looks like bits of wood chipped off," Ridley said.

Keelan inspected the edge of the door, then stood and did the same around the sides and top. Nothing looked out of order. He turned around with his back to the door to get a view of the walkway that led up to the building. There were no marks or broken bits. No scuffs. Nothing.

He lost himself in thought and leaned back against the

door. Nothing was out of place, but something didn't feel right. He'd learned to trust his gut in his years with the Guard—and it was churning. Without warning, the door swung inward, and Keelan had to catch himself against the frame to keep from falling. He motioned for Ridley to stay quiet and follow him in, drawing the short sword he carried at his side.

Dim moonlight streaming through the open door provided the only light in the dark foyer. Keelan paused and listened, then crept into one of the exam rooms, at the same time motioning Ridley to check out the other one. After a quick search, Keelan called out, "The place is empty. Light some lamps and let's look around."

Nothing appeared out of place, so Keelan walked back to the front door that still stood open to the night air. As he held a lamp close and examined the inside edge, he noticed small chip marks around the door lock's latch. The latch itself appeared newly scratched and dented, and Keelan saw similar scratch marks on the strike plate attached to the inside of the doorframe.

"Ridley, go back to the compound and let the duty watch know that there's been a break in. Have them send a couple of men to Tiana's house to make sure she's ok. And Ridley—tell them I said to keep this low key."

"On my way, sir. Do you need anything here?"

"No. I'll check out the rest of the building and head back up to the complex. Until we hear what the men find at Tiana's house, there's not much more we can do here."

Keelan walked through one of the exam rooms into the storage closet in the back. Earlier in the week, when Keelan had seen this room last, the walls were covered with cabinets and shelves that contained bottles, boxes, and jars of varying sizes and shapes. Everything was meticulously organized, with neatly printed labels on each jar and bottle, labels facing outward. Keelan had wondered then at how Tiana kept everything in such perfect order.

Now the room was in complete disarray. A couple of the shelves were nearly empty with most of their contents scattered across the floor. There was a strange, noxious odor coming from several of the now-broken jars and bottles whose contents had mixed. Keelan took a quick look around the room and stepped back. Before he could head for the front door, something caught his eye. Stuck under the foot of the exam table facing the storage room was a small piece of woven brown cloth. The thumb-sized scrap was silky smooth and had a sheen that made Keelan think it was torn from some expensive cloak or dress. He wouldn't have given it much thought, but it was unlike cloth produced and worn in the region. He stuffed it in his pocket, gave the other exam room one last inspection, and then headed back to the Guard complex.

Keelan rode straight to the headquarters building where Ridley was waiting. Two others stood with him, the Captain-Commander and another Guardsman who also wore a golden Lieutenant's chevron.

Before Keelan could say anything, a man in long deep-blue robes with a double line of gold around his collar and cuff stepped from behind the giant Commander. In the center of the Mage's robe was a golden version of the Phoenix. Keelan immediately recognized Arch Mage

Velius Quin, one of the Triad that ruled Melucia and the leader of Mages throughout the world.

Quin stood a little over seventeen hands tall with a slim but sturdy build. His sandy-blond hair was cut short to a military length, except for a sprout on top meant to cover his crown—unsuccessfully. His eyes were a deep shade of blue that swirled with otherworldly flecks of glittering gold. While his stare was unsettling, what Keelan found most remarkable about the man was that he looked to be only a few years older than himself, even though he had been Melucia's Arch Mage for decades before Keelan was born.

The Captain-Commander spoke before Keelan reached the top step. "Lieutenant Rea, Ridley told us what you found at the infirmary. Arch Mage Quin and I need to brief you on some additional information he received over the past couple of hours. Let's go inside where we can have a little more privacy."

Keelan cocked a brow at Ridley. He thought the need for privacy was odd, considering that they were standing in the heart of the Guard complex, but he followed without a word.

The group walked through the empty headquarters building, passing several administrative areas before approaching the door to the Captain-Commander's private office. Keelan had only been here a few times, and it gave him a nervous thrill. The man was a legend.

They walked through the outer office where the Captain-Commander's clerks controlled access to those seeking his time. There were two modest wooden desks, and a few simple chairs lined the walls. The most remarkable thing about the room was its thirty-six-hand ceiling, much taller than any other in the headquarters building, giving the suite an air of importance and command. The immense wooden door that stood between the two clerks' desks rose nearly to the ceiling and contained an intricate carved replica of the Shield of Melucia.

The duty clerk nodded and grinned at Keelan's poorly disguised awe as they entered. In direct contrast to the grandeur of the giant carved door, the Captain-Commander's office was simple, bordering on bare. One wall looked out onto the training grounds through a glass window that spanned the length of the entire wall. Glass wasn't uncommon, but windows this large were a luxury enjoyed only by royalty. Keelan smiled to himself as he surveyed the simple furniture, thinking that his plain-spoken Commander wouldn't have those windows if he hadn't inherited them from a predecessor who enjoyed finer things.

Aside from the window, the only piece of furniture that truly displayed the power of the Commander's office was a large ornate desk and chair that sat at the opposite end of the room. The desk had been used by Captain-Commanders for generations. Legend claimed that a distant Arch Mage had crafted the desk using powerful magic to commemorate the only Captain-Commander who had also belonged to the Mage's Guild. It was an enormous twenty-four-hand-long piece of wooden art carved from a single tree, a single piece of wood. The same intricate Crest of Melucia they saw on the office's door covered the front of the desk but with one significant difference—the Phoenix symbol was inlaid with gold, making it practically fly off the wood. On the desk's top, under a cover of clear glass, was a remarkable carved map of the Melucian Empire, complete with mountains, streams, and lakes. The entire piece radiated power.

Quin held a distant smile as he ran his fingers across the desk's wooden edge. Keelan swore he saw *pride* in the man's expression.

"Gentlemen, please take a seat." Albius motioned to the chairs around a conference table in the corner.

"Lieutenant Rea, let's start with you. Guardsman Doa reported the break in at the infirmary. Did you find anything in your inspection?"

"Sir, as I'm sure Ridley reported, we found scratch marks and dents on the lock and surrounding areas on the front door of the building. Small wooden chips were scattered at the base of the door. This was clearly a forced entry. The storage room where Tiana … sorry, sir … the Healer kept her potions, salves, and other equipment had been ransacked. There were broken bottles and jars everywhere, giving off an almost unbearable smell. I couldn't tell if anything had been taken, but it did not appear so. Nothing in the other rooms had been disturbed, including a very expensive tapestry that hung on the wall of the foyer. There was likely a struggle, rather than a theft."

Keelan took a drink of water before reaching into his pocket and continuing his report. "I found this scrap of cloth stuck to the corner of one of the exam tables. Its unusual quality made me take a closer look. I don't recall seeing anyone wearing material like this before." He handed the cloth to Albius who looked at it, then passed it around the room.

"There was nothing unusual in the perimeter, on the grounds?" Albius asked.

"No, sir. Ridley and I both inspected them and found nothing out of order. There were two packages that had been delivered and were still in the post box behind the building, but nothing appeared tampered with."

The room breathed as silence fell over the group.

"Sir, while I conducted my search, Ridley returned with instructions for two Guardsmen to visit the Healer's home. Do you know if they've returned?"

Before Albius could answer, the large door opened, and his clerk ushered in a Guardsman who looked a bit out of breath.

"Captain-Commander, your additional guest," the clerk said.

"Thank you, Del. Please close the door behind you," Albius said before turning to the new arrival. "Guardsman, report."

The slight tremor in the man's voice and the bead of sweat forming on his forehead gave away his anxiety at facing both the Captain-Commander and Arch Mage. Keelan sympathized.

"Sir, the Healer's home was empty," he said without further explanation.

"And?"

"It was ... just *empty*, sir. The door was standing open, and there was no furniture, no clothing, nothing on the walls except mounted lamps. The place had been cleaned out. It was too dark to do a more thorough search of the grounds, but the interior was bare."

The group asked a few questions of the Guardsman before Albius dismissed him.

Before resuming the briefing, Albius turned to Quin. "Arch Mage, a little more privacy?"

"Certainly." Quin removed a small box from the pocket in his robe. He opened the box and gurgled strange words before looking up toward Albius, nodding once.

"Thank you," Albius said, turning to the rest of the group around the table. "Gentlemen, two things from this point forward. First, the Arch Mage has just extended a magical barrier around this office so we can speak without being overheard. Hold nothing back. Second, what's said in this room stays here, understand?" He punctuated the last word with a stern glare, and everyone nodded.

"Arch Mage?"

Quin leaned forward and paced his elbows on the table. "The Mages of the various cities often share information that may be useful or have impact across the Empire. Earlier this week, I received word from our Guildmaster in Freeport that a young woman was reported missing in that city. While tragic, this wouldn't usually raise the alarm of the magicians across cities, but this girl is a member of our local Guild and the daughter of a prominent Merchant family. The family provided a few personal items from the girl's dressing chamber—her hairbrush, a silver ring she often wore, and a small journal containing poetry that she had written by hand. With more than one item, and the personal nature of each of these, the Mages should have been able to locate her even if she was traveling the ocean on the other side of the world. But their scrying failed. That is when they reached out to me."

He cleared his throat and continued. "It is a closely guarded secret that the Saltstone Mages' compound is built at the base of the Silver Mountains for a very specific reason. There is a vein of natural magic that bubbles like a well deep beneath its stones. This well of untamed magic gives our compound's buildings more strength and our Mages far greater power when they act within our walls. The tower in the back of the compound serves as a focal point for that magical well, greater than any other location in the known world.

"I enlisted the aid of our Mage with the greatest scrying ability and led him to the top of the tower. He worked through most of yesterday and into last night with no success, not even a hint of the missing woman's where-abouts. In all my years, I have never seen him fail."

Quin paused and looked around the room, finding Keelan's eyes before continuing, "We had no reason to believe the disappearance of Saltstone's Healer was related to the missing woman in the South, but something tugged at my mind. We attempted to scry for the Healer a few moments ago, but for the second time in two days, we failed to sense *anything*, much less discover her location."

The room was quiet as the possibilities sank in.

The Captain-Commander broke the silence. "Lieutenant Rea, I know you only took command of the Academy a few months ago, but this situation has implications far beyond our city. You are our best investigator and I'm putting you in charge of these cases, effective immediately. Lieutenant Del, you will take over temporary leadership of the Academy until Rea is finished with these cases."

"Yes, sir," both Lieutenants said in unison.

Albius then turned to Keelan. "Rea, there is no higher priority for the Guard than solving these cases and recovering the women alive and well. We've already lost a week on both disappearances."

Keelan nodded and began to speak, but the Arch Mage interrupted, "Keelan, as a member of the Mages' Guild, you already have access to our complex, our Mages, and many of our resources. Due to the sensitivity of this situation, and what we believe may be broader implications, you will also have my personal assistance if you need it. The full power of the Empire's Mages' Guild is at your disposal."

Keelan was taken aback by Quin's offer. "Thank you, sirs. Commander, I would like to assemble a small team, including Ridley and a few other Constables."

"Fine. Just keep me posted. Good night, everyone." Albius stood, dismissing the group. "Rea, Arch Mage, please stay a minute."

When the heavy door clapped shut, Albius looked at the Arch Mage, who nodded. Then he turned to Keelan. "Rea, this stays here. Not a word to your team or anyone else, understand?"

"Yes, sir."

Commander Albius walked to the large glass window, looked out at the night-shrouded practice yard, and lost himself in thought. After several minutes, he spoke into the glass in a low voice that Keelan strained to hear, "Keelan, report your findings only to the Arch Mage or me. The offices of the Triad, the Army command, even the Guard, have been compromised. We've only found one spy so far, but we believe that there are others—many others. Trust no one. Do you understand?"

Keelan's head spun. "Sir, what would spies have to do with a kidnapping? What am I missing?"

Albius turned to face him. "We don't know that the two situations are connected, only that more than one fact seems to cross paths with the other, and I stopped believing in coincidence a long time ago, especially where magic is concerned. I can't read you into the specifics, so you're going to have to trust me. Keep this thing quiet. Any information you learn stays between the three of us. Got it?"

"Yes, sir. Understood,"

Keelan thought a moment, then turned to the Arch Mage. "Who can I speak with in Freeport? I need to gather information regarding the missing woman and everything surrounding her disappearance. Also, has any of this gone public? If so, we should think through a cover for why investigators from the capital are being called into a local matter. Our presence will stir the rumor mill."

Quin turned to Keelan. "The second question is easier than the first. Yes, the disappearance in Freeport hit the local papers, and there is talk of little else. Serious crimes, especially kidnappings, are rare. Our greatest advantage is that reporters in Freeport don't know Saltstone may also have a kidnapping. Furthermore, the woman from Freeport is prominent in her community, the sole heir to a significant family holding, and her father commands political influence throughout Melucia. It would not be unusual for him to call in a favor to get someone from Saltstone to help find his daughter.

"As to your investigation, we have already assembled some notes, including names of interested parties and reports from the local constables who began their own investigations." Quin said, as he handed Keelan a folder.

"Now, Lieutenant, go figure out your teams and how you want to divide up the searches. There's a lot of land between Saltstone and Freeport, and you will need men you can trust to lead the various efforts. The Arch Mage and I will meet you at the Mages' Guild tomorrow at noon to review," Albius said with a formal tone of dismissal.

Keelan took his leave and walked out of the headquarters building. His mind raced at the enormity of what he had just learned and the task before him. He had never seen the Captain-Commander so ashen as when he gave the order to keep information between the Arch Mage and himself. He shuddered remembering the sound of his voice. Albius hadn't said that the members of the Triad *themselves* had been compromised—only their offices—but he also didn't rule it out. Keelan understood the sensitivity of a high-profile investigation, especially when a noble's daughter was a victim, but the whole spy thing made his head hurt. Why would a spy care about a few missing women? Who even wanted to spy on a country like Melucia? The Empire barely had a standing army and had never been a threat to its smaller neighbors to the east, who were more like sprawling city-states than nations. Sure, Melucia was a rich trading nation, perhaps the wealthiest in the world, but who spies on merchants?

Keelan shook his head. "Kee, you're doing it again. The Mages always said, 'If you focus all your energy on the problem, you'll never find the solution.' Knock this off and focus on the girls."

He started thinking through who he wanted on his team and the various assignments involved; then something struck him, and he stopped walking and stared at the cloudy night sky above. This wasn't some case involving strangers. In the excitement and strangeness of the last few hours, he had nearly forgotten how it all started, with *Tiana* disappearing. The same Tiana he had just spent an evening with. The same Tiana he couldn't stop thinking about.

Keelan's old childhood companion, that nagging little voice, started chattering again, asking more painful questions and threatening to overwhelm him. What happened to her? Why would someone take such an amazing woman who only wanted to help other people? Is she hurt? Is she still alive? If she is, how long does she have?

*How long do I have before …?*

## 5

### JESS

"Crown Princess Jessia Vester, Heir to the Throne of the Kingdom of Spires, and Second of her Name," the royal doorman announced in a booming voice. Massive bronze doors flew open, and Jess ran into the throne room at a full sprint. She streaked past the assembled members of the Privy Council, skidding to a stop at the foot of her father's throne.

"Father, you *can't* let her do this to me! You just can't!" she screamed through tears, completely oblivious to her mother's presence on the dais beside her father's throne.

Before either the King or Queen could respond, Jess threw a crumpled wad of parchment into her father's lap and ran out the side door that led to the royal residences. The assembled Council gawked in silence while King Alfred and Queen Isabel looked at each other with exasperated eyes.

"I swear that girl will be the end of me," Isabel whispered, anger seeping through every word.

Alfred couldn't hold back a chuckle, though he knew there would be a price to pay later. His wife and daughter had been at each other's throats for the better part of three years, and no one was brave enough to negotiate a peace, least of all Alfred. He adored them both, but he'd been head of state long enough to know when to back away from an unwinnable conflict.

"My dear, she'll grow out of this. I seem to recall another sixteen-year-old girl with a fiery temper some years ago … uh … a *few* years ago," he corrected quickly, before earning another icy glare.

Everyone in the room snapped to their feet as the Queen rose, mindful to avoid her eyes. "I need some air. The betrothal will be complete by the end of this week, no matter what our precious little Princess thinks."

She offered a sloppy curtsy to the King and stormed out.

The assembled Ministers exchanged glances. Some offered the King a sympathetic grin at the scene they witnessed several times each week. The royal family put on a unified public face, but the rift between Queen and Crown Princess was one of the worst-kept secrets in the Kingdom. Alfred did his best to referee larger squabbles but had resigned himself to more of a "duck and cover" approach with smaller tiffs.

Alfred turned to the Council with a heavy sigh. "Please forgive the interruption. Where were we?"

"The letter from the Triad, Your Majesty," High Chancellor Danai Thorn cleared his throat as the members sat.

"Right." The King fumbled through a stack of papers

on the table beside his throne before lifting the letter in question. He broke the deep-blue wax seal bearing the crest of the Melucian Empire, a shield containing a quill, sword, and Phoenix, representing the three chief Guilds of their neighbor to the east. The leader of each of the Merchants', Mages', and Armsmen's Guilds formed the nation's ruling body known as the Triad. Alfred scanned the letter and handed it to Thorn.

"It appears the Melucians would like to put a horse in our little race. They propose we marry Jess to their Master of Arms, Titus Vre."

"Vre? Isn't he nearly fifty now? Are they thinking we'll marry her off to an old man just to secure better trade deals?" asked Stephan Bril, Minister of War who had served the King for more than twenty years and was one of his closest friends and most trusted advisors.

The King's brows creased as he chuckled. "He's younger than you, Stephan."

"Perhaps … but I'm *much* younger than my King, Your Most Aged Majesty!" Bril said with mock offense.

"Your Majesty, forgive me for interrupting your vital engagement, but I think we should take this offer seriously. Melucia is our largest trading partner by a factor of a hundred. Securing a stronger alliance could only boost the flow between our nations." Destin Carver leaned forward. Carver was a fairly new member of Council, appointed by the King to serve as Minister of Trade.

Thorn nodded at Carver's statement. "Your Majesty, I agree with Minister Carver about taking this seriously. Our Gifted ranks are extremely thin. Less than twenty percent of our population now wear the gold, and we believe fewer will in this next generation. Without increased trade and movement between our countries, our Gift may die out when your grandchildren reign."

Danai Thorn served as High Chancellor and leader of the Kingdom's Hall of Mages, similar to the Arch Mage in Melucia. His long black robe looked like a military jacket above the waist but flared into a robe below. Highly polished golden buttons formed three rows, running from his shoulders to his belt, and the high collar was adorned with two rows of rich, silky gold. Thorn was a powerful Mage with hundreds of years of experience, but looked only thirty. While his public role focused on magic and its users, the Council knew that he also served the King and Queen as their master of spies, administering the most widely respected network of informants throughout the known world.

Thorn continued, "I don't need to remind this Council of the precarious balance of power between our two countries. We're significantly stronger in arms, but the sheer proliferation of the Gift among their population is a clear threat to our security. That doesn't even take into account the everyday useful things like enhanced farming and fishing, healing, and a hundred other abilities we used to take for granted that are now rare in our land. We need Melucia's *bloodline* as much as we need their trade if we are to secure our people's future."

The King regarded him as everyone else seemed transfixed by the shine on the table in front of them. The grand chamber fell silent.

After a few minutes, the King rose. "Thank you, everyone. You've given me a lot to think about. It's been a long day, and I have a family dispute waiting behind those doors. Let's resume tomorrow."

The assembled counselors gathered their notes, bowed respectfully to the King, and filed out, leaving Alfred lost in thought before his throne. He barely noticed them leave. The Triad's letter was staring back at him, daring him to decide. It pained him to think about betrothing his daughter to anyone, let alone someone who lived months of travel from home. His relationship with the Melucian rulers had always been strong and didn't really need a boost, but he understood the arguments in favor of the marriage. No one understood why, but the Kingdom's line was definitely losing its magic, and that long-term threat to his nation was painfully clear. The cynical part of him worried that Jess might actually make matters worse. She had always been spirited, but in her teen years she had become an unmitigated disaster. A dark cloud of resentment and rebellion followed her into every room. A few weeks with her might turn a solid relationship into a full-blown international crisis. He chuckled to himself at the image of the Triad trying to tame his little girl. Talk about something backfiring!

He turned to leave. He had just enough time to make a quick change of clothes before dinner would be served. Tonight's dinner was supposed to be a rare, intimate "family only" meal, and he looked forward to relaxing after a busy day. He folded the Triad's letter and placed it in the ornate box that sat on the table by his throne, filled with an endless stream of requests and appeals. Then he touched his fore and middle fingers to its lid to activate the locking spell. Satisfied with the click of the magical lock, he turned to leave the throne room. The crumpled wad of parchment Jess had tossed in his lap crunched under his shoe. He'd forgotten about the note. He knelt, smoothed the paper, and read.

---

MOTHER'S MARRYING YOU TO THAT FAT OLD DUKE FROM *Huntcliff. You know, the one with the crossed eyes and squirrel on his head for hair? He's got to be at least forty. I heard Lord Sneak talking to her last night about it. – Justin*

---

THE KING SUCKED IN A DEEP, CALMING BREATH. PRINCE Justin was a year younger than Jess, and the pair were virtually inseparable. Reading the scrawl, Alfred's hope for a peaceful evening dimmed.

## 6

### JESS

Jess stalked back to her room and slammed the door, ensuring that anyone within earshot knew better than to disturb or risk her royal wrath. Ever since her sixteenth birthday some months ago, her mother was determined to marry her off. What was so magical about sixteen? She wasn't ready to get married to some stodgy old man who would force her into ridiculous, frilly dresses and parade her around like some perfumed animal. She was the Crown Princess, after all, and would be a Queen—one who didn't need some man's backside warming her throne. Now that her brother had overheard her mother's plan to ship her off to Huntcliff, she was more determined than ever find a way out of this mess.

She rummaged through her wardrobe, looking for something to wear to dinner, when a thought occurred to her. Could her father be in on this? Would he actually agree to something so disgusting? She had always been his little duckling, his favorite—well, only—daughter. Surely, he wouldn't be in on this plot, too. It had to be that weasel Thorn pushing her mother. The Chancellor was always skulking around her parents, whispering in their ears, and everyone knew he was rotten to his maggot-crawling core. She was sure he was trying to get her out of the way so her brother could take the throne—someone Thorn and her mother could better control. The first thing she'd do when she wore the Crown was exile that conniving weasel.

A soft knock snapped Jess out of her fuming daydream.

"Jess, it's me. Open up," her brother whispered through the door.

She cracked the door open to make sure he was alone, then let him in. He saw the look on her face, then the scattering of dresses on the floor … and the bed … and the dresser. He stayed out of range, landing on the foot of her bed. She returned to her wardrobe, tossing more dresses across the back of a chair.

"Sis, calm down. I don't think they've decided anything yet. As long as nothing's been announced publicly, we have time to change their minds." He ducked as her dress tossing escalated to a near-violent activity.

Justin Vester was the middle child in the royal family, squeezed between Jess and their younger brother, Kendall, and at fifteen, he was wholly unremarkable—average height, slim build, and a face that would blend into any crowd. Despite his ordinary appearance, Justin's crystal-blue eyes and his general good nature, combined with his burgeoning Gift of Persuasion, made him hard to refuse and even harder to dislike.

"You just don't get it, Justin. Nobody's trying to marry

*you* off or make *you* move to some backwards town buried under a mountain of snow. I've spent my entire life with one tutor or another, learning geography and languages and politics and … well … how to be Queen. Now they want me to throw that away and roll around in the mud with some fat old pig?" She flopped facedown on the bed beside her brother.

Justin gently rubbed her back. "C'mon, Jess. We'll figure this out. Who have you heard is on the list?"

She mumbled something unintelligible into the pillow.

"You can either eat that pillow or sit up and talk. I don't think you can do both."

She flipped over and sat up, glaring at his infectious grin. "Well, there's Lord Piggy in Huntcliff. Spirits, I would kill myself."

"Stop that. Who else?"

"Barnabus Dask, Father's Crown Treasurer."

"Well, he's not terrible. The ladies at court seem to think he's handsome enough. And he's rich," he winked.

"Justin, he's forty. I'm sixteen. Besides, I will be Queen. What do I need with a rich husband?" She motioned to the graveyard of dresses.

"Ok, ok. I get it. Who else?"

"General Marks. He's actually pretty handsome if you like that sulky, stone-faced military look combined with the personality of a corpse." She rolled her eyes.

"Hmm. So no General's staff in your future?" he snickered.

Jess barked out a laugh despite her foul mood and punched Justin in the arm. "You're such a moron."

"Yeah, but you love me and you know it." His grin widened.

"I'll never know why, but I do, my dear little brother." She mussed his hair with one hand while putting the other around his shoulder. They sat in silence for a long moment before she asked, "What am I going to do, Justin? This is a disaster, and Mother won't listen to me."

"Have you tried not yelling at her? She doesn't respond well to screeching. Well, unless it's her own." He scrunched up his face, mocking his Mother when she was angry and earning himself another punch in the arm.

Justin tried another approach. "What about Father? Everybody knows you're his favorite. He'd listen to you."

She flopped backwards onto the bed again. "I guess. I just wish they'd ask what I want, let me be a part of the decision. If I'm supposed to be the future of the Crown, don't you think I should be part of choosing the man I'll rule with?"

"Do you even know what you want? All I've heard you say is what you don't want, not what you *do*."

Jess stared at the ceiling. "Little brother, you can actually be pretty smart sometimes. I have no idea what I want, just that it's not to be married off to some old man and treated like an ornament. Any girl would deserve better, but especially a future Queen."

Justin's eyes dropped to his hands. He agreed with Jess but had also listened in court for countless hours and knew the alliances a marriage could forge were invaluable to the Kingdom, especially one made with the Heir. Their parents weren't wrong about that.

A quick, firm double knock on the door made them bolt upright. The Queen bustled into the room, all business. "Alright you two, dinner in twenty minutes. Get dressed. Tonight is just the family, so you don't have to worry about court business or picking the right fork. Your Father had a long day and needs a relaxing night with his children."

Queen Isabel swept out of the room without waiting for a response.

Jess didn't move for the next few minutes, just sat staring at the fire in the hearth across from her bed as if it would offer answers. The flames danced and popped but refused to speak.

---

DINNER WAS EXCRUCIATING. JESS SULKED SILENTLY IN HER spot between Justin and Kendall. Her parents liked to sit next to each other so they could keep their entire flock in view without having to look back and forth. The round wooden table was large enough to fit ten, but their family of five made it feel crowded. Jess couldn't wait to escape.

For over an hour, the King and Queen held court. Thankfully, Justin played his role and commanded the stage for most of the meal. He talked about his training with the Crown Royal Guard, his studies with both the Mages and Scholars, and his tour of the National Treasury with the other high-ranking students. As he walked everyone through his day's adventures, Jess stared in wonder at how passionate he was about the simplest things, and how he held his audience in thrall. His Gift of Persuasion had to help, but Justin didn't need magic to enchant a room. Jess couldn't imagine a world without her brother in it, but was also quietly jealous of his easy manner and ability to draw people to him. She would be Queen, but he would always be the leader people admired. The one they were drawn to. Sometimes life just wasn't fair.

Kendall stepped into the conversation, asking question after question ... after question. When he ran out of questions, he would take a bite and think of another. As Justin turned the conversation to his martial practice, Kendall practically leapt out of his chair before the Queen's glare introduced him to the Gift of Gravity wielded only by a mother. As soon as Justin paused to take a bite of pork, Kendall resumed his questioning, drilling his older brother about the Royal Guard. He was fascinated with anyone who wore a uniform, and couldn't imagine actually getting to train with a real Protector. One day, he wanted to join the Royal Guard, the next he was planning a pirate raid on one of the islands. Who knew what wild interest would catch his fancy next? If Jess had half the imagination of that little boy, she might change the world one day.

Dinner finally ended when servants cleared the table, Justin ran out of stories, and Kendall, somehow, ran out of questions. Jess fidgeted.

"May we be excused?" She gave her father a dovish look.

"I suppose. But Jess, tomorrow we need to have a serious talk, Sovereign to a soon-to-be-Sovereign. Alright?"

The King's tone sent a chill down her spine. He was rarely formal with her, especially in private.

"I am in Your Majesty's service," she said, standing from the table and offering a deep, formal curtsy, never dropping eye contact with her father.

The King watched his baby girl walk out and shook his head. He wasn't supposed to have a favorite, but there she went. Watching Jess grow and change, develop her own personality and independence, had been the greatest joy of his life. And the most frightening thing he had ever witnessed. She was evolving into a strong-willed, intelligent, independent woman—everything he had hoped for—but that iron backbone of hers was strong enough to get her into serious trouble. The way she looked at him when she really wanted something definitely got *him* into trouble! He sighed. He wasn't looking forward to tomorrow any more than she was. *I just hope she'll forgive me one day.*

———

JESS DASHED BACK TO HER ROOM AND CHANGED INTO THE riding clothes she'd laid out on the chair by her armoire. She wanted to avoid attention tonight, and these were the most common-looking clothes she owned. Besides, the Royal Guard wouldn't think twice about her going out for an evening ride, even this late. With the war brewing between the Princess and her mother, she fled the palace most evenings to think or decompress or stew—whatever fit her mood in that moment.

Careful to avoid contact with her brothers, whose rooms were on either side of hers, Jess crept down the hallway toward the door at the end. She begged the door for silence as she pulled it open, peeking through to ensure no one was in the throne room. Nothing stirred. She bolted through to the door opposite the two ornate thrones. She sucked in one last breath as she stared at the towering golden doors. Two Royal Guards stood vigil on the other side, but had her story ready—besides, no one questioned a Princess, right?

She threw back her shoulders and raised her nose into the air, her best imitation of the "royal face." Then she opened the left side of the large double doors … and was greeted with crossed pikes in her path.

"Princess, forgive us, but where are you going without your detail?" A stern, chiseled man in gleaming armor peered down.

"Where I am going is none of your concern. If I needed guards tonight, I would've asked for them. Clear my path. Now!" The last word cracked like a whip, daughter the spitting image of her mother.

The cocky guard's eyebrows rose, then knitted. He looked to his partner, who simply shrugged. Technically, the Princess was too young to give a Protector orders, per the Queen. But both men understood, in painful clarity, what it meant to be caught between *that* mother and her blessed daughter. The pikes snapped away. As she passed, both guardsmen gave her a crisp head bob before resuming their statue-like pose.

"I'll be late. Don't wait up," she said with a coy smile

over her shoulder. She hustled toward the outer door that led to the stables. The guards shared another look.

It was nearly 23:00, and darkness cloaked the night sky. The stable boys would already be settled into their rooms at the end of the stalls, so Jess expected an easy getaway. Still, she crept as quietly as possible, offering each horse she passed a small piece of apple she had stashed away in a tiny pouch on her belt. She rubbed their noses affectionately, and each leaned into her palm in return. Jess might struggle with people, but she adored animals, and they adored her back.

She made it to the stall that held her Cretian stallion, Dittler. Consistently stronger, taller, faster, and smarter than other lines, there was a nobility to Cretian horses that was impossible to identify but equally impossible to miss. In all the Kingdom, there were only five Cretian horses known to exist, one owned by each of the principles of the royal family. Dittler's sheer size made the stable masters in the Royal Guard and army jealous, as he eclipsed even the largest war horses in their herds. His sleek silver mane shimmered in the light and turned to a dazzling, rippling quicksilver when he poured his endless strength into a run. Dittler stood alone in grace and beauty, even when compared to the other Cretians belonging to the family. Jess worshiped every moment she spent with him.

She pulled the last of the apple from her pouch and fed it to Dittler. It always amazed her that a beast so full of raw power could be gentle, even loving. While Dittler chomped, she gave him a quick brushing and then placed the saddle on his back. He gave a little dance in anticipation of the ride he knew was coming.

Jess wasn't like the others. Her family was so afraid of someone getting hurt that they would barely canter around the grounds. Even her brother, the great future-Royal Guardsman, seemed afraid of the horse's bulk. But not Jess. She'd break from everyone, giving Dittler a nudge, and howled with ecstasy as he flew across the wide meadows of the Palace grounds. She loved the way the air rushed across her face, how her hair whipped and flew, and the sense of reckless, wild abandon that came with Dittler's incredible speed. This was the only time Jess felt completely free.

"No racing tonight, baby boy. We have to be quiet, ok?" She rubbed the inside of Dittler's ear with her thumb in the spot that made his eyes roll backward.

Jess scanned the stalls before mounting Dittler and trotting out of the stables. She cleared the perimeter of the Palace, entering the large arboreal area that bordered the wide-open meadows they normally preferred. Dittler slowed and looked back at her, as if questioning the wisdom of a trek into the woods at night.

"It's ok, Dit. We're going to see Danym. You like him, remember?"

The image of the seventeen-year-old made a smile light up her face and a tingle snake down her arms.

The trees were tall and old, but the canopy was thin enough for a well-lit stroll by moonlight. Jess knew they had left the Palace grounds when she passed a series of hunting stands in the trees. Her father and brother spent hour after hour staring out of those treehouses, hoping to spot something to shoot. Jess couldn't understand how something so incredibly boring could seem so exciting to them. *Men are nuts.*

They trotted for another few minutes before reaching their final destination—a small clearing by a stream that ran down from the neighboring mountain and through the entire wooded area bordering the Palace grounds. Danym sat on a small boulder, staring into the bubbling water when they rode up. A quiet moment passed as Jess watched him. A nervous energy rippled through her chest. Dittler, sensing her shift in mood, danced and let out a snort, causing Danym's head to snap up. Their eyes connected, and his smile lit up the forest.

At seventeen, Danym stood a little over eighteen-and-a-half hands tall. Lean, corded muscles ran throughout his arms, shoulders, and chest. Deep emeralds peered from behind a floppy curtain of sandy-brown hair that hung to his shoulders and never seemed to land in the same place twice. But the thing that made Jess's heart skip a beat was his smile. Oh, that smile. It was wide and bright and, well, it made his eyes sparkle and laugh. And it made Jess lose all sense of time or reason. *He's so perfect.*

Danym stood slowly, brushed his tan leather leggings, and walked over to give Dittler a gentle stroke on the neck. He looked up at Jess and extended his hand. "May a humble subject offer Her Royal Highness a hand?"

*Spirits, he has to stop looking at me like that. Please, don't let him stop looking at me like that.*

She tried to come up with a sharp retort, something that flowed so easily with her brothers or father—and *especially* with her mother. But this demon had cast his spell, and she couldn't speak. She nodded, smiled, and took his hand, allowing him to help her down from Dittler's back. She stumbled as she landed, forcing him to wrap her in his strong arms and hold her close to keep her from falling.

*Oh, that worked well. Gotta remember that one!*

Danym let her go, stepped back, and gave her a formal bow. "Welcome, my lady. May I tether your magnificent horse?"

She gave Danym her most regal stare. "Oh, my boy, of course. But be careful. He is a keen judge of character, and we're still deciding about yours."

Once Dittler was cared for, Danym took Jess's hand and led her around behind the boulder, revealing a perfectly laid blanket scattered with glasses, a bottle of wine, and a small wooden plate containing cut meats and cheeses. In the center of the plate was some sort of fruit hidden in a delicate shell of chocolate, something he knew was her favorite.

"You think of everything, don't you?" She reached up and gave him a long kiss, all pretense forgotten.

He wrapped her in his arms again, and they kissed for a few blissful minutes, after which Jess pulled away and knelt to examine her offering.

They talked and enjoyed the cool evening and smooth wine. Danym caught her up on news outside the Palace and the routine of his days. After a brief pause to feed each other a bite of cheese and pour more wine, Danym reached up and moved a stray lock of hair from her eyes. "I've missed you. I know the Palace can be a crazy place, but I worried when I didn't hear anything for a week."

"Danym, I'm so sorry. It's been awful. My mother is a demon. I just hate her. All they can talk about is who they're going to marry me off to. Now they're even thinking about some fat old duke from Huntcliff!"

"Lord Parna? The one who picks his nose and farts at court? They call him 'the ostrich' because he can stick his head up his own—"

"Danym!" She slapped his arm playfully.

He laughed. "Well, that's what they say. Is your father seriously considering him? Isn't he thirty years older than you?"

"Yeah, but he's a Duke. They're worried about securing alliances, and trade, and who knows what else? And I get it. I will be Queen, and my hand is a powerful trading chip. But I hate being treated like some cow at the auction. I should have a say in this. No. I should *decide* who I want to be with—who I want to rule with. All I want is for us to be together." She buried her head in his shoulder as tears fell.

He wrapped his arms around her again, and she listened to his heart quicken as she pressed close against his chest. There was no sound in the world that calmed her like Danym's heart. She felt so *safe* with that rhythmic beating, his strong arms around her. Why couldn't her parents see that Danym was who she was meant to be with?

An eternity passed before he gently pulled her away, holding her shoulders in his hands at arm's length. "I love you, Jess Vester. We'll find a way to be together. But I need to get back before my father realizes I left. It's not easy being the High Sheriff's son. It's like he knows when I'm up to something without even asking."

"I know. I need to get back, too. Mother would love an excuse to confine me to the Palace—and she has a whole army to keep me there if she sets her mind to it."

Danym helped her mount Dittler again, giving her a kiss on the curve of her neck as he lifted her up. She bent her neck to wrap his face in her scent and shivered at the intimate touch. *This man will be the death of me. Spirits, I love him.*

As she rode back to the Palace, Danym packed up the remnants of their picnic and started his trek back to his father's estate. The moon was now high and full in the sky. Despite the moon's best efforts, neither of the two teens noticed the man in the shadows who had been listening and now watched them leave. He muttered a few words and disappeared, leaving no trace of his presence in the woods.

# 7

## JESS

Thorn held a deep bow, waiting to see how the Queen would respond before rising. He had spent the better part of twenty minutes recounting the events of the evening, starting with the report from the throne room guards of the Princess's departure. "Your Majesty, they had clearly met at this location many times. They spoke with a commoners' familiarity and held each other most of the night, but there was no carnal knowledge. I believe the Princess is still intact."

The Queen's crystal-blue eyes brimmed with fire as she listened.

"Are you sure the boy was the High Sheriff's son?"

"Yes, Your Majesty. He even spoke of his father as they parted." He slowly straightened, eyes cast toward the floor in front of Isabel.

She reached up and shook her inky black hair from its tightly woven chignon, allowing it to fall freely below her shoulders, then rose and walked to stare into the roaring fire in the massive stone fireplace of her study. She had been patient with Jess for months—years really—but it was past time the girl grew up. If she ever hoped to be Queen, Jess needed to accept her role and do what was demanded of an heir.

This childish crush had to end.

"Danai, I need to speak with the High Sheriff … *privately*. It is imperative that no one, not even the King, knows we are meeting. I will impress upon our chief constable the importance of proper succession and the need for alliances above petty, childish love stories. Sebastiano is a reasonable man, loyal to the Crown; I'm sure he'll come around and tame that son of his."

Thorn remained silent a heartbeat too long, and the Queen turned with an impatient brow raised. When he finally spoke, his voice was a low murmur that carried more than a hint of malice. "Your Majesty, we *could* go with a more direct—more *permanent*—solution."

Isabel nodded pensively. "That is one option, but let's try diplomacy first. I know your skills and am sure you would make it look like an accident, but we can't risk angering the High Sheriff. He's too influential, both at court and across the country."

"Before the Crown gets involved directly, perhaps I could give diplomacy a try, as you said." Thorn inclined his head.

She steepled her fingers, giving Thorn a sidelong glare. "Go on."

He drew a deep breath. "We should save the royal presence as a trump card in case other efforts fail. Allow me to speak with the High Sheriff. We are both members of Council, and no one will look twice at a meeting between us. It would be difficult to hide a meeting with the Queen, especially from your daughter. I think we both know how poorly things might turn if the Crown Princess learned of her mother's … involvement … in this matter."

"Fine. You have one opportunity, but I will squash this if you fail, no matter how messy things might get for Her Royal Highness." Her voice lowered to a near-whisper. "Come back tomorrow after the dinner hour and report. I want this tied up quickly. The King intends to put candidates for betrothal before the Princess tomorrow, and we can't have the Sheriff's boy spoiling the plan."

She turned toward the fire before tears could escape and crack her precious facade of invincibility. *Why does everything have to be* so *hard with that girl? Why is it always a battle?* She missed the days when Jess looked up at her as if there were nothing and no one else in the world. When she was her whole universe. *Spirits, she was so beautiful and fragile.* Isabel smiled at the memory. But that sweet little girl had grown into a willful, obnoxious, frustratingly cunning young woman. All Isabel saw in her eyes now was resentment and bitterness. Deep down, she knew this happened with many girls and mothers, but it had hurt when it happened with her own precious baby.

Thorn bowed respectfully to his Queen's back and slipped out the door, leaving her to ponder the flames.

THE NEXT MORNING, THE STAFF ENSURED THE BOYS WERE shuffled off, freeing the King and Queen to manage their daughter and the day's agenda. Alfred had previously asked Chancellor Thorn to clear the royal calendar, determined that they would finally settle the question of betrothal.

He took Isabel's hand. "Issy, she's only a few minutes late. Take a deep breath."

She crushed his fingers in her vice-like grip. "You have no idea what I've had to do to get all the candidates together on the same day. If that ungrateful child so much as whimpers—"

"Deep breath. Please." He squeezed her hand and carefully pried his from her grip, returning it to the safety of his lap.

They had been watching the side door that led to the residence and were surprised when the massive golden double doors at the end of the chamber swung open. A page in royal green livery appeared and bellowed formally, "Her Royal Highness, Crown Princess Jessia Vester."

Jess walked through, and the King stood, mouth agape. The Queen's eyes narrowed into thin lines.

The Princess wore a flowing sky-blue gown trimmed in glistening gold, with a deep purple sash crossing her chest in the formal, royal style. Her normally ruffled hair was brushed to lustrous perfection and bound tightly behind her neck by a thin silver net that sparkled in the light. One lustrous trickle of hair fell down her right shoulder. Blue and white diamonds glittered from the tiara on her brow, the one normally reserved for official State functions.

The King looked at Isabel with a boyish grin and

hopped to his feet. He'd hoped Jess would show up and represent them well, but he never dreamed she'd make such a stunning effort.

The Queen reached up and pinched his arm. "Not a word out of you until this day is won." He couldn't hold the chuckle back, earning him another pinch.

Jess strolled down the center of the chamber, head and shoulders high, every inch a queen surveying her domain. When she reached the bottom step of the dais, she offered the King a deep, formal curtsy and held it a moment longer that was usually expected, a sign of subservience in any royal court.

"My Lord Father and Lady Mother, I am here at your command."

The King looked at the Queen out of the side of his eye and raised a brow. The Queen was a stone, staring ice through her prostrated child.

Alfred beamed down at his daughter. "Jess, you are absolutely radiant. I've never seen you more—"

Isabel broke protocol, interrupting the King, her voice crisp, "Rise and take your place, Daughter. We decide the fate of the Kingdom—and our line—today."

Jess didn't flinch or give her mother a second look. She simply rose and took her place on the right side of her father's throne, one hand resting on his shoulder. The King smiled, assuming the gesture showed affection, and placed his hand over hers. Jess meant it as a plea for help and leaned down to whisper in his ear, "Father, I will make *you* proud, but please don't give me away to some old man. I love you, Papa."

The King's breath caught, and he swallowed his guilt as he felt his daughter's hand tremble under his own. His heart broke to feel her fear, her dread. But he knew what had to be done.

The Queen nodded to the High Chancellor who seemed to appear out of nowhere.

*How does he do that? Lord Sneak indeed!* Jess thought as she sneaked a peek at the Chancellor.

"Your Majesties, I present you with the list of proposed suitors for the hand of the Crown Princess Jessia. Members of the Privy Council have reviewed each name on this list, and, after many days of furious debate, agreed on a few finalists. We submit them for your review and sincerely hope the Princess is well pleased." As he said that last part, he looked at Jess and maintained eye contact throughout the deep bow that followed.

*Not Lord Sneak—Lord Weasel!*

Thorn turned to the page at the door and nodded.

The boy disappeared, returned, and announced, "His Excellency, Kinsley Parna, Duke of Huntcliff, Warden of the East."

A short balding man whose width nearly outpaced his height waddled into the room. His tiny brown eyes were so close together Jess thought they might blend into his pinched, upturned nose. The effect was punctuated by the largest, bushiest eyebrows she had ever seen. The Duke's face was clean shaven, and his once black hair now swirled on top of his head to form a vortex of failed camouflage for his pale, flaky scalp. Most of it refused to stay in place and flopped down the front of his face as he walked, forcing him to shove it back every few seconds with an irritated scowl.

The Duke shuffled to the foot of the throne and offered the King and Queen the deepest bow his knees and massive belly allowed, then turned his gaze toward Jess with a predatory grin. The man had been comical until she held his gaze. Now she felt only fear.

"Duke Parna, welcome. We are pleased to see you again," the King said.

"Thank you, Your Majesty. Huntcliff can be so tedious. One welcomes the change," Parna said in a high-pitched squeal that caught Jess so off guard a small chortle escaped, earning a stern look from her mother.

"How are the borderlands these days?" the Queen asked.

"My Queen," Parna began with a flourish toward Isabel. "One observes trees and mountains. Traders pass through headed to other destinations, rarely stopping in town, and the men and women who live in Huntcliff are tough as the mountain stones and friendly as the lions that live in their heights. One does miss the capital."

Isabel sucked a deep breath and pursed her lips. "We understand too well. But how are things on the border with Melucia? How are relations with their Rangers?"

"One would *never* wish to speak with those barbarians, Your Majesty. Filthy ruffians, they are."

The King intervened, irritated. "Duke, are things peaceful? Is trade flowing normally through the pass?"

Parna offered another shallow bow. "My King, one has not seen a change in trade in years. One's patrols report multiple caravans each week and no disturbance within the pass, aside from the occasional wildlife attack one must expect in the wilderness."

Jess stifled a yawn, accidentally catching her father's eye.

"Duke, you must be exhausted from your travels. The page will show you to your rooms and help with anything you might need. We look forward to spending less formal time together this evening at dinner," Alfred said.

The Duke bowed toward the King again, then to the Queen, then seemed to remember Jess and gave her a shallow head bob. "One looks forward to it, Your Majesties, Highness."

Parna hadn't heard the page approach and nearly knocked him over as he took two backward steps, retreating from the throne. Jess laughed out loud and the Duke tried to stab her with his glare before he turned to leave the chamber.

Once the doors closed, Jess turned to her father and pleaded, "Papa, please no. Marry me to a goat, but not *that* man."

He turned and took her hand. "Baby girl, please just entertain our guests today with an open heart. Regardless of whom you marry, these are the nobles of our Kingdom, and we need their support and goodwill. *You* will need them one day as their Queen."

"Yes, Papa," was all she could say.

As Jess gathered herself again, the page barked out, "Lord Barnabus Dask, His Majesty's Crown Treasurer, and

Sir Ethan Marks, Lord General of His Majesty's Armed Forces, Lord Protector of the Realm."

The doors opened and admitted the chief banker and armsman, who walked side by side to the throne and bowed. General Marks wasn't a relative, but had been the King's closest friend for years. Marks covered his long frame in a black cloak and a fur shoulder wrap that almost masked the bright gold collar poking through around his neck. He looked more like a man on a hunt than a suitor.

In contrast, Treasurer Dask resembled some solitary monk more than the Kingdom's top financial official. He wore a simple black robe that bore no adornment save the golden collar of his Gift.

Jess's mood lifted as the men walked into the room, and her father smiled, noticing her sudden attentiveness. Dask and Marks stopped before the bottom step and gave the King deep, respectful bows.

"Gentlemen, rise and be at ease. We are pleased to formally introduce a lady you both know well. I present to you my daughter, the Crown Princess Jessia." Alfred beamed with pride as he gestured with an open palm toward Jess.

Both men offered Jess a bow. General Marks even attempted a smile, such that it was for the most somber man in the Kingdom.

Jess's mind raced as she watched the spectacle unfold before her. *They're both handsome. But Spirits, Dask is nearly twice my age and Uncle Ethan—he's UNCLE ETHAN!*

Jess schooled her face and returned her callers' bows

with a graceful curtsy of her own, swallowing her inner turmoil.

"General Marks. Lord Dask," she said tightly.

The King rescued her quickly. "Gentlemen, we look forward to seeing you both at dinner."

Recognizing the King's tone of dismissal, both men bowed, retreated backward two steps, then turned and exited the chamber.

The doors had barely closed when the Queen shot to her feet and turned to Jess. "Jess, did you see how handsome Ethan is in his furs? And he's so tall!"

Jess maintained her air of regal superiority, stepping off the dais and arching a brow toward the King. "Father, I believe Mother would like you to match her today. I'll gladly give her my betrothal if it pleases the Crown. After all, General Marks is quite tall." Jess said with a smirk, without breaking eye contact with her mother.

Isabel bristled and an accusing finger shot toward her daughter. But Alfred stood and cut her off before she could respond.

"Listen, you two. Not today," he admonished. "Jess, you'll learn more about these three at dinner tonight, but we need to discuss one more option that has come to our attention."

"Please tell me it involves the Sheriff's son." The plea escaped her lips on its own, and she was horrified, covering her mouth with both hands, eyes wide.

The King's brows knit together, and he looked questioningly to Isabel. "Sebastiano's boy?"

"Your daughter thinks her secret admirer is actually a

secret, my love," the Queen said, settling back onto her throne. "I imagine she hopes a match with him would appease us since Sheriff Wilfred is so widely respected. But I suppose it is worth a discussion."

Jess couldn't believe what she was hearing. *Is Mother really considering this?* Her heart raced and color flooded into her cheeks.

The King actually laughed. He laughed! And not the good deep belly laugh that meant he loved the idea. More the "you're absolutely out of your mind" laugh that crushed hopes and dreams.

"Ladies, be serious. Wilfred's boy is what, seventeen? There's even rumor he's a bastard." Jess shot him a mystified look, and he laughed again. "This decision will be at the heart of the reign of Queen Jessia Vester and must be treated with the utmost seriousness. The Kingdom's future turns on decisions such as this. The fate of the entire world will be affected by this choice. A boy barely old enough to grow whiskers or know his own desires can hardly guide a queen."

The hair on the back of Jess's neck shot to attention, and the pendulum of her emotions swung from hope to anger. "Guide? You want someone to *guide* me? Did you seriously just say that?"

"Jess, you know that's not what I—"

"No, father! I see it now. That's exactly what you meant. I've been *guided* my entire life." She paced furiously before the thrones. "I've been told what to wear, how to hold my head, when to speak—which is basically never. I've been *guided* through every tiny detail of every pointless day. Now you want to arrange a marriage with men more than twice my age because I'm too ignorant or stupid —or *too female*—to rule!

"I stood here all morning as you paraded potential buyers for your prize cow. I am your daughter, heir to your crown, not some mindless beast to be auctioned off to the highest bidder."

She took a deep breath, trying to calm herself, but the flames of her anger only grew hotter. "Father, this will be my husband ... my partner ... *my Kingdom*, not yours! When I am Queen, *I* will do the guiding and I won't need any man to tell me how to do it unless *I* choose him and allow for his guidance." She stormed out the side door toward her room.

The King slumped back into his throne. He removed his crown and held it in his lap, eyes downcast at the heavy symbol of office.

Isabel turned to him with a raised eyebrow and small chuckle. "That went well, dear. For once it's you and not me. I pity those poor men coming to dinner tonight."

## 8

## DANAI

High Sheriff Sebastiano Wilfred's office sat at the center of Fontaine's trade district in a large stone building with few windows and even fewer doors. The place looked more like a massive mausoleum than a functional government building. A set of small double doors were the only adornment on the front of the building. City Guardsmen, Royal Guards, and National Patrol could be seen entering and leaving through those doors in a constant stream that reminded Thorn of an anthill angered by the rain.

As he approached the building, the milling crowds of uniformed men and women offered shallow bows and parted to allow Thorn to pass, guided by some involuntary impulse to avoid contact with the Mage. He walked the short length of the lobby and bounded up the stairs to the third floor, where he found the offices of senior officers and bureaucrats. He approached the familiar desk of the High

Sheriff's clerk and smiled. "Kay, I'd like to see Sebastiano for a moment, please."

A woman in her fifties with spectacles and gray hair pinned in a tight bun looked up and stood quickly, offering a short curtsy. "Of course, High Chancellor. Please have a seat."

When Kay reappeared, she was followed by a tall man with long brown hair wearing a crisp green coat lined with two rows of highly polished gold buttons.

"Chancellor Thorn, what an odd time for a visit from the King's right hand. Is everything alright?" Sebastiano asked with genuine concern.

"All is well. Would you mind if we spoke in your office … *privately*?"

Sebastiano paused, then turned and motioned for Thorn to precede him into his office. At the far end of the room, next to one of the precious few windows, was an enormous desk littered with parchment stacked inches thick. Either the High Sheriff was seriously in demand or woefully behind on his paperwork.

The men sat at a small table just inside the door. "So, I take it this isn't a courtesy call. What's going on that we needed to talk privately outside of Council?"

Thorn spoke bluntly. "Are you aware that your son has engaged in private, unchaperoned rendezvous—sometimes very late at night—in the woods near the Palace grounds?"

Sebastiano leaned back, eyes wide. "No. I've been working all hours lately. What's he gotten himself mixed up in? He's a good boy but has been a little lost since his mother died last year. With those missing Gifted cases piling up, I haven't been home much."

"He's seeing Princess Jessia in secret."

The Sheriff's eyes threatened to pop out of their sockets as he searched for any sign of humor in the Chancellor's face.

"You're serious?"

"I'm afraid so. In fact, they were seen having a picnic last night in their regular spot in the woods, complete with wine, a cheese board, and large, comfortable blanket," Thorn peeked up to catch Wilfred's reaction while pretending to leaf through documents.

Sebastiano was used to crimes that perplexed, even shocked, but this was more than he could process. Danym and the Princess? *The Queen will have his head for this!*

"Does the King know?"

"No. But … *she* does."

"Gods, no!" Wilfred put his head in his hands.

Thorn leaned forward and placed a hand on the Sheriff's arm, "Relax, my friend. The Queen is pleased with this match."

Now Sebastiano's head really started spinning. "You're still serious, aren't you? Why would the Queen want the son of a lawman to be paired with the Heir to the Kingdom? That doesn't make any sense at all."

"It makes perfect sense when you know the Queen, as I do. She and Jess have been at each other's throats for years, and the betrothal has heightened tensions beyond measure. Even as we speak, the King is parading three more suitors in front of our Princess—including two members of Council," Thorn said with a meaningful look.

Wilfred laughed and a bit of tension released. "Members of Council? Which old men are they desperate enough to try now?"

"Dask and Marks."

He barked again. "You're kidding, right? Every rumor I've heard pegs Dask as favoring the Prince, not the Princess. And Marks ... well ... he's not as old as the rest of us, but do we really want the leader of our military sitting on the throne? And he's so serious all the time. I can't imagine Jess accepting either of them."

"They're better than Parno."

"Now I know you're joking. Parno? Parno the Porker?" he asked in disbelief. "One does love talking about oneself, doesn't one?"

Thorn actually cracked a smile.

*I don't think I've ever seen Thorn smile before. Now I know this is a nightmare*, Wilfred thought.

"So, back to Danym. You are well respected throughout the Kingdom. Your son is young and handsome, and the Princess seems genuinely enchanted. What's not to like about this match?"

"I suppose. But why all the sneaking? If the Queen approves, shouldn't the courtship be public? Or at least not hidden in the woods in the dead of night?"

"Quite right. Let's get through the last suitor dinner at the Palace, and Her Majesty will address the issue properly," Thorn said.

There was a pause as the Sheriff digested the implications of his son courting the Crown Princess. *Spirits, how is this possible?*

Thorn changed subjects abruptly. "While I'm here, do you have any update on the missing Gifted cases?"

Sebastiano snapped out of his fog, finally asked something within his professional purview. "A *fourth* was reported missing yesterday. That's four Gifted in the past nine weeks. The only common thread we've found is that all four have a Gift. The latest was taken from the small town of Crelt on the southern coast. Son of a local merchant. No one particularly important or famous."

"What was the boy's gift this time?" Thorn steepled his fingers.

Sebastiano stood and walked to his desk. He rifled through some of the stacked parchment, finally pulling a page. "Looks like he was Mental: Clairvoyance."

"So, Strength, Fire, Animal Control, and now Clairvoyance. Doesn't seem to follow a pattern, does it?" Thorn asked.

"I was hoping you'd have more insight, see some magical pattern. Even the locations where the victims were taken are random, many days' travel apart."

"Have you discovered a trail to follow in any of the cases? Any sign of where they were taken?" Thorn asked.

"No. Nothing we can positively identify is linked to our missing Gifted. We received some unrelated reports that caught my eye, though. Our Patrol Captain near Cradle in the East noted a recent increase in activity by The Children. He believes they are migrating further east, possibly over the mountains into Melucia."

"The Children? I haven't heard anyone mention them in years. They're a strange group. Harmless enough. But have always kept to themselves. Do you suspect their involvement?" Thorn asked.

"We don't have any information to connect them, just an odd increase in movement at the same time as the Gifted have gone missing. I have two units in the area, one in Cradle and the other in Huntcliff. If there's anything going on, we'll hear about it."

Thorn stood and nodded. "Thank you, Sebastiano. Please keep me informed as you learn more. The King and Queen are quite disturbed by these cases and are eager for their resolution."

"We all are, Chancellor. We all are."

———

TWO HOURS LATER, THORN STOOD IN THE QUEEN'S STUDY as she sat staring into her fireplace, anger seething in her eyes as she listened to the Chancellor's assurances.

"Yes, Your Majesty, the Sheriff understands completely."

She responded in a low, measured tone that was more intimidating than if her voice were raised. "I'd better never see his boy anywhere near the Palace or my daughter again. Do you understand me, Chancellor? Never. Again."

"I understand perfectly, Your Majesty," Thorn bowed low before leaving the Queen to ponder her flames. He couldn't decide which burned hotter in that moment, the ones in the hearth or her eyes.

# 9

## TIANA

The cart hit a bumpy patch and tossed Tiana against its hard wooden side. She was groggy and her head hurt, but she was alive. She remembered waking a couple other times as the cart would stop, the sudden change in motion jarring her senses.

Each time they stopped, one of the men opened the heavy wooden cover to the cart's shallow bed. He wore a strange carved mask that looked like the face of an angry bull with horns on either temple and a long beak that curved downward, ending in a point. Through her clouded senses, she thought to herself, *"Bulls don't have beaks, do they?"* The random thought almost made her laugh. Almost.

The man's dark-brown robes were so loose-fitting that she couldn't tell anything about his build, and the hood he kept pulled over his head obscured his hair. But she could see his murky almost black eyes through the holes in the mask. The man never spoke to her, just glared through those creepy little eye holes.

Bull-bird checked to make sure her ropes were still in place and offered her a waterskin. It seemed like an almost mechanical routine, performed each time in the same order and with no conversation. There was an odd distance in the man's eyes as he stepped through his little dance, as if he was staring at her from far away. If she refused the water, he would stand there until she relented and drank. Something in his bearing told Tiana that he didn't care how long he had to stand there as long as she downed the liquid. A Healer her whole life, she knew instantly what the sweet, almost syrupy taste in the water meant—at least, that's what she was thinking as she drifted away again.

Some hours later, maybe a day or more, she woke again. The air was cooler, almost crisp, and had the sticky-sweet smell of pine. The road beneath the cart's wheels had grown rougher, and she was sore from all the tossing in her rigid coffin. She couldn't see any daylight coming through the tiny cracks between the wood, but there were sounds of movement from other people and horses nearby. She tried to clear her head and gather her strength. This was her first opportunity to even think about escaping since she was taken. Her throat was sore, and she felt weak from a lack of food, but adrenaline was a magical force of its own, and the possibility of freedom jarred her senses into a heightened state.

The cart came to a crawl, then stopped.

"Hold. Where are ya headed and what's your business

crossing the border?" she heard a man ask with almost bored authority.

The low, raspy voice that answered sent a chill down her arms. It sounded strange, almost inhuman, and carried no hint of emotion. "We are Children returning home."

"What's in the cart?" the first voice asked.

Tiana found her own voice in that moment and began screaming through the wood. "Help me! I'm in the cart. Please help me!" she yelled again and again as loudly as her scratchy throat would allow. When no one responded, she tried to kick her rope-bound legs against the side of the cart, making a loud banging sound each time. Still nothing.

Suddenly the cart top popped open. Tiana could see the night sky peeking through a canopy of tall, thick fir trees. A moment later, a face she didn't recognize appeared over-head. The man was strikingly handsome, with a strong, chiseled jaw and wavy light-brown hair that curled in places, especially the one curl that fell across his forehead above his left eye. He wore a simple forest-green uniform. She could see the rich wood of a sturdy bow poking up from his back, which explained the brown leather strap that disturbed the green field of his coat. The only ornamenta-tion on his coat was a small silver pin shaped like an owl with its wings spread wide. And then there were his eyes. They were a brilliant, penetrating green that seemed to bore through Tiana as she looked into them. She had never seen eyes so clear and bright. For a moment, she forgot where she was and wanted nothing more than to reach up, twist that curl back into place, and stare into those dreamy eyes.

Then she came back to herself and pleaded, "I'm right here. You're looking right at me. HELP ME, PLEASE!"

The green-eyed man scanned the inside of the cart up and down, not seeming to see or hear her. He turned back to the robed man. "Going home empty-handed, it seems. Well, be careful in the mountains. We've had several traders go up and not return. Safe travels."

Then he walked away.

A couple of minutes passed before Tiana saw Bull-bird return overhead. "Illusion is my Gift. They see what I want them to see. They hear what I tell them to hear. You may scream if it makes you feel better, but no one will see or hear you," he rasped, and then handed her the ritual water-skin before sealing the lid to her coffin once more.

As the cart lurched forward, starting its assent through the mountain pass, a trickle of tears fell down Tiana's cheek. As with most storms, the light fall was followed by a torrent that caused her angry stomach to clench. Welcome drowsiness overtook fear and pain, and Tiana fell into a fitful, restless sleep.

## 10

## KEELAN

**K**eelan walked into his house and tossed his boots by the door. Something so simple shouldn't feel that good, but after a day like today, it was amazing. He'd missed another dinner in the Officers' Mess and was down to eating tidbits left in his pantry. He grabbed the last apple and somewhat edible crusty end of a loaf. He really had to get better at keeping the house stocked. Between bites, he opened the notes the Arch Mage had given him and began to read.

- - -

FREEPORT CONSTABLE NOTES, ADDENDUM TO FILE 4.327-8, Month 10, Day 1, Report Time 23:15

Sergeant Dav Colby, Investigative Lead

**Criminal Matter**: Missing Person

**Victim**: Bel Crim

**Description of Alleged Crime**: *Vic left Mages' Guild at approximately 18:00. Wtns at Guild state vic said she was leaving to meet her parents for dinner at Campfire Grille on East Doarn Avenue. Vic last seen exiting and walking east. Vic never arrived at destination. At 22:05, mother and father presented to Constable Beel (4301), who was patrolling area. Vic last seen by Mage-Apprentice Kirin Knight.*

**Physical Description of Victim**: *Female, 22, average height, slim build, waist-length blond hair/straight, blue eyes. At time of report, vic wore pale yellow ankle-length dress with white lace/Gifted gold trim on collar and cuffs, brown shoes with small silver buckles, small gold signet ring (Crim family seal–gull flying over ship with sails).*

**Additional Information:** *Vic's Gift–Mental, Empath, power level strong*

- - -

Freeport Constable Notes, Addendum to File 4.327-8, Month 10, Day 2, Report Time 11:15

Sergeant Dav Colby, Investigative Lead

**Criminal Matter**: Missing Person

**Victim**: Bel Crim

**Investigation Notes:**

1. ***Witness Interview: Mage-Apprentice Kirin Knight.*** *Wtns states vic was at Guild from apprx 11:00 to 18:00. Vic was studying with senior*

*Mages. Vic left Guild at apprx 18:00. Vic told Wtns she had dinner plans with parents (Lord Jereth Crim, Lady Fely Crim) at Campfire Grille on East Doarn Avenue. Vic excited b/c dinner to talk about betrothal. Wtns walked vic to door, saw her leave and head east. Vic not carrying anything. Wtns stated vic was upbeat, noted vic was singing as she left. Known vic for 3 years.*

2. ***Search of Route to Vic's Stated Destination.*** *Walked route twice. Spoke with multiple merchants along route & none reported seeing vic. Found nothing unusual.*

3. ***Search of Victim's Residence.*** *Vic lives with parents. Perimeter doors and windows to manor appear undisturbed. No unusual visitors or trespassers reported by staff. Interviewed cook, valet—neither reported anything unusual over past week at manor. Vic acting normal, seemed happy. Lord/Lady Crim allowed search of vic's rooms—Lady Crim accompanied to answer questions. Nothing appeared disturbed or out of place.*

4. ***Public Release.*** *Coordinated with Editor of Freeport News, included sketch of vic. No tips from public as of this report.*

- - -

Keelan rubbed his temples as a headache threatened.

There was so little to start with, and it was now Day 6, five days following the initial report. Stone cold trail.

———

THE SUN BROKE OVER THE HORIZON A FEW MINUTES LATER. At least that's how it felt to Keelan as he struggled to shake the fogginess out of his head. He started a small fire and hung an old blackened pot filled with water to boil. This morning desperately needed coffee—lots of coffee.

While the water heated, he reviewed the notes from Freeport again to see if he missed anything in his initial reading. There was nothing noteworthy, so he turned his attention to assembling his team. He had already put himself in charge of Tiana's investigation. His professional judgement told him to avoid any case where personal feelings might be involved, but he rationalized that he and Tiana had only spent one short evening together. There wasn't anything there to compromise. At least, that's what he kept telling himself.

He added a couple of Guards he trusted, then turned his attention to the Freeport search. He wrote Ridley's name and then *Lead?* beside it. He added another Guard and then wrote *Mage/Telepathy* on a blank line. The idea had come to him late in the night. They would need to coordinate with the team in Freeport, and having a Mage who could send updates mentally would be helpful. He made a note to ask the Arch Mage for a recommendation when they met later in the day. After some thought, he decided against adding any others to the teams, revisiting the Captain-

Commander's concern regarding spies who might be embedded in both the Guard and Mages' Guild.

Keelan jotted a few more notes, threw on his uniform, and headed to the Officer's Mess for breakfast. Ridley was already halfway through his meal when Keelan flopped down. As he surveyed the eggs, bacon, and biscuits stacked on plates in the middle of the table, his stomach reminded him he'd skipped too many meals.

"Morning, L.T." Ridley said, peeking over his mug of steaming tea.

Keelan grunted acknowledgement through a mouthful of biscuit. When he got the bite down, he looked up at Ridley and said in a quiet voice, "I want you leading the search down south. This thing is bigger than we realized, and I need someone I can trust. You'll have one other Guardsman, and I'll get a Mage assigned to your team as well."

"Just three of us? Seems kinda slim for a high-profile case, don't ya think, sir?" Ridley asked a little too loudly for Keelan's liking.

"Lower your voice—and no details here. I'll explain what I can later, but this has to be kept quiet. Bigger teams mean bigger leaks. We'll talk about reporting frequency and timing later, but whatever you report, it stays between the two of us, understand?"

Ridley stared at Keelan for a moment before speaking, turning the conversation over in his head. He'd been involved in sensitive cases before, but this level of secrecy was new.

"Understood. But what if the search needs more

people? Two constables and a Mage won't cut it if someone grabbed the victim and left town."

"We'll worry about that when we get to it. We might have to get a little creative with cover stories, but let's focus on what's in front of us right now. I'm briefing the Captain-Commander and Arch Mage at noon. Meet me at HQ at 14:00 to get things started. In the meantime, do a little digging into the political situation in Freeport. I haven't heard of anything unusual lately, but the vic is an heiress, and her father is politically powerful. Might as well learn what we can before splitting up. Your team will need to leave for Freeport tonight." Keelan stuffed a forkful of eggs into his mouth.

"I'll head over to the Merchants' Guild and see what I can learn. If anybody stays up on the politics of the cities, it's the money guys. See you at 14:00." Ridley downed the last of his tea and stood to leave.

"Ridley, one more thing before you go. Tell me about your Gift. I know it's Physical & endurance related, but we've never talked about it. Given what we're about to do, I need to know every arrow we have in the quiver."

"OK. Kinda personal, L.T.." Ridley chuckled uncomfortably as he avoided Keelan's eyes and shifted from one foot to the other. "No asking to court or meet my parents after."

He tugged at his suddenly itchy golden collar as he cleared his throat, meeting Keelan's steady gaze. "Yes, Physical. Endurance is one way to say it. I rarely need more than an hour or two of sleep and recover from physical activity within minutes. If we went on a long run, I guarantee you'd lose that big breakfast before I even breathed heavy. My Gift came in handy in recruit training. When everybody else was falling out, I didn't even break a sweat."

"Good to know. Thanks. And tell your parents I miss them," Keelan smirked, sending Ridley away chuckling to himself.

A FEW HOURS LATER, KEELAN SIGNED OUT A HORSE FROM the stables and made the short ride to the Mages' Guild. The small circular compound was ringed by an twenty-four-hand tall stacked stone wall that appeared more ornamental than protective, but Keelan knew that those stones had stood unaged and undisturbed for over five hundred years. Thanks to his childhood spent surrounded by Mages, he knew more about magic than most, but he couldn't wrap his head around the power it must have taken for that wall to remain standing for so many years. There was no gate to open and close, just an open archway in the stacked stone. The Phoenix symbol was engraved in gold at the top of the archway, and its glittering crystalline eyes followed Keelan as he passed through. The apparent lack of security of the complex stood in direct contrast to the secrecy he knew the Mages valued so highly. Spirits help the man who tries to enter that arch when the Mages wanted their privacy!

As Keelan rode into the complex, he saw the large L-shaped Academy building that housed classrooms, laboratories, and housing for the Student-Mages. All the buildings in the complex were made of the same stacked stone, giving the place a feeling of comfortable elegance, if there was such a thing. The other massive building in the complex, also L-shaped and sitting opposite the Academy, held the living quarters for the Mages and staff. Just looking at those two buildings brought back a flood of memories of kindly old Atikus and his bushy eyebrows. Keelan couldn't help but grin as he thought of how Declan terrorized the poor Mages. No place was safe from that tiny puffy-headed demon.

Looming above the other buildings from the back of the complex with the Silver Mountains as its backdrop stood the tallest building in Saltstone—the Mages' Tower. Students were never allowed to enter the Tower, and Keelan often wondered what magical adventures waited inside. It was the subject of many students' frustrated daydreams throughout the centuries.

To the right of the arch, opposite the stables, was Keelan's destination, the Guild Hall. The Hall, as the Mages called it, was a long rectangular building. While the other buildings lacked adornment beyond the simple beauty of their stone, the Hall displayed carved symbols every ten paces around the exterior of the building. Each symbol was coated in gold and glittered in the sunlight. A giant polished set of double doors rested on hinges in the middle of the western wall. The ever-present Phoenix was etched across the doors, spanning both and consuming over nine of the doors' thirty-hand height. It was breathtaking and gave the Hall's entrance a majesty often reserved for palaces and kings. Glittering eyes of fist-sized rubies flared brightly every time a Mage entered the hall, as if welcoming that son or daughter of magic home.

Keelan walked through the doors into the well-lit foyer. He lived within the walls of the Mages' complex for over eight years but had never been in the Guild Hall. The walls were paneled in immense pieces of rich wood that almost shimmered while the floors, a black marble swirling with gray tones, gave a sense of perpetual motion. Large basin-like braziers were mounted to the walls six hands from the floor and were polished to the point of mirror-like clarity. Out of the top of each brazier danced a bright blue and white flame that grew and brightened when Keelan entered the room. He was tall enough to look down into the bowl of one brazier and was amazed to find it empty and carrying the same polished finish as the exterior. The flame actually floated in the air above its brass bowl. The curious little boy in him grinned. *Magic is seriously cool.*

Before he could wander too far from the entryway, a short, overweight man in deep-blue robes appeared through a doorway on the far wall. The man's eyes locked with Keelan's, causing his face to split into a wide smile, and he took off at full waddle, nearly knocking Keelan off his feet as he wrapped him in an embrace—at least as much as his little arms could wrap around the giant Guardsman.

"Keelan, they sent *you*! We've missed you around this musty old place. Welcome home, my boy." The Mage's eyes glistened with moisture.

Keelan took a step back, looked down at the Mage, and said with as much authority and mock offense as possible, "Mage Fergus, as I'm certain you know, it's unlawful to place hands on a member of the Guard. I will have to report this physical aggression at once!"

Fergus straightened as tall as his pudgy frame would allow and scowled at Keelan. "Young man, pick on someone in your own weight class. It's taken me two hundred years to get fat enough to squash you—and I'm not afraid to. Well, maybe after supper!"

Both men broke into a fit of laughter, and Keelan embraced the old wizard again. When they let go, there was a hint of moisture in Keelan's eyes. For once, the troubled boy deep in his heart smiled and stayed quiet.

"Uncle Ferg! I've missed all of you so much."

"This place has been *so* quiet without you and your little brother. You breathed new life into these stale buildings—and into the crusty old men who live here. We never knew how badly we needed the laughter of young children until Declan the Terrible streaked through these halls, quite literally." Fergus chuckled. "It feels like just yesterday that you both landed in our laps. Where is Declan these days? What sort of ridiculous trouble has he gotten himself into?"

Keelan drew a deep breath. "I think Dec's doing ok … finally. It's been hard to watch him struggle to find a path. We haven't seen each other in the two years since he joined the green squad, and I'm not sure where they have him stationed these days.

"Uncle Ferg, he always seemed so alive when he had people to terrorize; now he's surrounded by nothing but animals and trees. It feels like he's run away, and I don't know how to get him back." He ran a hand over his short-cropped hair, searching one of the flaming braziers for answers.

"He's nineteen now and still hasn't manifested a Gift. That bothers him a lot more than he's willing to admit, especially since he watched me join the Guard and enjoy some success over the past few years."

"Oh, Keelan, give him time. He's young still. It takes a while for many to find their way." Fergus patted Keelan's arm. "As for the Gift, that is troubling. You say he's nineteen now?"

"That's right," Keelan nodded.

"Well, if it hasn't come by now, I can't see that it will. Maybe being out in the middle of nowhere is just what he needs, rather than living in some town surrounded by shiny golden reminders everywhere."

A bell tolled somewhere outside, and Fergus's eyes popped wide. "Oh, no. Seeing you again made me forget about who's waiting—you know, just the people who run the country! Come on, the others are waiting for you in the Marble Room."

He led Keelan through a short hallway. There were no doors or openings in the wooden walkway, leaving Keelan with the impression that they were trapped in a richly appointed mahogany box. The only thing on the walls, other than braziers and their magical blue flames, were two small marble squares on each wall. Fergus placed his palm on the square to the left and a section of wood paneling shimmered out of existence.

Keelan's jaw dropped.

Fergus noticed and let out a chortle.

At the center of the room they entered stood an impossibly large marble table with puffy leather chairs that looked like they wanted to consume anyone who sat in them. As they walked further into the room, Keelan froze and stared at the table in disbelief. There were no seams, no joints, nothing to reveal how one piece fit into another. In fact, there was only *one* stone. He couldn't imagine what work of magic was used to craft such a piece from a single block. Now that he thought about it, how did they even get the thing into this room?

"So, the Beekeeper returns to the hive, does he?" A tall man in deep-blue robes mused over his shoulder from across the room without turning around, then took a sip of brownish liquor and sighed loudly.

The man set his glass down just quick enough to save it from imminent danger as Keelan bounded across the room, weaving in and out of the chairs, to wrap the old Mage in a tight hug. From the side of the room, Fergus's quiet sniffling turned into full-blown blubbering.

"Atikus, you're old as dirt!" Keelan lifted his adopted father off the ground.

"I *am* old as dirt!" Atikus bellowed, prying himself loose.

He held both of Keelan's shoulders, eyeing him up and down. His eyes settled into Keelan's, and his hands offered a fatherly squeeze. "And from the look of things, you are becoming the best of us. I'm so proud of you, Keelan."

That was all it took. Keelan lost it.

He gripped the old Mage again and wept with unbridled joy at the reunion. Despite their proximity in the city, they hadn't seen each other in nine years, since Keelan was sixteen and joined the Guard. He vowed at the time to return often, but the well-intended promises of youth often go unfulfilled when real life intervenes.

As Keelan was gathering himself, the wall opposite shimmered and the Arch Mage entered, followed by the Captain-Commander. Both wore serious expressions but pulled up short when they saw the scene before them. "Dev, it appears we've stepped into the middle of a family reunion. Keelan, are those tears staining your Guard blues?" Arch Mage Quin cracked a wry smile.

Keelan cleared his head and turned to Albius. "Sirs, forgive me. I wasn't expecting these two. Given the work in front of us, this is a welcome surprise."

Albius gave Keelan a rare smile and surveyed the group. "We thought you might enjoy this visit—at least this part of it. Now, Mage Fergus, if you would excuse us, we need to get started."

Fergus gave Keelan a wink, then a quick head bob to the Arch Mage, and walked out of the room, making the wall reappear in his wake.

Commander Albius walked to the large table. "Gentlemen, please take your seats. Lieutenant, why don't you start with your review of the Freeport notes?"

"Well, sir, there isn't much there. It appears the local constables did a cursory search of the route the victim took and spoke with a few shopkeepers whose businesses are along the way. No one reported seeing the victim or anything out of the ordinary. Like you said last night, it's been five days, and witnesses will be useless unless we're lucky enough to have a Gifted Memory among them. My team will head down there today, start with the local Guardsmen, and then conduct a more thorough investigation. But sir, this is going to be a tough one."

Albius nodded. "That's how I read the notes, too, but it was worth a shot to see if you would pick up on something I missed. You mentioned your teams. What were you thinking?"

Keelan shuffled his notes until he found the page with his teams. "For Freeport, I want Ridley Doa to take lead. He's a solid investigator, and I can trust him. Given the sensitivity of these cases, trust is at the top of the requirements. Arch Mage, I would like a Mage to join Ridley's team, preferably one with Telepathy so I can receive regular reports. If we discover that these cases are linked, coordination between the investigative teams will be important. Liv Went is my choice for the third Freeport team member.

"I'll lead the Saltstone investigation, along with Sil Wesser and Wil Buros. Wesser grew up tracking small game between here and Grove's Pass, while Buros has a Physical Gift with arms, specifically archery. He's the best marksman in the Guard. The Freeport team has some traveling ahead of them, but our team will get started on the local investigation as quickly as possible. If our timeline is accurate, we're already two days past the disappearance and I don't want to fall further behind."

The Arch Mage leaned forward. "Let me fill in your missing link. I anticipated your need for a Mage to accompany your investigation. I asked Atikus to step in."

Keelan had been wondering why Atikus was still in the meeting. His expression brightened at the mention of the old Mage being involved, but asked, "Arch Mage, I appreciate Atikus joining the team, but why choose a Mage with the Memory Gift rather than Telepathy?"

"Keelan, I know it's hard for you to believe after all this time, but I do have my secrets," Atikus said, his eyes twinkling. "Do you remember all those years ago, when you first came to us, I told you about magic and my Gift? You surprised me by asking about my double gold collar, so I explained what it meant and told you about my Gift for Memory. Then you surprised me again by failing to ask about my second Gift, which happens to be Telepathy."

Atikus grinned as if he'd pulled some grand prank on Keelan.

"That explains a lot." Keelan chuckled and rolled his eyes.

"Now that that's settled, we have one additional piece of information we need to give you before you start. I'm not even sure what it means. Atikus?" Albius passed the conversation to Atikus.

"We've identified that piece of cloth you found." Atikus tossed the scrap on the table.

Keelan leaned forward. This was the first likely lead, and it got his blood pumping.

"Are you familiar with The Children?" Atikus asked.

When Keelan shook his head no, Atikus continued, "They are a small, semi-religious cult that dates back to the time of the Kingdom War, over a thousand years ago. They were established after Empress Irina died and have persisted ever since. Between the Kingdom, Melucia, and our neighbors to the east, The Children are only estimated to have hundreds, perhaps a thousand members. There's no history of them causing trouble or even spreading whatever their beliefs are to others. They are small, secretive, and until now, were of no concern to anyone. The only thing noteworthy about them is that their members wear full-length brown robes made of the expensive material you found.

"We have no idea why one of The Children would visit Tiana's infirmary, or why they would be involved in her disappearance. But there is no doubt that the scrap belongs to one of them. I recognize it from my studies years ago and you know I never forget a detail. More importantly, another of our Mages also verified this information. This Mage can take an item, use a scrying bowl, and generate a weak image of the item's owner in the water. It doesn't last long and is often difficult to see, but this time there was no mistake. When he performed this magic on your scrap, the image of a man in a brown robe appeared. He was standing in a group of five others also wearing robes of The Children."

## 11

___

## BEL

After endless days stuffed in the false floor of a carriage, Bel was stiff, sore, mentally drained, and frightened. She was only lucid for a few minutes at a time before the man in the strange brown robe and twisted fox mask, whom she dubbed Fox-face, would force her back to sleep. Aside from fear, that man was her constant companion on the journey.

She lost track of the days early on but thought they had been traveling for a week when the carriage pulled to a stop and she was lifted out of her little cubbyhole. Two of her three captors had to hold her upright because her weakened legs refused to obey. Fox-face slipped a silky black hood over her head and drew it tight with a cord to keep it from slipping off. Even if she hadn't been so groggy and her vision so blurry, she wouldn't have had time to see much around her before the blackness of the hood blinded her.

Bel's Empathic Gift was in overdrive, and she was too tired to shut out the emotions slamming into her mind. Her three captors had shifted from wariness tinged with fear to excitement and something else. Anticipation? Yes, that's what it was. She shuddered.

As they moved from the carriage, Bel could also sense a shift in the air. Freeport was always warm, bordering on tropical in the summer months. In contrast, the air here was crisp and cool. If she hadn't been in constant fear for her life, the change might have been refreshing. She heard a door creak open and was shuffled inside a building, through a series of hallways, before reaching their destination. Her hood was removed, and she watched as Fox-face took out a long, sharp-looking dagger. Bel jumped back, bumping against the wall behind her. The man held up the knife and an open palm in a gesture of peace. He used the knife to mimic the motion of cutting her rope, as if it were on his own wrists. Bel breathed deeply and leaned forward with her arms in front of her. She was a little surprised when Fox-face sliced her bonds, freeing her angry, raw wrists. Without a word or gesture, he bent down and did the same with the rope around her legs. She rubbed her wrists to get the blood flowing as the man gave her a deep bow and backed out of the room, leaving her alone. The last thing she heard before his footsteps faded was the thud of a large metal bar sliding into place across the outside of the door.

Bel took a few deep breaths to steady herself. She'd spent so many days and nights in the bottom of a carriage that it felt a little strange standing still without the ground moving underneath. She imagined that's how sailors felt when they came home after a long voyage. That thought conjured daydreams of home in her mind's eye—the harbor, the squawking gulls, the crystal-blue water and bright-white sails—scenes that made tears fall once again.

She looked around the room and realized she was in a suite appointed with every luxury imaginable. The floors and walls were made of interlocking gray stone blocks. While the walls were rough, the stone of the floors had been polished smooth, giving it an almost mirror-like sheen. A massive bed rested against one wall. Four tall pillars of wood at each corner were carved with intricate vines and leaves running the entire length of the wood. But it was the headboard that took her breath. The enormous wooden piece was more art than furniture, stretching nearly to the ceiling. Carved into the rich wood was an artistic representation of the Phoenix symbol of magic. The breast feathers and eyes of the hallowed bird were inlaid with a pearl-like stone that sparkled in the candlelight, while the four flames at the base were decorated with deep-maroon gemstones, giving the symbolic fire a life and intensity she had never before seen in the emblem. The bed itself was covered in rich cloths of gold, maroon, and black. Small tables of the same cherry wood sat to either side and held lit candles cradled in polished golden stands shaped like giant leaves.

A massive fireplace made of exquisite marble that swirled with white, black, and bluish waves consumed the opposite wall. Someone had anticipated her arrival as there was a pleasant fire crackling warmth through the room. In front of the fireplace sprawled an elegant couch and a pair of puffy side chairs, creating a cozy sitting area that Bel thought odd since no one in the masked group seemed to speak much. Against the back wall sat an extravagant dressing table with a towering mirror. This was a room made for royalty, not a prisoner.

Bel was baffled.

The stillness of the large room was unsettling, yet also oddly comforting after so many days on the road in a cramped compartment. Bel tossed her shoes in the corner, frowning at one that was now missing its ornate silver buckle, then pulled the lush bedspread back and stretched out on the bed, staring at the rough stone ceiling.

This was the first time she could really think clearly without the blue poison clouding her mind. She thought back to the day she was captured, trying to piece together what had happened. It felt like trying to grab fog with her hands, but she forced herself to concentrate.

She remembered being excited. She was supposed to meet her parents for dinner for … something.

She rubbed her eyes and took a few deep breaths. The fog finally cleared.

*It felt strange, watching herself walk up to the entrance of the Freeport Mages' Guild as the day replayed in her mind. The sun shone brightly in the cloudless sky, and there was a salty tang in the air. A perfect day.*

She tried to focus on what happened next, what she did that day, but her memories were hazy, her mind clouded … waking in a wooden prison. A carriage? The *bottom* of a carriage.

*The carriage rattled endlessly, climbing hour after hour, up a twisty road before starting a slow descent. She was awake for most of the trek and could smell pine every-*

*where. When they finally leveled out, Fox-face opened her
cage and made her drink that syrupy water again, this time
a full canteen rather than just a mug. She nearly gagged.*

Everything between that moment and when she arrived
in this room was blank. Sleep rescued her from the
memory, and she lost herself in a dream of crystal water
and white sails.

———————

THE GRINDING SOUND OF THE HEAVY BAR MOVING FROM ITS
resting place pried her awake. She bolted upright in the bed
and stared at the door as two brown-robed figures entered
the room, one wearing a mask of an angry-faced eagle and
the other a snarling wolf with feathered wings for ears.
Wolf carried a shimmering golden gown, beautiful in its
simplicity and the unnatural way light glinted off its fabric.
Eagle carried a small basket with two different soaps, a
round orange sponge, an ornate silver hairbrush, fluffy
white towels embroidered with the Phoenix in golden
thread, and several pins that Bel assumed were for her hair.
They motioned for her to join them at the washing basin
where they bathed her from head to toe. There was an odd
gentleness in the way they washed her, a strange reverence.
What she felt through her Empathic Gift was more baffling
than anything so far. The masked figures' emotions over-
flowed with *respect* and *awe* … for her.

*Nothing makes sense anymore.*

Satisfied with the bathing ritual, Wolf picked up the
brush and began wrestling with the tangles that had devel-

oped during her time in the carriage. She—Bel assumed Wolf was a woman from her smooth hands—brushed out her tiara of braids, leaving her vibrant hair to fall past her shoulders. Bel was again surprised at the caress of the brushstrokes, the gentleness of her jailers. She was their prisoner, and yet it was almost like a sister was caring for her.

They helped her dress in the silky gown that fit perfectly. The fabric was exotic and smooth, perhaps the most comfortable thing she had ever worn. She looked down and was stunned to see the crest of the Phoenix interwoven across the front of the dress in a lighter shade of gold. Despite everything, one question popped into her head. *Will they let me keep the gown when this is all over?*

Bel rolled her eyes at her own silliness and looked down at the marks on her wrists, and her humor vanished.

Eagle took her elbow gently and walked her to the giant mirror so Bel could see their finished product. Her hands flew to her mouth as she scanned her reflection. The woman staring back was stunning, the elegant simplicity of the gown accentuating her well-proportioned frame. For the crowning touch, Eagle reached into a pocket and pulled out a necklace that made Bel's eyes pop. The entire chain of the necklace sparkled with inlaid diamonds, leading to a fist-sized sapphire pendant. The sapphire was cut into a teardrop and surrounded by diamonds. As she looked closer, Bel noticed that the sapphire shimmered faintly with some sort of magical aura.

Eagle reached around Bel and placed the piece over her neck, snapping it into place, then spoke a few words in a language Bel didn't recognize. The sapphire's aura grew into a bright, warm light, and the stone hummed against her chest. Eagle reached into the other pocket and presented Bel with a small vial filled with a clear bluish liquid, motioning for her to drink. She hesitated a moment but saw no alternative and downed the vial. Rivulets of warmth trickled down her body.

Wolf placed one hand on Bel's shoulder and motioned toward the door with the other, then Eagle led the way, with Wolf trailing behind her. The stones of the floor in the halls were smooth and cold against Bel's bare feet, but walking felt good to her knotted muscles. They went about twenty paces before turning right into a massive hallway. Hung along the walls were detailed paintings of various masks like the ones worn by the robed figures. Bel strolled slowly, taking in every painting, before stopping when she saw one of Eagle's mask. She reached up and traced the lines of the painting with her fingers and turned a questioning look to Eagle. Eagle remained silent, but Bel thought her eyes hinted at a grin.

When they reached the end of the hallway, the trio was greeted by a pair of massive highly polished doors. At the center of each door, about eye-level, the familiar form of the Phoenix rising from its four-plumed fire was deeply etched—but with one significant addition to this version. At the top of each Phoenix, inlaid in silver, gold, and glittering diamonds, was a crown.

The Phoenix always gave Bel chills, but the crown puzzled her. First, it was against the law to change *anything* in that symbol. It was practically religious and was treated with reverence around the world, unlike any other emblem. Second, Bel had always been taught by the Mages that magic was a tool, a servant in the hands of its master. Putting a crown on the Phoenix made magic the master— and that was *heresy*!

The doors opened and Bel's jaw dropped.

The room she now faced was at least three hundred paces long. Lining both sides of the chamber, massive columns made of polished black-and-white marble swirled up into the darkness. In front of each column was a large brazier lit with a flickering blue flame. Somewhere above, there must have been more hanging braziers or an oculus, because the opposite end of the room was well lit. The space between the columns and the side walls were dark and shadowy, contrasting with the brightness of the rest of the room.

At the far end, a two-tiered stage that spanned two-thirds of the width of the room captured her eye. Three steps led from the floor to the first tier. Two braziers stood against the far wall at the back of this landing while two others were positioned near its front. In the center of the stage, reigning over the massive chamber, was an enormous throne made of pure-white stone.

Another set of three steps led from the throne to another landing that held an immense statue of a woman. She stared into the distance as if gazing at the peak of a faraway mountain. The statue was made of the same pure-white marble as the throne and wore a flowing golden gown exactly like the one Bel wore. A crown like the one Bel saw on the doors rested on her brow. In her right hand, she held a long silver staff, and in her left, held high above her head, an orb that glowed a deep, bloody crimson. A flash of color around the statue's neck made the last of Bel's breath catch. It was a teardrop of brilliant blue that glowed brighter than anything else in the room.

As they stood in the doorway, Eagle motioned for Bel to wait, then pulled a tasseled cord that hung just inside. From somewhere high above, a bell pealed, sending vibrations through the floor and making the light of the braziers dance. The doors on the side walls opened, and masked figures filed into the room in orderly lines. By the time the footfalls ceased, over four hundred had assembled in the hall that somehow still seemed vast and empty. The figures formed into lines that ran the length of the chamber and were facing inward, creating the impression of a grand walkway from the doors to the marble throne. Each figure wore a robe and mask like the ones Bel had seen before— wolves, birds of prey, stalking cats, and variations of many other beasts. Most were combinations of various animals and birds, creating an eerie landscape.

Just when Bel thought things couldn't get any stranger, a tall, slim figure emerged from behind the statue wearing the same robes as the others in the room, with one exception—they were bloody red like the orb in the statue's hand. Instead of an animal's face, this figure wore a mask of blank skin with only eye holes to break up the featureless face.

Skin-mask, as Bel named her, strolled purposefully around the statue and down the stairs to stand behind the throne. Once in place, she raised both arms, palms toward the ceiling as if lifting some heavy burden. The hundreds of assembled figures erupted in a discordant hum that undulated like the dying cry of some ancient beast.

Eagle came to life, gently placing a hand in the small of Bel's back and motioning her forward, and the trio paraded toward the altar, with Bel's robed escorts careful to ensure she was always in the lead. As they reached the first row of humming observers, the robed figures on either side dropped to one knee, whispered "Mistress," and bowed their heads. Bel faltered a step but continued the march, and by the time they reached the first set of stairs, everyone except Bel, her escorts, and Skin-mask was on bended knee.

The humming vanished.

The snapping of the magical flames disappeared.

Silence blanketed every corner of the massive hall.

Bel had forgotten about the vial of blue liquid, but it had not forgotten her, and she started feeling dizzy and seeing double. Eagle nudged her up the stairs but remained on floor level. Once she reached the throne, both Eagle and Wolf dropped to a knee and bowed their heads.

Bel tried to focus.

Skin-mask stared at her, but not with the emptiness of the other figures. There was a spark of life in her eyes as she watched Bel with hungry interest. Now that they were close, Bel could see the mask she wore—such perfect, blank detail, as if actual skin …

Time stood still as the magical potion seized control of Bel's body, yet leaving her mind free to process everything around her. Skin-mask surveyed the room and clapped once, and everyone stood and moved into large semi-circular rows facing the throne, hemming Bel and her two escorts in. Wolf and Eagle were suddenly at her side on the top step, holding her limp body upright.

The humming of hundreds began again, somehow amplified. Somewhere in the distance, the rhythmic booming of drums added urgency to the jarring humming that filled the hall. She tried to resist, but her body betrayed her.

Terror gripped her heart.

Tears formed.

She erupted in a soundless scream as her eyes darted back and forth.

Eagle and Wolf sat her on the throne, crossing her hands in her lap so they stayed in place. From a distance, Bel looked like a queen holding court, with hundreds of besotted followers surrounding the base of her majestic throne. Inside, her Empathic Gift was bombarded by primal feelings of hunger and excitement and anticipation from the surrounding mob. But what she sensed from the Skin-mask chilled her soul—pure, unrelenting hatred and desire to dominate.

Skin-mask began muttering.

The chanting swelled.

The drums beat louder and faster …

As Bel's consciousness faded from her grasp, Skin-mask walked around the throne carrying a crown, a replica of the one she had seen on the giant doors above the Phoenix. She stood facing the throne, placed the crown on Bel's head, and dropped to both knees, touching her forehead to the second step of the dais. The sound of hundreds kneeling flooded her ears.

The room held its breath.

There was no sound but the beating of those incessant drums that thrummed faster and faster.

Without warning, Skin-mask reached into her robe and drew a long, needle thin blade. She plunged it with all her strength into Bel's chest, twisting the dagger as she pushed. Pain screamed through Bel's already weakened body as her heart seized at the sudden intrusion. Her vision blurred, and she lost all balance, toppling from the throne to the steps. Eagle snatched the crown from her head before it could fall and held it with outstretched arms toward Skin-mask.

Immobile on the cold stone stair, Bel stared up at the orb held high in the statue's hand, and watched in horror as it grew in brilliance, until its red-black light enveloped the massive chamber in a pulsing glow that mirrored the rhythm of *her* slowing heartbeat. The room dimmed in Bel's eyes, and her limbs numbed. Adrenaline drove a steady flow of blood from the wound in her chest to the stairs, her beleaguered heart racing toward its end.

Skin-mask took the crown from Eagle, held it high for all to see, and placed it on her own head. She turned to face her congregation. The crowd chanted and undulated in a frenzied ecstasy that swelled and sped in cadence with the drums. Bel glimpsed the crown and the seven enormous diamonds embedded in its base, four of which were pulsing dark crimson like the statue's orb.

She was awake through it all, thanks to the bluish potion. She couldn't feel her life draining away, but the blood flowing on the stairs below told her she was dying. In that nightmarish moment, a peaceful calm entered her soul. Her pain and fear and racing heart stilled. She closed her eyes. Unbidden, her mind carried her to the docks of her home, and she stared lovingly at the soaring white birds and billowing sails. The rush of waves rolling and crashing echoed in her ears. In odd contrast to the surrounding horror, she smiled.

When Bel's spirit finally fled her lifeless body, the fifth stone on Skin-mask's crown turned from diamond-clear to bloody red, then flared in unison with its brethren. The last sound Bel heard was the deafening cheers of the robed mob and the frenzied chanting of one name.

"Irina … Irina … Irina …"

# 12

## ATIKUS

A few hours after the meeting at the Mages' Guild, the trio of Ridley, Atikus, and Liv rode out of Saltstone's southern gate toward Freeport. Atikus's Gift had already proved useful when he sent word to the Guildmaster of the Freeport Guild that they were on their way and asked him to make preparations with a few of the local mages. Unfortunately, the Gift of Telepathy's one-way nature limited the conversation—Freeport Mages couldn't respond or even acknowledge the instructions.

The team arrived at the stables of the Freeport Guild several hours after dark. A young boy in a dusty-blue Mage-Apprentice robe took their horses, while a middle-aged snow-topped man wearing Mage's robes walked out to greet them.

"Mage Atikus Dani, in the flesh!" he beamed. "It's been at least thirty years since you've graced our door. Come, let's knock the dust off and put some whisky in."

Atikus returned the warm smile and clasped arms with his brother-Mage. "Pel, it has been too long. Please allow me to introduce our illustrious leader, Guardsman Ridley Doa, and his associate, Guardsman Liv Wint. I know Lord Crim requested the best Saltstone could offer, but we're all you get," Atikus added with a theatrical wink. "And that whisky sounds wonderful if it might also come with a side of pork. I'm starving, and I'll bet you've never seen anyone eat like young Ridley here. He's ready to chew on his horse after that ride. Good thing your young groom took the poor animal before he could do any damage."

Liv gave Ridley a questioning look. He was struggling to maintain his composure after Atikus's little act and shrugged his shoulders before grabbing their bags and following the Mages into the hall.

As they walked through the entryway, Pel turned to the group. "I'm sure you'd like to clean up a bit before supper, maybe even change. I know *we'd* like you to. That should give cook time to get something hot on the table. Let's say thirty minutes in the dining hall?"

Pel showed each of them to their rooms, then explained that the door at the end of the hallway led to the dining hall.

Ridley walked into his room and set his pack down by a square table in the corner. The room was simple, yet well appointed. A small stone fireplace had been lit in anticipation of their arrival. A stack of cut wood rested in a black metal basket, and the dancing flames in the fireplace gave the room a warm, cozy feeling.

Ever the constable, Ridley took a moment to inspect

every corner. Finding nothing unusual, he turned to the washbasin on the table and was surprised to find warm, almost steaming water. He rinsed off and changed into a pair of tan trousers, a simple white long-sleeve shirt, and a blue coat. The team had discussed the need for some discretion while investigating in the port city and decided that both Ridley and Liv should wear civilian clothing. Answers would be easier to get out of people if they weren't intimidated by a uniform bearing the capital's crest.

Satisfied with his change, Ridley sat on the bed and turned to his constant companion—a small leather-bound notebook. He reviewed the information they had received from local investigators and scribbled a list of questions for Pel and his Mages. A knock on his door startled him out of his thoughts.

"Ridley, you ready? Atikus and I are walking to the dining room," Liv called through the door.

When the door opened, he froze. Plain, ordinary, almost manly Liv was stunningly beautiful. She had changed out of her uniform and now wore a floor-length light-blue dress that accented her azure eyes. Her boxy uniform hid her figure, but the dress did the exact opposite, clinging to every well-toned curve. Dark rusty curls fell to her shoulders, with one landing dangerously near the wide open neckline that teased what lay beneath.

"Uh … Liv. You … uh … don't look like a constable." Ridley struggled to keep his eyes above her shoulders.

"I think that was a compliment. Thanks?" she smirked. "I hate this thing. Makes it hard to ride and even harder to run, but it should help us blend in down here. We can play the husband-and-wife routine, and Atikus can be our doting grandfather."

"Hey! Let's make that *father*, young lady. Any more cracks about my age and you'll go to bed hungry." He wiggled his bushy brows before turning toward the dining room.

"Sure, Pop. Whatever you say," Liv replied.

Atikus barked a laugh as Ridley shook his head and smiled. This wasn't like any investigation he could remember.

The smell of roasted chicken slammed into them as they entered the dining room. A wide variety of cooked vegetables covered the center of a long rectangular table that sat beside two similar tables. The light wood paneling and large candles held in silver mounted brackets created a welcoming, comfortable atmosphere. The flame on each candle was the same magical blue fire Ridley had seen in the braziers of the Guild in Saltstone, though he had never seen it atop a candle before.

Pel and two other Mages came through the door on the opposite wall and greeted their guests. The only conversation that survived the start of the meal was that of a fork and knife arguing over a piece of chicken. Maybe he was just starving after a long day on a horse, but Ridley couldn't remember a roasted chicken that tasted so good— and don't get him started on those buttery, garlicky, peppery potatoes and other veggies.

Pel noticed the rapture on his face. "So, Constable Ridley, do you find our cook acceptable?"

It took Ridley a few seconds to clear that last bite. "If I didn't know better, I might think someone used magic to make this taste so good. Mage Pel, this is the best meal I've had in a long time."

"Oh, but magic *was* used in your meal. Our cook has a unique Gift that none of us quite understand. It involves enhancement of flavors. He can't alter what something tastes like, but he can accentuate what is already there. I guess that's why we call him Mage Salt," Pel said, raising a glass of wine to his lips.

"Salt? I like that. Funny little Guild. I might have to trade in my uniform for a robe if this is what Guild life is like." Ridley stabbed another potato.

"We have our moments—and you would be welcome."

They finished the meal with a blueberry pie that made Ridley's eyes roll backward. Atikus, perpetually consumed with thoughts of food, never said a word as he focused on crushing his meal as though it were an enemy of the state. He licked blueberry juice off his fingers and noticed the group staring at him.

He turned to Liv, who was sitting to his left. "Dear daughter, I believe you've embarrassed us with your table etiquette."

"Oh, dear *father*, the blueberry clinging desperately to that beard of yours might tell a different tale."

Ridley spit a mouthful of wine as a laugh escaped, and the rest of the table's occupants devolved into fits of laughter.

After a few minutes, everyone caught their breath, and the conversation turned to the reason for their visit.

"So, Atikus, I understand you're here asking after Bel. She's a sweet girl. I've worked with her since she was a young thing, helping her learn to navigate her Gift," Pel said.

Atikus leaned forward and put his elbows on the table. "I suppose we should talk business. Ridley, you're leading this investigation, so why don't you start. We can jump in as we have questions."

While this wasn't their rehearsed introduction, Ridley appreciated the way Atikus steered the conversation and deferred to him, despite how much younger he was than the Mage.

He pulled out his leather journal and leafed through a few pages before looking up at Pel. "I've read the reports from the local Constables. They did a decent job with what little they had but didn't find much that would be helpful in picking up a trail. Has the Guild learned anything new since you were alerted of our visit? And do any of your Mages have a Gift that might help us locate Bel or recreate her route after she left this hall?"

Pel nodded. "Yes, but the information we gathered was not obtained by any magical means. A girl on staff who was a close friend to Bel stepped forward. She said she saw Bel leave through the back door of the Guild Hall and walk down the alleyway that runs behind the buildings, parallel to the main road,"

Ridley sat back. "That doesn't make any sense. The local Guards have a witness who said she walked Bel out the front door and watched her go down the main road. That was around 15:00."

"Yes, that's what we were told, but this girl is unequivocal. And her version of events makes more sense, as the main road is well lit and surrounded by people walking in and out of the shops. Even with magic, it would've been difficult for someone to take Bel from that road without anyone seeing something. The alley is quiet, unlit, and faces a large wooded area,"

Ridley scribbled notes. The conversation continued with Ridley and Liv peppering the Mages regarding the alley, the businesses along that route, and who else in the Guild might have seen Bel and lied about it. After an hour, Atikus stretched and yawned, hinting that it might be time to free their hosts for the evening.

Ridley caught the hint. "Mage Pel, you have been most gracious and helpful. Thank you."

He then turned to Atikus and Liv. "The meal and conversation have my mind racing, and I won't be able to sleep. I think I'll go walk the alley Pel described and see if anything jumps out. Why don't you two get some rest so we can start early in the morning?"

Everyone rose and took their leave while Atikus tried to sneak another piece of pie from the table.

Liv turned with a grin. "Pop, Ma would never let you have another piece this late. You know how gassy you get."

Laughter echoed in the dining room as the group walked out.

Ridley escorted Atikus and Liv to their rooms, then went outside where he found a bin with torches, lit one, and walked around to the back of the building in search of the door that Bel had exited. The back of the Guild Hall opened to a dirt alleyway. Across the alley was a densely wooded area that ran the length of the alley, as far as he could see in the dark.

He turned and walked down the alley in the direction Bel would have traveled. It would be impossible to conduct a thorough search by torchlight, but he wanted to at least get a feel for the place.

The Guild sat apart from the row of shops, and Ridley had to walk some fifty yards before reaching the back side of the first one. From there, the narrow buildings were packed together tightly with only a foot or two between them. This was the most upscale Merchant area in Freeport, where the elite came to shop and dine, but the back of the shops looked the same as those in the poorest neighborhood. Flecked paint, chipped wood, and overflowing rubbish bins gave the alley a grungy look. Each building had back door, but only a few of the doors held any label or marking.

The alley itself was mostly dirt and pebbles and appeared to be infrequently traveled. With each step, the path gripped his print and held it, letting Ridley know that tracks would remain if undisturbed. It was dry, so he didn't think there had been any rain in the last couple of days to erase possible prints.

He walked past a building marked *Cobbler*, then *Moira's Naughty Nighties*, then *Men's Grooming House*.

The next few doors were blank until he reached a door with chipped blue paint that read, *"Gil's Royal Tailoring"* in faded black script. This was the building the serving girl said was Bel's destination. He searched the outer wall of the building, then held his torch in between the building and its neighbors on either side. There wasn't enough space for a person to squeeze through, and nothing looked like it had moved in years.

He turned away from the building toward the woods. When looked down, something caught his eye. Deep grooves in the dirt headed off the trail and into the woods. He couldn't see the tracks continue on the forest floor, but he could tell by broken branches and disturbed leaves that the tracks led in that direction. When he knelt to get a closer look at the tracks, something small reflected a glint of torchlight back at him. He brushed leaves away, revealing a gold signet ring engraved with a crest he recognized from the conversation at dinner. It belonged to his missing victim. She must have dropped it for someone to find, leaving behind the only clue she could. *Good girl, Bel*, thought Ridley, scooping up his prize.

He pocketed the ring and took another walk around the back of the tailor's shop before deciding to return in the morning with his team. The walk back passed quickly as his mind raced. The leads weren't much, but they were more than they had a few hours ago.

---

THE NEXT MORNING, ATIKUS, LIV, AND RIDLEY WERE greeted in the dining room by spicy smoked bacon and biscuits. The table was also littered with platters of eggs and an assortment of fruit and bowls of nuts. Pel was already seated, attacking an overfilled plate that struggled to contain a sample of everything on the table. Atikus grabbed a plate from the stack and began piling mountains of food.

As the group ate, Ridley filled them in on what he saw the night before.

He turned to Pel. "Would you ask the local Guard to return to the rear of the tailor's shop with an experienced tracker and see if they can follow the wheel marks? That may at least give us an idea of the direction the kidnappers went."

"Let me send someone to do that right now." Pel wiped his mouth with a napkin as he stood.

He motioned to the serving boy who was leaning by the door and instructed him to find his apprentice. When the boy left the room, he turned back to Ridley. "Let's talk about that ring you found. I know the Saltstone Mages failed to learn anything with their scrying, but I'd like to try again using that ring. We don't have a focus tower like they do, but I believe an item that was so highly personal to Bel might yield more information."

"Anything you find will be more than we have right now. Atikus?" Ridley turned a questioning glance at the old Mage.

Atikus nodded slowly. "It's worth a try. When our Mages used the scrying bowl in the tower, we didn't even get a ripple, much less a picture. They believed Bel was alive at the time based on the energy given off by the items, but something was blocking their scrying sight, and they couldn't break through. Even if we can't pinpoint a location, the ring may give us some additional clues and confirm that Bel is still alive. Pel, I would like to help with the scrying, link with the Mage performing the spell. With my Telepathy and greater magical strength, we may be able to break through whatever is shielding our sight."

"Alright. We will need to make some preparations. Meet me in the lab in an hour. You remember where it is?" Pel asked.

"Ha. The one thing I can't remember is the last time someone asked me 'Do you remember?'" Atikus snorted. "You forget that I can't forget, even the things you've forgotten."

*Mage humor. Hilarious,* Ridley thought to himself as he rolled his eyes at Liv, despite the wide smiles that escaped both of their lips.

According to Atikus, the scrying would take about an hour to prepare and then another hour or two to complete, so Liv and Ridley decided to pursue the other lines of inquiry and return to hear the Mages' results later in the day. They began with interviews of both the serving girl who had revealed Bel's backdoor departure and the young apprentice who'd lied to the local constables about showing Bel to the front door. The latter was in tears, horrified that her deception might've brought harm to her friend. She explained that Bel was meeting her parents for a very important dinner to discuss her betrothal, so she'd sneaked out the side door to visit the tailor's shop. She'd wanted a new gown for the occasion, and she'd hoped to surprise her parents. She had asked the apprentice to cover for her. The girl was clearly worried about Bel and offered to do anything to help in their search. Unfortunately, those interviews were dead ends in their search for new leads.

The pair of investigators then retraced the back-alley route, looking for any clues Ridley might have missed under torchlight. When they reached the tailor's shop door, Liv walked over to the ruts in the dirt and began following them into the woods. With daylight, the pair could see that the trees were old and tall, spaced several paces apart, allowing their roots to grow and intertwine. The floor of the little forest was leaves, dirt, and the occasional shrub or tangle of vines, leaving a visible path of the wheel marks.

After a few minutes, Liv turned back to Ridley. "The locals should've been able to follow those tracks to a major road. They'll at least be able to give us an idea which direction they headed. I doubt we'll get much more than that."

"That might be useful if this case is linked to the missing Healer in Saltstone."

Liv walked to where Ridley stood, careful to not disturb the tracks. After a brief re-inspection of the back side of the building, they walked a block before finding a break in the buildings that allowed them to access the storefronts. Not long after, they walked through the front door of the tailor's shop where they were greeted by a short graying woman wearing thick spectacles and a tangle of measuring tape around her neck.

"Please come in and make yourselves comfortable. I'm

right in the middle of a measurement, so look around a bit and I'll be back in a few moments," the woman smiled graciously.

Liv immediately liked this woman.

The walls were lined with dresses and coats, display items illustrating what might be possible for Freeport's wealthy customers.

Sometime later, the woman who'd greeted them returned and curtsied. "Please forgive the wait. It's the busy season for us, and so many young women are getting married this year. Now, young miss, is that what's brought you my way?"

Ridley chuckled a little too loudly at the brightness of Liv's blush, earning him a stern look and a raised eyebrow. "On, no, ma'am. We are here on official business. Guard business," Liv said.

"Oh. My goodness. I just assumed with your fine dress and handsome escort that you were a couple. I hope I haven't stepped in something." She straightened her dress and began fidgeting with a thimble that materialized from her pocket.

"No, ma'am." Liv smiled and softened her voice to put the woman at ease. "Not at all. Do you recall making a dress for Bel Crim recently? She's the daughter of Lord Crim."

"Oh yes, I do. That family has been a loyal customer for many years. We spent hours with her just the other day, even brought in a hairdresser. She was so excited and couldn't stop babbling about some dinner she had that evening. I wasn't paying much attention. Such a sweet girl but could talk your ears off. I saw in the papers she's gone missing. You don't think that had anything to do with my shop, surely?"

"That's what we're trying to learn—and to make sure she gets home safely to her parents. They're worried sick, as you might imagine," Liv said. "Would you mind telling us about her visit that day? We never know what little detail might fit with other things we've learned."

It took the dressmaker a minute to gather herself and recount the events of that day. Liv and Ridley were impressed with the level of detail she could recall, down to the stitch patterns Bel preferred, but there was nothing surprising in her recitation. The one thing she told them that stood out was that Bel asked to leave through the back door rather than the front, stating that she wanted to avoid running into her parents and ruining her grand entrance.

Liv stayed with the dressmaker as Ridley spoke with her assistant in the back of the shop, who confirmed the same series of events and became emotional talking about Bel's disappearance. He returned to the front and nodded toward the door at Liv. They thanked the dressmaker and asked her to seek them at the Mages' Guild if she remembered anything else, then took their leave.

As they walked back to the Guild Hall, Ridley asked, "So, any read on either of those two?"

"They're sincere. No whiff of deception. I think the shop's a dead end, other than the tracks out back and the ring."

It was lunchtime when they walked into the Guild Hall, so they headed straight for the dining room again. Atikus,

Pel, and two other mages were already devouring large plates of food. Atikus used his fork, still saddled with a roasted turnip, to motion them to sit.

"Father, we met the most skilled seamstress today. Perhaps, after all these wonderful meals, she might let a little room out of those robes of yours. I believe the twins are kicking down there." Liv poked Atikus with her elbow as she sat next to him.

Pel was so caught by the comment that a piece of turkey shot out of his laughing mouth and caught Atikus square in the forehead. The room erupted.

The next half hour was spent eating and laughing, the group having bonded over the flying turkey.

After a half hour, Atikus reined in the conversation. "Ridley, Liv, I'm afraid we were successful in our efforts with the ring."

"That's great … Why don't you sound happy about it?"

Pel stepped in to explain. "Our Mage was successful in creating a scrying link using the ring. He could sense Bel's presence and even ascertain a general direction and distance. Just when we were feeling good, his link snapped. Worse, the ring's aura faded in front of us, as if Bel's life drained away before our eyes."

"I'm sorry, Pel, my Gift has nothing to do with scrying. Can you explain that to an amateur?" Liv asked.

"Of course. Of course," he said, gathering his thoughts. "When an item is personal to someone, it takes on the aura of that person. The longer it is worn or used, the stronger the pairing of the auras becomes. In simple terms, the ring's natural aura, which is very weak to begin with, is replaced by a linked version of Bel's aura. Think of it as a mirror of her own."

Pel lost himself for a minute before continuing. "She had worn the ring only a few days ago. It was a family heirloom, and their auras were intertwined. What we witnessed in the scrying was Bel's life force fading. Her location and distance were hazy, but we know one thing for certain. Bel is dead."

Ridley and Liv both sat back in their chairs, shoulders slumped. Their mission was to locate and save Bel, yet here they were on day two, and she was dead.

Pel and Atikus spent the next hour explaining the process of scrying and the information they had gathered. Bel had been taken from Freeport, traveling west to somewhere beyond the mountains at the border of Melucia and the Kingdom. They explained that as the distance grew, the accuracy of the scrying became more unclear and "beyond the mountains" was about as specific as they could get.

Pel and his Mages excused themselves, allowing Atikus, Ridley and Liv to discuss their next steps alone. Ridley first asked Atikus to send word to Keelan via his Telepathy. The one-way nature of that communication was frustrating and wouldn't allow Keelan to give them direction, but at least he would know what they had learned. They hoped that the information might help save the Saltstone Healer, since Bel was now lost to them. The trio then decided that there wasn't any point to remaining in Freeport and they would return to the capital. It was just a couple of hours past noon, and each of them wanted to get home before it got too late.

A quick half-hour later, they had gathered their packs and thanked their hosts. Pel presented each of them with a small bag of bread, dried fruit, meats, and vegetables that Mage Salt had prepared for their ride home. Atikus grinned like a schoolboy as he tied his little bag of goodies to his horse. By 21:00, they were back in the capital and headed to their respective homes.

## 13

### KEELAN

Keelan's team revisited the infirmary, then spent the rest of the afternoon combing Tiana's house and the grounds surrounding it. The difference in how the two locations were treated by the intruders was confounding. In the infirmary, the team found nothing missing, even though the storage room had been ransacked. But Tiana's house was stripped bare, without even a piece of furniture left. It was as if she had never lived there.

As they walked around the back of the property, a brown and white horse snorted and walked toward them, burying its nose into Keelan's chest.

"Friendly guy, aren't ya?" Keelan scratched its head between the ears.

Sil walked up and ran her hand along the horse's back. "She's a beauty. Tiana had good taste."

"Bet she knows what happened here. Wish she could talk."

Sil looked up. "About that, sir …"

"You're kidding, right?" Keelan gaped.

Sil shrugged sheepishly.

"I spent years as a tracker. That's well documented, and we talked about it when you picked me for the team. But you never asked about my Gift, which isn't tracking," Sil gave him a little smirk. "My Gift allows me to talk with wildlife."

Keelan whistled. "Don't think I've ever known anyone with that one. Care to make introductions?"

"That's not quite how it works. *Talk* is a word used by people who don't understand the Gift. It's more like sharing images, impressions, or emotions. I can visualize things or people and share those images with an animal. Unless the beast is particularly stubborn, they'll return images or emotions in reply. The intelligence of the animal is the crucial factor in how clear or understandable the images are. Sometimes, I can even send emotions to get an animal to calm or react in different ways." Sil continued stroking the horse's neck.

"OK. Not sure I get all that, but why don't you talk to Bessie here and see what we can learn?"

The horse snorted and turned from Keelan toward Sil.

"Sure. But she didn't like being called Bessie. No idea what her name is, but she didn't like that, sir." Sil grinned.

Keelan smiled and shook his head.

Sil removed a glove and placed her hand on the horse's neck. *Not*-Bessie leaned into the contact, having decided she trusted her. Sil closed her eyes and was motionless for several minutes.

Sil first thought of Tiana, conjuring images of the Healer

in her blue smock, willing them into the horse's mind. A feeling of intense warmth flowed back through the link, then changed to something akin to longing. Sil changed tactics and thought of the empty house, mentally walking through the now bare rooms. The horse's emotions shifted to frenzied fear. Fuzzy images of three men in simple shirts and trousers carrying furniture fluttered to mind. Behind the men, Sil saw something odd. Another man stood watching the others. He wore a brown robe and mask that she couldn't see clearly. The horse fidgeted and danced, breaking the link.

Sil relayed what she had seen and felt to Keelan. "The man in the mask was strange. It was clear the horse was afraid of him. I didn't get the impression she knew him, but he definitely made her uncomfortable."

"That confirms some other information we received." Keelan said. "Any chance she can give us anything else? We've got so little right now."

Sil spent a minute calming the horse before placing her had on her neck again. The horse sent a feeling of hunger into Sil's gut but refused to revisit the house or the men who cleaned it out.

"Well, she didn't want to think about the men anymore. But we know she's hungry," Sil said.

A quick search revealed a barrel with feed grain beside the horse's water trough. Sil fed the hungry beast while Keelan finished his fruitless inspection.

"They picked this place clean, and we're running out of light. Let's head back to HQ and see if the Freeport team reported anything," Keelan dusted off his shirt.

"What do you want to do with her horse?"

"We can't leave her to starve. Bring her with us, and we'll stable her until we learn more. Hopefully, we'll be giving her back to Tiana soon," he said.

They rode back to the Guard compound with Tiana's horse in tow. It was dark when they arrived, so they stabled the horses and called it a day. Keelan made it to the Officer's mess just as they were shutting things down for the night, but one of the cooks caught his dejected look and took pity on him, wrapping up a small plate of fried fish and roasted potatoes. Keelan took his dinner home and made a few notes. Albius would want a report first thing in the morning.

---

THE NEXT DAY, KEELAN MADE HIS WAY TO THE HQ building to give his report. He was ushered through the giant doors where Albius was seated at his ornate desk, reading from a towering stack of papers. The Captain-Commander scribbled something on the page, then set it down to turn his attention to Keelan.

"So, anything?" he asked without preamble.

Keelan detailed the visit to the infirmary and Tiana's house. The only substantive lead was the "conversation" Sil had with Tiana's horse. Albius sat back in his chair, digesting.

"I'd think this was little more than a very thorough robbery if we didn't have the link to The Children popping up everywhere. I'm changing this case from missing person to kidnapping."

"Agreed, sir," Keelan nodded. "I'm not sure where we go from here, though. The road to the Healer's house is so well traveled that we'll never find a trail. Sil didn't think so, and she's the best tracker we've got. Atikus should make contact on the Freeport investigation soon. With your permission, I'd like to visit the Arch Mage again and see if he has any other ideas."

"Of course. Report back this afternoon and let's review Freeport's status," Albius said, dismissing Keelan.

Keelan headed across the river to the Mage's compound and walked Arch Mage Quin through what he'd found. At the mention of Sil's communication with the horse, Quin perked up. "Now that's interesting."

Quin bolted from his chair and called to his clerk. "Jon, have Daris join us in my office, please."

A few minutes passed before a Mage's head poked tentatively through the doorway. "You asked for me, Arch Mage?"

"Daris, don't stand there. Come in." Quin looked at Keelan and rolled his eyes. "Any chance you can scry using a living animal? Say, a horse?"

The young Mage scratched his balding head for a minute, staring blankly at Quin. "I guess. Sure … but I don't know what we'll get. Living emotions and thoughts jumble when mixed with scrying magic. Add to that, animals don't think or hold memories in chronological order. They respond in the moment. The horse may give us memories or emotions from years ago—or yesterday—

depending on which is stronger in the animal's mind in that moment. If there's a strong enough emotional tie between the beast and human, we might get emotions the animal has for its owner. Could be fun to try, though. Why do you ask?"

"The missing Healer situation. You tried scrying for her a few days ago. Lieutenant Rea found her horse and a Natural linked to it and communed."

Daris's face lit up and he tapped a finger against his chin. "That's a twist. If the Natural were to join in the scrying, it might get us more information, better images. I've never done it before, but you've got me very curious."

"Keelan, I recommend we try the scrying with your Natural and the horse, but it's your call. I don't believe there's any danger to either of them if that helps," Quin said.

Keelan nodded. "Alright. We don't have any other solid leads. I'll get both the horse and Sil. When can you be ready?"

"By the time you return, we should be ready. I'll start setting things up right now," Daris said.

Later that afternoon, Keelan, Sil, and Not-Bessie strode into the Arch Mage's office, earning confused looks from passing Mages. It was even stranger when they ushered the horse through the entrance of the tower and struggled to get her to make the winding trek up the narrow stone stairs. Keelan had never been in the tower and was surprised by how large it was. The circular scrying room at the tower's peak held a handful of simple chairs set against the walls. In the center stood a pedestal with a wide but shallow silver bowl attached to the top. The shiny bowl reflected light from magically lit braziers stationed throughout the room. On the floor surrounding the pedestal, concentric circles of pearly stone encased a ring of magical symbols that were inlaid in alternating gold and silver, reminding Keelan of other magical markings throughout the Mages' Guild compound. The circle stretched ten paces in diameter with the pedestal at its center. No one was actively using magic when they entered, but the circle made the hair on Keelan's arms stand at attention. Not-Bessie appeared disinterested.

Arch Mage Quin and Daris greeted them as they entered the room. "Please, bring the horse inside the circle."

The group gathered around the bowl. Once everyone was in position, Quin poured the contents of the pitcher he was carrying into the bowl.

Daris turned to Sil. "Please place your hand on the horse—it doesn't matter where—and don't remove it until we're finished. The flow of magic may make her jumpy, and we'll need you to help keep her calm. I'll hold your other hand to create the link between the three of us. I have no idea what we might see, and you may experience strange sensations or images through your Gift. When I stop chanting, maintain contact, keep your eyes closed, and tell us what you see and feel. I will need to concentrate on the casting, so the Arch Mage will guide you."

Sil did as instructed, and the Mage took her hand. He closed his eyes and began muttering in the strange, guttural language of Mages. He swayed from side to side, and the water in the scrying bowl rippled. Not-Bessie stepped nervously, but Sil touched her forehead to the horse's neck, and she calmed.

Fuzzy images materialized in the bowl's water as the ripples settled. At first, the images were so faded that all they could make out were colors and rough shapes that changed every few seconds. Daris chanted a melodic phrase, and the images sharpened. A view of the back of Tiana's house from a distance. A huge silver stallion. Tiana's face.

Daris stopped chanting.

"Sil, what do you see?" Quin asked.

She concentrated, and the horse's emotions came to life inside her chest. Feelings of longing and loneliness almost overwhelmed her. In her mind's eye were flashes of Tiana's face. It was hard for her to focus as the mare's mind flitted from one thought to another, so Sil tried something. She used her Gift to press deeper into the horse's mind, causing emotions to surge and Sil to stagger. Keelan wrapped an arm around her waist to keep her upright.

Sil pushed further, seeking the horse's memories. The images in the scrying bowl shifted so rapidly that it was impossible to process one before the next appeared, then the water rippled so violently it threatened to spill over the edges. Sil focused her thoughts on Tiana, driving the horse's mind to comply, and was rewarded with images of the men who stripped Tiana's house bare … then a campfire somewhere in a large field surrounded by the same men. The images shifted, and she felt intense fear as wooden walls closed in around her. Darkness enveloped her. Her head swam.

In the next moment, her senses were nearly over-whelmed by the sweet scent of pine. She shivered at the crisp, cool air.

A face looked down at her. It was a quick flash, but she could see the squareness of his jawline and the intense green of his eyes. He appeared to be searching for something.

Everything stopped.

Sil's visions and the images vanished.

The water stilled.

The room was quiet for about two seconds before Sil's consciousness fled, and she fell to the cold stone floor. She shook violently, swinging her arms at the air around her. She muttered in her sleep-like state, pleading over and over as tears flooded her face. Her muttering swelled into screams. "Save me. Please. Save me. I'm right here in front of you! PLEASE…"

# 14

## JESS

S he had planned to be the perfect daughter, the perfect Princess. Today was important to her Father, and she desperately wanted to see approval in his eyes. That's all she'd ever wanted. Her father had taught her to be brave and independent. He had instilled a sense of strength in her, making her believe that one day she would be a great queen. He had painted images of her coronation in her mind that captivated her dreams and made her believe that anything was possible.

But then he made that comment about her *needing to be guided*. Today, in one careless comment, he'd shattered his little girl's fantasy. Maybe it wasn't careless. Maybe it was what he really thought. That she needed some *man* to guide her. That she couldn't think for herself. It made her blood boil.

These couldn't be the words of her father. Maybe they were those of the King, but not the father who said he believed in her. No, he would never! *Mother is behind this somehow.* She'd wanted to be rid of her troublesome daughter for years now. Betrothal to some faraway lord was the perfect opportunity to get her out of the Palace and out of their lives. What had she ever done to deserve to be tossed aside, to be sold off? She couldn't believe this was happening.

She paced, wearing a path of anger and hurt into the rug that covered the stone floors of her room. Then it came. The knock. The summons. The executioner had come to escort her to the gallows. Well, to dinner, but it felt like the gallows. How was she going to get through this night?

"Stop knocking! I'm coming!" she yelled at the door.

"The King and Queen request your presence in the formal dining room, Your Highness," the royal porter called from the other side. He was used to Jess's outbursts and barely flinched as she threw the door open and stormed past.

A trail of fury stalked Jess's path as she wound her way through the ancient hallways of the Palace toward the dining room. When she entered, everyone was already seated and talking quietly. Servants in long formal coats lined the walls awaiting the tiniest royal desire. Unlike the intimacy of the family's private dining chamber, this room was vast and contained a table long enough to hold fifty guests comfortably. The King sat in his usual place at the head of the table. The Queen, who usually occupied the seat opposite the King at the table's foot some leagues away, was now seated to his right at the same end. Treasurer Dask sat beside the Queen on her right.

The chair to the King's left remained empty, awaiting her royal presence. Beside the empty chair sat Duke Kinsley Parna.

*Empty chair beside an empty shirt. So glad they saved me the place of honor by Lord Piggy.*

Jess stopped at the far end of the table and stared. She couldn't move.

"Jess, please come join us. The cook made your favorite tonight, and I'm sure these gentlemen are eager to get to know you," her father said in a tone she thought might contain a bit of contrition.

*Good. He should feel guilty.*

Jess walked as slowly as she could until her chair appeared before her. She took her seat. The King handed her a glass of mulled wine and raised his own, "To the future of the realm. To my beautiful daughter, Crown Princess Jessia Vester."

"To the Crown Princess," the men said in broken unison, each raising his own glass then taking a sip.

And so it began.

Lord Parna spent the night trying to whisper in Jess's ear. He reeked of stale musk, and his breath was worse than that of their twelve-year-old hound. Every time a servant brought a new dish or different wine, the Duke would spend the next eternal moments telling Jess how wines or beef or vegetables or anything from the East were better, and how, in great detail, the masters of that region made them so. She might've found the lectures somewhat educational if the Duke would've spoken in anything other than third person. *One can only take so much of one referring to one's own person in the third!*

Oh, and that infernal piece of meat lodged between his two front teeth threatened to fly out every time he lisped an *s* or tutted a *t*. Jess kept her napkin at the ready in case of an unexpected shot across her bow. As he droned, she daydreamed the image of a little naval cannon shooting roast beef out of the Duke's mouth. That made her chuckle, drawing a sharp, questioning look from Lord Piggy.

Treasurer Dask was actually quite handsome and might've been a worthy candidate if he hadn't been so incredibly offensive. He tried a fresh approach at impressing the bride-to-be, offering one inappropriate joke after another. As the servants began placing large platters of various meats and vegetables on the table, he sprang from his seat, commanding everyone's attention.

*"I KNEW AN OLD BISHOP WHO HAD LOST SOME OF HIS TEETH and complained that others were so loose they might fall out.*

*'Never fear,' said one friend. 'They won't fall.'*

*'And why not?' the Bishop asked.*

*His friend replied, 'Because my testicles have been hanging loose for the last forty years, as if they were going to fall off, and yet, they are still there!'"*

THE KING OFFERED A NERVOUS LAUGH, EYES DARTING TO the Queen, who was staring daggers through the Crown

Treasurer. Dask seemed pleased with his effort and laughed deeply before downing more wine and taking his seat again. Everyone else looked uneasily around the table, seeking some guide for how to react.

General Marks never spoke. Not. One. Word. He seemed to assess those seated around the table as if they were players on some battlefield board game, waiting to be moved or attacked or dismissed. He barely looked at Jess. When he did, a look of pity and sadness filled his eyes. In that moment, he looked as trapped by circumstance as she was. *Interesting.*

As the servants entered the hall carrying trays of decadent desserts, Duke Parna ran his hand up Jess's leg for the third time, adding a little extra squeeze when he approached the upper part of her thigh. She had finally reached her limit. She took her two-pronged shrimp fork and stabbed him in the wrist. He pulled back quickly and howled in pain, jumping from the table with a small splatter of blood following in his wake.

"That wicked, awful girl! She stabbed me!" he squealed.

"Jess! What have you done?" The Queen rushed to the Duke's aid.

Jess shot to her feet and threw her napkin and bloody fork onto the table. She screamed back, "What have I done? I did what *you* should have done. I protected myself from this disgusting pig and his wandering hands and foul breath. Of course, *you* didn't see or do anything. All *you* can see is how to get rid of me. Fine. I'll go. You get your wish, YOUR MAJESTY!"

Jess ran out of the room, knocking a steaming platter of vegetables out of the hands of a servant who was entering the hall. When she made it to her room, she bolted the door and practically tore off her gown. After a few moments of boiling rage, she donned her leather riding clothes, then grabbed a small travel bag and packed as many things as possible. When it wouldn't hold anything else, she fastened the top and threw it over her shoulder. She was almost out the door when she thought of her brother. She sat and scrawled a quick note to Justin, which she left on her pillow.

The Queen had given most of the Palace staff the night off in anticipation of a long dinner and evening of entertaining the small group. For once, Jess was thankful for her mother's thorough planning. It only took ten minutes to sneak through the corridors to the throne room, then perform the dance with the guards and exit the Palace. For the second night in a row, Jess found the stables empty of people and quickly saddled Dittler. She had no idea where she was going, but she would get there as fast as she could!

Tears streamed down her face, and she could barely see as they entered the forest. The darkness that folded around her was comforting, and she relished the feeling of aloneness, of freedom.

She was so lost in her own emotions that she barely noticed where Dittler was taking her until she looked up and saw the familiar break in the trees that led to the riverside she loved so much—the place she would meet Danym. Her tears subsided and Jess actually smiled as she thought about last night, Danym holding her for hours, making her feel safe and warm and loved. She dismounted and led Dittler to the bubbling stream so he could have a drink, then aimlessly walked around the area, grasping for some sight or scent that would evoke Danym's memory.

*I really am under his spell, aren't I?* Her rage vanished and she giggled.

She took her waterskin out of the bag on Dittler's back and drank deeply. The adrenaline that fueled her escape was wearing off. Thirst and exhaustion crawled through her.

As she knelt to refill her skin from the stream, Dittler snorted nervously and began nudging her with his nose.

"What is it, boy? There's nobody out here. Easy."

The moon wasn't as full tonight as it was when she'd met Danym, and she could only see a few paces away. She put the stopper on her skin and walked around Dittler, looking into the forest darkness. Something moved off to her left, causing her head to snap in that direction. Then the leaves rustled.

"Who's there? Show yourself," she said, trying to sound brave as a lightning bolt of fear traveled up her spine.

Another snap behind made her spin around, and she saw a tall man in a brown robe creeping toward her, now only a few paces away. Their eyes locked through the odd mask he wore. The man bolted forward, arms outstretched.

Jess leapt onto Dittler's back and spurred him forward into the robed man, who dove out of the way with a muffled curse. He grabbed one of her boots and nearly pulled her out of the saddle, but it yanked free as her horse gained speed. A second man appeared to her right and reached out for Dittler's reins, but the horse was quicker, bolting further into the forest.

Jess heard another horse whinny in the distance. She looked backwards every few seconds as the sound of the other horse edged closer. Her heart felt like it was going to beat out of her chest. She came to a clearing and wove between several large boulders. The path was blocked by fallen trees. Dittler reared high on his back legs, throwing Jess to the ground where she lay dazed. Her horse leapt over her prone body and bounded off into the darkness, leaving her surrounded by large chunks of stone and towering trees, alone in the woods.

She shook off the fall and looked around. The taste of salt from newly flowing tears tickled her senses. She could hear hooves crushing leaves, sounds of the horse getting closer. Then a man's voice called out, "I think she went this way. Over here."

Jess had lost track of where she was in the woods, so she stayed as still as possible, hoping the robed men would just go away. The leaves were thinning, coating the forest floor and making stealth difficult. She could hear them searching, no longer concerned for secrecy as they crunched through the woods.

She tried to slow her breathing, to be quiet and still. *Spirits, what have I done? All I wanted was to get away. Nice job, Jess.*

The sounds of pursuit finally faded into the distance.

Jess released the tension she held, taking deep breaths

to calm her racing heart. She was lying on a rough bed of sharp twigs. Cold rocks dug into her side. Clouds had obscured the moon and near-total darkness descended upon the forest, leaving her confused, scared, and virtually blind. Ever so gently, she pushed herself up into a sitting position, careful to make as little noise as possible.

Suddenly another twig snapped behind her.

She froze.

A warm hand reached around from behind and covered her mouth while a strong arm encircled her waist. She squirmed and struggled.

"Jess, stop, it's me," a familiar voice whispered.

"Danym?"

He loosened his grip enough to let her head turn. Jess's eyes widened. She threw her arms around his neck and buried her head into his shoulder.

"Shhh. Quiet. Those men are still out here looking for you. I found Dittler wandering through the woods and tied him up by my horse. If we can get back to them, we can get out of here."

She nodded into his shoulder, still squeezing him with all of her strength. He had never felt so good.

Nearly an hour passed as they slowly wound their way through the trees to the waiting horses. Only once did they spot one of the robed men, forcing them to duck down behind a large tree and hold their breath until he passed. Jess could make out the edges of his mask, an odd deer or gazelle with angry eyes and devil-like horns. *Who are these people?*

When they reached the horses, Danym pulled her close

and whispered in her ear, "Do you want me to take you back to the Palace?"

She stared into his eyes and whispered back, "No. I never want to go back there again. Take me somewhere safe, just you and me."

## 15

### ISABEL

The Queen sat simmering over her daughter's outrageous performance. The King stared into the rich wood of the table in front of him. All their guests had been dismissed to relax in their quarters while servants cleared the table and retreated from the obvious ire of their monarchs.

"I'm going to wring her pompous, spoiled little neck," Isabel fumed. "How could she show us up like that in front of two members of Council and the Warden of the East? Does she have no idea what it means to rule, to be subject to the needs and whims of the nobles? Tongues will wag across the whole country before this week is done, mark my words."

The King knew he stood on dangerous ground. If he defended Jess, Isabel would turn her anger in his direction and there wouldn't be peace in the Palace for weeks. But if he condoned the Duke's actions and failed to defend his daughter's honor, he would betray her and send a signal that the King didn't have the strength—or the will—to protect his own family and heir. It could damage the Crown and would definitely hurt Jess's credibility before she ever even wore it. Why did impossible decisions always find their way before him? There were never good or easy answers, only miserable choices, and he had to choose the least miserable among them. Some days the Crown was just too heavy, even for him.

"Issy, she was out of line, especially stabbing the Duke like that. But did you see what he was doing all night? At one point, he practically licked her ear."

"Alfred, don't you dare go there. Do you think I've never had to put up with a noble whose hands decided to explore a bit? Or had to face the humiliation of a man looking down his nose at my judgement simply because I'm a woman?"

The King looked shocked. No one would dare touch the Queen in that way.

"Of course I have! Every woman has. It's not right, but it's the way of far too many men, and we understand it. We learn to deal with it in our own way, one that maintains peace and order in the household. What we *never* do is embarrass our King and Queen in front of the most important men in the Kingdom! Just one night, that little brat could deal with a touch of degradation and support the bigger picture. Just. One. Night." Her voice rose with each word.

Alfred took a deep breath before taking Isabel's hand in his own. He waited for her to make eye contact and spoke in a low, measured tone. "My Queen ... my love ... if *any* man ever touches you the way the Duke touched our daughter, promise me you won't 'deal with it in your own way.' Promise you'll tell me so I can see him locked in the tower while his offending hand is fed to our hounds.

"I'm not naïve enough to think that men always behave well. But I won't allow anyone to dishonor you or our daughter—ever. Am I clear?"

Isabel wasn't often at a loss for words, but in that moment her voice faltered. She stared into her husband's eyes and saw a passion—a justified, protective rage—that she had never seen before. In that moment, she loved him more than any day she could remember, and a tear fell to her cheek for the first time in years. Alfred gently reached up and wiped the tear, then pulled her hand to his lips and kissed it.

"None of these men are right for our daughter. The Crown can wait until we find the right match. A match who will offer her the respect and love she deserves."

Isabel felt like her heart would burst. How had this man stolen her anger and turned it into something so beautiful? She cupped his cheek with her hand. "My King is far wiser than his Queen."

"Nonsense. My Queen gives me strength. Unburdens my heart. Makes me wise." He stood. "We've had enough for one night. Let's get some rest and start fresh in the morning. We're young still, and Jess won't inherit the throne for many years. I don't know why we were in such a rush that we'd ever consider Lord Piggy."

Isabel snorted a laugh and playfully slapped his arm. "Now who's besmirching honor, Your Majesty?"

"My dear, being a sovereign has its privileges. If I say he's Lord Piggy, then that is who he is," he said with a wide grin. "Sometimes it's actually good to be the King."

---

THE NEXT MORNING, AS THE KING AND QUEEN WERE eating breakfast, a page scurried into the room and whispered into Alfred's ear. The King's face darkened as the page stepped back, waiting for instructions.

"Show them in at once," he said.

Isabel set her fork down and gave her husband a sharp, questioning stare. Before he could respond, Chancellor Thorn, Minister of War Bril, and Sheriff Wilfred marched into the room and offered a quick bow.

"Your Majesty," Thorn began, "forgive the interruption, but this couldn't wait for Council this afternoon."

"It's alright, Danai. What do you have?"

Thorn nodded to Wilfred and Bril. The Sheriff fixed his eyes on the King, "Your Majesty, we know some things with certainty, and we suspect others based on those facts. I'll start with what we know.

"As you are aware, four Gifted have been kidnapped from various locations throughout the Kingdom. Chancellor Thorn and his Mages worked closely with my team to ascertain some pattern for the kidnappings but came up empty. Both men and women were taken, their Gifts varied widely, and each individual was taken from their home city or town, which are hundreds of leagues apart. We traced the victims' families, some of which were prominent, others not, some wealthy, others poor.

"We found only three common threads. One, each victim was Gifted. Two, every trail we could follow led east. Three, brown-robed members of The Children were seen in two of the four cases." He paused to allow for questions, but the King remained silent.

"Based on these facts, and some witness statements, Chancellor Thorn and I believe the victims are being taken through the mountain pass into Melucia."

The King's expression changed to disbelief. The Queen leaned forward. "Melucia? Surely you don't think the Melucian government is behind the kidnappings?"

"We don't know enough to be sure, but that is exactly what we fear," Thorn said.

Bril cleared his throat, drawing the monarch's eye. "Sir, our border forces posted at Huntcliff have reported an unusual level of activity by Melucian Rangers in the mountains. Several trading caravans were recently stopped and inspected as they made their way back home from their trading runs. Two of the merchants interviewed said they had never been stopped and inspected before, that the Rangers appeared to be anxious and looking for something specific."

"Do you think our caravans are at risk? Were they threatened?" the King asked.

"There were no explicit threats, but in each case, several Rangers were involved in the stops. They separated the merchants from their carts and carriages and had a pair of heavily armed men stand guard while others conducted their search. We've never seen such aggressive measures by the Melucians and have no idea what sparked this escalation. On the advice of the Merchant's Guild, we have ceased all outbound trade through the pass until we can better understand the situation."

Thorn inserted himself again, "Your Majesty, it is reasonable to assume the two situations may be connected, that the Melucian Rangers had knowledge of the kidnappings and were searching for our missing Gifted."

The Queen leaned back, one brow raised. "That's quite a leap, Danai. For all we know, there was theft or some other crime, and they're simply being cautious."

Sheriff Wilfred beat Thorn to respond. "I would agree with Your Majesty if we had not also received reports of unusual movement of The Children along the pass. Nearly a dozen robed men were seen going to and from Melucia in the same time period. In my years as High Sheriff, I have never heard a single report of that tiny faction traveling abroad. They have rarely been seen traveling within our own country."

The King steepled his fingers and tried to process everything he'd just heard. After a thousand years of peace, why would the Melucians provoke hostilities? Their military was weak—practically non-existent. The country focused its efforts almost exclusively on trade. Sure, they had a significant magical advantage, but they'd never appeared interested in applying their magic toward aggressive measures. None of this made sense.

"Do you have a recommendation?" the King asked.

The Minister of War was normally reserved and rarely

spoke at Council but didn't hesitate. "Yes, Your Majesty. We recommend full closure of our Eastern border, and reinforcement. The Third Infantry and Sixth Archery divisions are posted nearby and could be positioned at Huntcliff within the week. There is already a complement of scouts stationed within Huntcliff. We should increase patrols in the mountains and gather intelligence on Melucian Ranger numbers and movements. Additionally, we recommend a team of engineers be dispatched to assess the structural defenses along the border."

"Are you sure we shouldn't just invade?" the Queen said in a mocking tone.

"Your Majesties, these are our scaled down recommendations. Our teams preferred a more … how should I say this … *robust* approach," Thorn said.

"Fine. Do it. But gentlemen, keep these suppositions quiet. Come up with some war game or training mission as a cover. I don't want the entire country rallying to war before we even know what's going on here," the King said.

"Right away, Your Majesty," Bril said.

The three men bowed respectfully and exited, leaving the King and Queen staring at each other in disbelief. A moment passed before the Queen reached for her tea and took a sip to steady her quivering hand.

"Let's hope one of those scouts doesn't get nervous and take a shot at a Ranger. One scared soldier could bring a thousand years of peace to an end—and there would be nothing we could do about it," the King grumbled.

## 16

# JESS

Danym led Jess to his home on the eastern end of the city. Despite his exalted station, his father was a humble man, preferring to let his performance as High Sheriff impress rather than the size or grandiosity of his manor. Danym walked them around to the back of the modest house, revealing a small barn at the far end of a large grassy field. The Sheriff might not go for grand, but he appeared to like having plenty of space.

They walked the horses to the barn, removed their saddles, and brushed them out. The ride from the forest had been uneventful, but they were exhausted by the night's excursion, both physically and emotionally. Jess helped feed and water the horses before she and Danym closed the barn and headed to the house.

"My father won't be back until late. There's something going on that he won't talk about, but it's big enough to keep him at his office, sometimes overnight. We can get a good night's rest and leave before sunrise," Danym said.

Jess was still reeling from her escape from the robed men and reached over to take Danym's hand as they walked. When they entered the house, she was surprised to see the modest outside matched by an equally modest and tasteful interior. The walls were mostly bare with an occasional painting depicting a family member or pastoral scene. They passed through a sizeable sitting room with several comfortable looking chairs facing a large hearth. On the wall above was the head of a deer with a giant rack of antlers. The deer's eyes seemed to stare accusingly at Jess, and she looked away to escape its scrutiny.

As they entered a bedroom, Danym offered a bow and a smile. "The royal suite, Your Majesty."

Jess slapped his arm playfully. "None of that. Remember, we're trying to *not* be recognized. We've both got to forget my titles, maybe even come up with different names until we're safe somewhere."

"You're probably right, but you will always be my Princess." He gave her a peck on the cheek before backing out of the room and closing the door.

Jess sat on the small neatly made bed and looked around the room. She couldn't stop replaying everything in her mind. The smugness in her mother's eyes as she paraded those men through the throne room. The smell of the Duke's breath as he whispered against her ear. The feeling of his hand penetrating her personal space, insinuating his intentions should they ever actually be alone together. That thought made her shiver despite the warmth of the room.

Then her mind strayed to the robed men in the woods

and the frantic flight that led her into Danym's arms. Who were those men, and what were they doing in the woods at night? It almost seemed like they were waiting for her. But she didn't even know she would be out there that night. How could they? Then there were those strange, twisted animal masks. She understood the need to hide your identity better than most, but to pick something so hideous struck her as bordering on insane. That thought made the men's eyes pop into her head. Those dull, lifeless eyes that stared at everything and nothing. Another shiver.

She tried to calm herself with less complicated things. Getting ready for bed. Brushing her hair. Little things that always comforted her in the simplicity of routine. She pushed the covers on the bed back and climbed in, reveling in the fluffy warmth of the multi-colored comforter. As she finally drifted into a fitful sleep, Danym's smile overtook her dreams.

---

HOURS LATER, JESS WOKE TO A GENTLE TAPPING AT HER door. She rubbed her eyes and stretched, finally giving up the warmth of the comforter to answer the incessant knocks. Danym had his finger over his lips when she cracked the door and peered through.

"My father came home a couple hours after we got here. He should be sound asleep, but we need to leave as quietly as possible," he whispered.

She nodded and closed the door. After changing into her riding clothes, she made her bed and skimmed the room to erase any sign that she had stayed there. The last thing they needed was for the chief constable of the whole country to spot something and spoil their escape.

Once satisfied, she grabbed her travel bag and walked into the hallway where Danym was waiting. They crept through the house and out the back door to their horses in the barn. Dittler seemed irritated at the early start but overcame his annoyance at the sight of an apple in Danym's hand. He was starting to like the Sheriff's son.

They saddled the horses and strapped their travel bags into place. Danym turned to Jess. "Are you sure you want to do this? To leave? You're going to be the next Queen. Running away like this may make your father think twice about your place in the succession."

"I can't go back. I just can't," she said in a small voice. It took her a moment to gather her strength and look up to find his eyes. "Danym, I need to be free to make my own future. My own choices. Nobody outside our family sees the invisible chains attached to the Crown, chains that bind our every move or word or thought. When I was little, I wanted to be Queen more than anything, to rule over a glorious nation. But I've seen what ruling does to my father —what it's doing to my whole family. I can't wear those chains anymore."

Danym took her in his arms and held her close against his chest, kissing the top of her head. "You don't have to go back. I'll help you be free. I'll protect you."

They stood there for a long moment enjoying the simple peace and comfort of an embrace, the safety they found in each other's arms.

Finally, he stepped back. "So, where would Your Majesty like to go?"

"Danym, stop that!" she said, smirking. "Let's think this through for a minute. We could follow the coast through Clude and Oliver, maybe to Cooper on the Hook. I love the tiny coastal villages with their dirty sand beaches and amazing sunsets. But Cooper is the only town of any size west of the mountains. I'd probably be recognized when we passed through the smaller ones that sit closer to Fontaine."

"We can't give anyone a trail to follow. Let's rule that one out for now," he said.

"Ok, that leaves the King's Road through the Spires toward Spoke, or east toward Featherstone on the northern coast."

Danym thought for a minute, trying to remember his geography lessons. Swordplay was so much more fun than dusty old maps.

"I don't care for Featherstone. My father talks about pirate raids from Riz and how his teams struggle to keep the peace along that coast. The thought of having to fight our way to freedom is almost as scary as staying here," he said.

"Agreed. So that leaves the King's Road." She stroked Dittler's neck as they talked. "It's pretty heavily traveled, but that might actually be good. There'll be more people to blend in with, and it should be well patrolled. We'll be ok as long as we can get some distance between us and the capital before anyone realizes that I'm gone."

"The King's Road winds through the Spires, and those

are some cold mountains. We'll need better gear and warmer clothing if we're making that trip. Why don't you keep Dittler company while I go back into the house for a few minutes?" He turned to walk out of the barn.

"Danym," Jess said, causing him to turn back as he stood halfway through the open door. "I just want to say thank you. You saved me from more than you'll ever know."

"No, Jess. You saved me, and you don't even know it." He smiled and closed the door behind him.

Dittler snorted, and Jess let out a deep sigh, resting her head against his strong back. "I know, he's amazing."

Barely a minute passed before Danym returned, struggling to catch his breath as he raced through the door. "We have to go. Now! There are two of those robed men looking around the front of the house. I don't think they saw me, so let's sneak out behind the barn and cut through the neighbor's field."

He helped Jess mount Dittler, then walked to the back of the barn and opened a small sliding door, letting Jess pass. He walked his horse through and latched the door closed, mounting and leading Jess to the back of the property. The barn was still in their line of sight, and they couldn't see if the robed men had made it to the back of the house or not. Assuming the worst, they moved quickly to put distance between them and their pursuers.

When they got to the neighbor's rickety wooden fence, Danym took a piece of meat out of his pocket. Jess's questioning expression was quickly satisfied as a giant gray mastiff thundered toward them. Danym held the meat out so the dog could see his prize, hoping desperately it wouldn't bark and alert everyone within leagues to their presence. That beast could make the mountains shake with his howl.

"Timber, come here, boy! Treat!" Danym half-whispered, half-shouted.

At the mention of the *T* word, Timber's loping canter turned into a full sprint. An enormous slobbery smile forced his tongue to loll out the side of his mouth. Jess was relieved to see that he recognized Danym and accepted the bribe with gusto and affection. Danym scratched the giant behind his ears as he chomped, earning a moan of ecstasy and a bit of an eye roll. Now that a silent peace had been established, Danym dug into his saddlebag, retrieving a large meaty bone, and gave it to Timber to keep him occupied.

Jess smiled and shook her head in wonder. *He thinks of everything!*

They made it through the neighbor's large field and the gate on the other side of his sprawling one-story log cabin before they heard a man call out. "Over here! I've got fresh tracks."

Jess's eyes popped wide, and Danym spurred his horse into a gallop. They made it to a rough side road that ran through neighboring properties. The sun had yet to make an appearance, and the quarter-moon offered only milky light that Danym thanked the Spirits for. They could see well enough to travel without risk to the horses, but their pursuers would have trouble picking them up in the murky light. *Finally, a little luck.*

They moved quickly through the outskirts of town, Danym nervously peering over his shoulder at Jess every few minutes. When they finally reached the Cathedral of the One, the last major landmark before crossing beyond the borders of Fontaine, Jess suggested they make a quick stop.

"We shouldn't stay here long. The sun is coming up, and people will head to the Cathedral for morning prayers. The last thing we need is for someone to recognize you as we're standing on the border of town," Danym said.

They found a wooded area to the eastern side of the Cathedral, out of the general sight line of anyone who might be headed into the massive stone building, and ate a quick breakfast of dried fruit and flat bread. Jess fed the horses while Danym marveled at how the animals took to her, gently eating out of her hand and nuzzling her neck with their noses. Jess looked back and caught him smiling at her.

The capital's eastern border was guarded by the Spires, a massive mountain chain that contained some of the tallest peaks in the world. The King's Road crossed from one end of the Kingdom to the other and was wide and well maintained once travelers made it past the Spires. But within the shadow of the mountains, the road was narrow, winding, and often covered in ice as it rose sharply in elevation. From their vantage point behind the Cathedral, they could see the western leg of the mountains, and Jess felt a slight chill in the air that heralded the onset of the northern winter. Thirty minutes passed before they were mounted and headed toward the King's Road, which was visible from their spot behind the Cathedral. It was still early, and only a few could be seen walking or riding along the nation's chief artery.

Danym noticed her staring at the frosty peaks. "That's what we have to pass through. You sure you still want to go through with this? Last chance to change your mind."

"No turning back. They're beautiful."

"Tell me that after a few days of riding through them," he smirked. "Alright, here we go. It should take about an hour to get to the base of the mountains, then another four or five days to Spoke."

"That long? I've never made the trip, but it doesn't look that far on my father's maps."

"It's not that far, but the road winds up and down and around and through. You'll see. It's a challenging trip, and we risk laming the horses if we push too hard, especially in places where rocks or limbs have fallen onto the road. In another month, snow and ice will cover everything and it'll be nearly impassable," he said.

"Well, good thing we're leaving now. Lead on, my dear boy." She waved her hand in a commanding gesture.

Danym gave a half bow from his saddle, "Yes, Your— my lady."

She winked at his quick catch and flashed him that smile that made his skin tingle.

# 17

## ISABEL

What should have been a peaceful morning filled with walks through the gardens or forests, chaperoning Jess and her suitors, turned into a circus of activity with a constant parade of generals and advisors seeking the King's counsel or approval. Alfred spent much of his time in his sprawling study staring at the detailed maps he'd spread across the large conference table. Minister Bril, General Marks, and Chancellor Thorn buzzed around him like angry hornets waiting to sting anything that met with their displeasure.

Zumi Bacras, Minister of Foreign Affairs, joined the discussions around midday and objected to every step recommended by the military leaders. "Your Majesty, none of my envoys in the other countries have reported anything beyond peaceful trade and negotiations. There has been no talk—not even a rumor—of hostilities by anyone. Please, let me go to Saltstone and speak with the Triad, see what I can learn before we destroy over a thousand years of peace."

"If war is coming, we can't give up the initiative. The Minister's talks could tip our hand and give away a significant advantage." Bril said.

Marks nodded to support his Minister. "I agree. If it comes to a fight, I'd rather hit an enemy who is still ill prepared. Anything we do beyond readying our troops will give them time to dig in and fortify, possibly even rally the small border nations to their side."

Bacras snorted derisively. "The border nations barely stir among themselves. They spend their days squabbling over fishing rights and whose Gifted farmers raise the largest cows. They wouldn't know what to do with a sword if you handed it to them."

Thorn wormed his way into the debate. "Their Magic makes them powerful. We have no idea what martial talents they've developed. Our Mages in Saltstone have been monitoring the research their Guild has been conducting in concert with their military command. It's troubling. We have nothing to match what they can do with Magic."

Alfred had listened to this argument for hours. His head was throbbing. "Gentlemen, that's enough. No one is going to war. We're repositioning a few units to conduct military exercises designed to hone their skills. War games, nothing more. The fields near the mountains are the perfect location for those exercises. There's no need to engage in any abnormal talks because we're not doing anything abnormal."

Bacras pressed. "But we are, Your Majesty. In your

twenty-three years on the throne, we have *never* conducted such war games. At least let me notify the Triad of these exercises and their peaceful intent, allay any fears sparked by our troop movements along their border."

"That might actually work to our advantage, Your Majesty. If they think the games are peaceful, they won't try to respond or prepare when they see the buildup," Bril said.

"Minister Bril, these are *defensive* maneuvers. Period. No more talk of war," the King snapped. He turned back to Bacras. "Send word to our Ambassador in Saltstone of the war games but say nothing of the increased patrols in the mountains. Our scouts need to see what's going on, and I don't want the Rangers masking their movements because we've tipped them off."

"Yes, Your Majesty." He bowed low and backed out of the room.

As the door closed behind Bacras, Justin walked in. Alfred's eyes widened.

The Queen, who had been watching quietly from a large chair at the other end of the conference table, rose to intercept her son.

"Justin, we're really busy right now." She reached to stop him.

"Mother, it's important, and I don't think it can wait," he said nervously.

The King watched the exchange and held up a hand to his advisors, silencing the room. "Justin, come here."

Everyone took a step back to allow the Prince to walk sheepishly toward his father. "What is it, son? I don't think you've ever interrupted Council. And you look terrified. Take a breath and tell me what's going on."

Justin looked up with tear-stained eyes, "Dad … Jess is gone. She … ran away."

"Why do you think that?

Justin handed a folded note to his father. "I found this on her pillow. None of the staff have seen her today, and the guards are acting weird and won't give me a straight answer."

The King read the note, a look of concern creasing his face. He handed it to the Queen and turned to a page. "Ask the guards at the throne room door to come here immediately."

The page gave a quick head bob and scurried to obey the King.

The Queen threw the note onto the map-strewn table. "I really am going to wring her little neck."

"Can we make sure she's *safe* before we start plotting her death?" Alfred's icy glare silenced her.

The page returned with a Protector sporting Captain's epaulets.

"Captain, what do you have for me?" the King asked.

The man offered a crisp bob. "Your Majesty, the two men who were on duty last night are not in the Palace. I've sent for them and expect their arrival shortly. But sir, your page told me about the Princess, and I doubt my men will be much help. We are charged with keeping people *out* of the Palace, not keeping them in. Your daughter is … well … rather forthright in giving instructions to the staff and guards, and rarely offers much explanation. I made a quick inquiry with the duty watch, and they confirmed that she hasn't been seen since leaving the grounds late last night."

"Very well, Captain. Let me know if the guards remember anything that might be useful," the King said, dismissing the Captain. He turned back to the page. "Send for the High Sheriff and let him know that it's urgent."

Isabel's eyes snapped to Alfred's. "What do you want with him?"

"We have to assume Jess is on the run and need to alert every uniformed man in the country. The Sheriff controls more watchful eyes than anyone outside of the military. Even if the local constables maintain their distance, we can offer Jess *some* protection as she roams the countryside. The thought of her out there … alone … It makes me sick."

"Uh, Father, she might not be alone." Justin struggled to meet his father's eyes.

They'd nearly forgotten that Justin was still in the room. Alfred turned toward his son. "And who do you think she has with her?"

Justin stared at his shoes. It felt like he was about to betray his sister's trust, something he never thought he'd do willingly. But she was in trouble, right? He had to help somehow.

"She's … umm … well …"

"Out with it, Justin. We don't have time for this. Say what you know." At the familiar sound of their Queen's whip-crack, the Ministers mirrored Justin's shoe-staring routine.

"I think … she's with Danym, the High Sheriff's son.

They've been seeing each other in secret. Almost every night."

The King's mouth fell open. When he looked up and found the Queen's eyes, his shock deepened.

"You *knew* about this?" he asked her.

"I suspected."

Alfred couldn't decide if he was more worried for his daughter or angry at his wife for keeping this from him. They never kept secrets, especially about the children. The Sheriff's son seemed like a fine boy. Why would she keep that from him? *Focus, Alfred. She's missing, and that's more important than placing blame right now.*

"What's done is done. Right now, we need to focus on finding her," he said. He took a deep breath to calm himself, then began barking orders.

"General Marks, this isn't just some wayward girl. It's the heir to the throne. I want flyers with her picture and description distributed to every man in our military. With the movements to come, their eyes may be as useful as any."

"Yes, Your Majesty."

"Chancellor Thorn, have your best scrying Mage search for her. Justin, take the Chancellor to Jess's bedroom and find something personal of hers," the King continued. "Minister Bril, send word to the officers on the border to be on the lookout. Everywhere else, our men should just observe at a distance; but if they make it to Huntcliff, I want those units to detain them. Under no circumstance are they to be allowed into Melucia."

Everyone stared at the King, waiting for further instructions that never came.

"*Now!* We're behind by a good twelve hours and need to move quickly," he snapped, causing a flurry of activity.

When the room finally quieted again, the King and Queen stood alone with Foreign Minister Bacras. Alfred took a seat at the large table and leaned back with a deep sigh. His mind sorted through one terrible possibility after another. He still couldn't believe Jess would actually run away. In the middle of everything else, how could she add to the chaos?

He looked inward and grappled with his part in pushing her away. He had always been closer to Jess than any of his children. They had a special bond he knew went far beyond most father-daughter relationships. She was his heir and the only person in the world who would ever understand the weight of the Crown. Sure, the Queen shared power with him, but only another sovereign could truly understand. To rule meant committing to a lifetime of service to everyone else—service that could break one's back under the weight of such responsibility.

Unlike his other children, Jess actually enjoyed watching Council meetings, regardless of how long or tedious they became. They often talked at the end of long days, walking through what she had seen and how he'd handled situations. He loved her endless questions, especially when she would ask about the intrigue between ministers. She was starting to understand the complexity in governing, with so many ambitious men harboring widely divergent goals and views.

Her judgements about courtiers or petitioners were often accurate and insightful. Sure, she could be headstrong, volatile, and selfish. What sixteen-year-old couldn't be all of those things? But she was also more mature, more intellectually curious, and far more poised than her younger brothers. She would make a good Queen one day.

Minister Bacras coughed, waking the King from his thoughts. "Your Majesty, if there is nothing else, I would like to get my envoys on the road before the military units move."

"Of course. Thank you, Zumi." The King nodded, his eyes never leaving the smooth table's wood.

When the door closed again, Isabel walked around the table and placed her hands on Alfred's shoulders. She spoke in a soft, almost pleading voice. "What are we going to do with her? Jess understands her responsibility, *her duty*. If she would run now, what would stop her from trying to escape the Crown in the future? Maybe one of the boys would be better suited to wear it."

He gave her a pointed look. "She's still young. Unless you have some other plans you haven't mentioned, we'll be wearing the Crown a few more years. There's plenty of time to help her grow into her role. I've felt like running away a time or two myself."

"But you didn't. You honored your commitment, your duty to the Kingdom above your own desires, or hopes, or fears. I'm starting to think she'll never put anything above her own desires."

Before the King could respond, another page walked

into the room with High Sheriff Wilfred. He bowed respectfully. "Your Majesties."

The Queen started to speak, but Alfred patted her hand and stood, indicating that he wanted to lead the conversation. He locked eyes with the Sheriff and held his gaze for a moment before speaking in a slow, measured tone. "Sebastiano, we have another situation. Jess is missing, and we believe she may have run away ... and that *Danym* may be with her."

The Sheriff staggered back a step, bracing himself on a chair. "Your Majesty, I just heard about the Princess, but had no idea *Danym* might be involved. I got home late last night, well past midnight, and he was asleep in his room. Nothing seemed out of place."

Alfred took the note from the table and handed it to Sebastiano. "This was found in Jess's room. It doesn't reference Danym, but Justin seemed to know quite a lot about the pair and their little rendezvous over the past few months, far more than *we* knew. He believes they've become serious, and their relationship drove her to rebel against our betrothal efforts."

"I ... I don't know what to say, Your Majesty. I would *never* encourage or condone ..."

"We know, Sebastiano. Our concern right now is locating Jess and Danym and ensuring their safety. We'll figure out how to deal with the pair once we know they're back." Alfred tried to reassure the Sheriff. "How would you suggest we best use the constables throughout the Kingdom? General Marks and Minister Bril have the military angle covered and will be on alert at the border in case they get that far."

"We'll send word to the Chief Constable in every town right away. Our resident Mage is a telepath and can get the word out quickly. Every office should already have likenesses of the royal family, but we'll work up a new flyer and get it distributed quickly. We'll also increase our patrols on the major arteries. They're bound to use the roads at some point," Wilfred said.

"Good. If the Mage's scrying turns up anything, we'll make sure you're informed. Let us know immediately if you learn even the smallest detail. And Sheriff, start with a thorough search of your house. We believe they left early this morning. If Danym slept in his own bed, as you say, Jess might've been somewhere nearby. That would at least give us a place to start."

"Good idea, Majesty. With your permission, I'll get started now." The Sheriff barely finished before the King nodded his dismissal.

Alfred reached out and took Isabel's hand, pulling her into his chest, where he held her close. The world seemed to spin out of control around them, but he took comfort in her warmth and constant support. *I don't know how I would do any of this without you, Issy.*

## 18

### TIANA

Tiana woke from a fitful sleep realizing she was no longer in her cramped wooden prison. She lay curled on a bed of pine needles and leaves beside a small campfire. Both her wrists and ankles were secured by scratchy ropes that left angry red lines across her skin. The crisp air was filled with the scent of mountain pine.

As her mind cleared, she looked around and saw the cart just off the dirt road, tethered to a tree by a heavy rope. But the horses and masked men were gone. In fact, she couldn't hear anything other than the usual sounds of a forest at night.

She tested the ropes on her wrists and sighed as they refused to budge. Her captors had taken great care in re-securing the bonds on her wrists when she was removed from the cart. She turned her focus to the rope around her ankles and realized there was room to move her legs within the bonds. She wiggled her foot and bent it as straight as she could. After a few minutes of panicked squirming, her left foot was rewarded with freedom, followed by the right as the rope slipped to the ground. She blinked a few times at her now unbound feet, barely believing her good fortune, then attempted to stand under her own strength for the first time in days. The world wobbled. She leaned against a tree and waited for feeling to return to her legs before moving again.

Now alert, Tiana ran into the closest opening in the trees. Her mind raced with images of everything she was running from: the men in robes and strange masks, the rolling coffin that had been her home for days, the endless possibilities for how her journey might end if she didn't free herself. What did they want with her? Where were they going?

Tears ran down her cheeks, and the cold of the forest penetrated her skin.

She shivered.

She imagined the glassy, blank eyes of the men in their masks behind every tree as she ran, her mind tormenting her with what might happen if they found her again. Small twigs lashed her arms and face, causing trickles of blood to flow. She felt none of it. She was *free* . . . and not going back!

It was dark and tough to navigate in the thick woods, but slivers of moonlight poking through the forest canopy guided her way. She made it a half mile from the campfire when she heard someone headed her way clomping through the forest with little care for silence. She scurried toward a clearing in the trees that was littered with large rounded boulders, then threw herself behind the biggest stone she could find. She tucked into a ball as the rustling grew closer. Her breath caught as torchlight revealed the surrounding forest. She was hungry, weak, and cold, causing her breathing to labor loud enough for the approaching guest to hear.

"Whoever's there, come out now and you won't be harmed," a stern male voice ordered.

Tiana tried to quiet her breathing and remain still. She would *not* go back in that box; they'd have to kill her first. She sucked in another deep breath.

After a moment of silence, the man's voice darkened. "Don't make me come back there. Rangers don't like surprises in our mountains, especially after dark."

Tiana sat up and looked over the top of the boulder, but just as she gained her footing, two of the robed men came blundering through the foliage, breathing heavily from their chase. Tiana's heart threatened to beat out of her chest as she ducked her head down and pressed her body against the cold stone.

The Ranger drew his bow and faced the two men who stood about six paces in front of Tiana's boulder, facing him. "Stay where you are, gentlemen. What are you doing in the woods after dark—and why you're wearing those masks?"

"We lost one of our own—a young woman. She wandered from our campsite some time ago, and we're worried for her safety in these dark woods," the man in the bull-bird mask said in his scratchy, toneless voice.

The ranger cocked his head, trying to process the strangeness in the masked man's tone. Tiana found her courage and peeked over the boulder, only the top of her head and eyes now visible. Tears streaked down her face, and she struggled to control her shivering. She stared at the backs of the robed men. The second her head appeared above the boulder, the Ranger sensed her movement and looked up, locking eyes with her. Her eyes popped wide, but she kept quiet and gave him a panicked head shake. She ducked back into her hiding place.

The robed men didn't notice the exchange.

The Ranger hesitated only a second. "I've been patrolling these woods all night and haven't seen anyone, but it's a vast range and she could be anywhere. I can help you look for her, but it will be morning before I can get more of the Rangers to join us. From the looks of your robes and shoes, you're not really dressed for a mountain search."

"We cannot return without her," was all bull-bird said in reply.

"She'll be cold by now—and lost. I'll go back to the station and get my pack, along with some medical supplies, water, and a blanket. We'll need all those things when we find her. You'll slow me down more than help. Go back to your camp and wait. I know this mountain well and can cover it quickly. I'll let you know when I find her."

Bull-bird stared at the Ranger, never blinking. After an eternity of silence, he nodded and the two robed men turned and left, heading toward their camp.

Tiana stirred, but the Ranger whispered, "Stay where you are. They stopped close by and are watching."

He continued his faux search of the area, kneeling as if looking to the forest floor for answers.

Another twenty minutes crawled by before the Ranger's calming voice reached over the boulder. "They've gone now. You can come out."

Tiana untangled her tight, sore legs and peered over the boulder. The Ranger was looking straight at her, his bright grey eyes assessing. He wasn't tall, and his green uniform drooped off his lanky frame. Unkempt straight black hair sprouted from under his murky brown cap. A quiver of arrows rose over his shoulder, and a long knife in its scabbard clung to his belt.

"It's ok, ma'am. Come on out and let's get you warm. I'm Ranger Wilk. Donovan Wilk."

That cautious, protective voice inside Tiana's head vanished as she hurtled out from behind the boulder and blundered into Wilk, knocking him back. He had to wrap her in his arms just to stay upright. She pressed herself close and sobbed uncontrollably.

Startled by the woman with bound hands now in his arms, Wilk whispered. "Miss, what happened to you? You're safe now, but I need to know what we're dealing with before it tries to deal with *us*."

While Tiana gathered her breath, he pulled the dagger from its sheath and reached behind her to cut the rope. She pulled back at the sight of the blade before realizing what he was doing, then let him free her angry red wrists.

"Thank you. Spirits, that hurt," a distant, tiny voice escaped as she tried to rub life back into her hands. "Please take me somewhere safe. There are three men in brown robes who kidnapped me as I was walking home a few days ago. I've lost track of how many have passed because they kept me drugged in the bed of a cart. I woke up about an hour ago by a campfire. The cart was there, but the horses and men weren't. The rope holding my ankles was loose, so I wiggled out and made it into the forest. I hid when I heard you coming … and you know the rest."

"Alright. My station's not too far from here, up this mountain. It's not the easiest climb, but I'll help you. I want to hear everything, but not until we're back at the station. Last question for now. What's your name?"

"I'm Tiana."

"Tiana, everybody calls me Donny. Well, that's what I think the animals call me. They're about all I see these days." He chuckled with a comforting smile. "Let's stay quiet until we get to the station. I'm going to snuff this torch to make it harder to follow us. My Gift is iNght Vision, so we'll be fine without it, and I'll know if anyone else is out here long before they reach us. Just stay close and follow my steps."

As Donny led them on a winding trek through the forest, Tiana's mind raced. She saw robed men behind every tree they passed, and she stumbled twice when she heard some animal running from their approach.

Donny reached out and took her hand, guiding her forward. He was at home in these mountains, but they moved slowly to help reduce the noise of their passing and to ensure they didn't get split up. It took a little more than an hour to make it to the guard station that looked like a tiny house on stilts. Tiana dropped into a chair and began sobbing again, a storm of emotions threatening to over-power her.

Donny grabbed a blanket and wrapped it around her shoulders, then placed his firm hand on her right arm while using his left to lift her chin. "Tiana, you're safe now. I promise. Just try to breathe while I start a fire and make us something hot to drink."

She placed her hand over his and whispered, "Thank you, Donny. Thank you."

He went to work starting a fire in the stone hearth. By the time he hung a pot of water over the flames, Tiana was feeling some of her old heart return.

She found her voice as Donny tended the fire. "I'm a Healer in Saltstone. They took me on my walk home from the infirmary a few nights ago."

Tiana relived her journey for Donny, at least what she could remember of it through the perpetual drug-induced haze she'd endured. He listened without interrupting her, occasionally closing his eyes as he visualized her painful trip and marveled at her strength and quick thinking in her escape. After so many days in a traveling box, most would have given up.

Tiana ran out of words and yawned, so they decided she should rest. Donny gave her his bed and told her he would stand watch throughout the night in case her robed pursuers returned. For the first time in days, she slept peacefully and dreamed of her little house with the picket fence in Saltstone.

## 19

------

## JESS

On their first two days of traveling through the Spires, Jess and Danym barely saw any wildlife, much less other travelers. The road's elevation soared, and the air turned crisp. Most of the leaves had fallen from the trees, masking the edges of the road and forcing the pace to slow even more. Despite these challenges, Jess's worries over her mother's reaction and their robed pursuers were beginning to fade. For the first time in her life, Jess could taste freedom, and she savored every moment.

Danym was quiet. At first Jess thought he was just being cautious, not wanting to be heard by anyone who might be on the road. But as they traveled farther from the capital, she suspected his silence was more thought than caution. He was always thinking, working through all the crazy things that might happen and planning for them.

The third day was brutal as the road steepened sharply, and the air became thin, making their breathing labored. Danym struggled with the altitude more than Jess and needed to stop every hour to rest. Around midday, they pulled off the road into a small clearing that butted against a rocky cliff. Lunch was the same monotonous travel rations: dried meat, nuts, and the last of their bread. Jess daydreamed about stealing steaming, freshly made bread from the Palace kitchens. Life in the Palace might've felt like a prison, but the food was amazing.

She finished her last scrap of bread and stood to look around. The view over the cliff was breathtaking, with brushstrokes of brilliant blue clouds and bristly green mountain peaks in every direction. Standing there on what felt like the edge of the world, Jess understood why the ancients had named this land the Kingdom of Spires. There couldn't possibly be anything more beautiful and majestic than these mountains. Danym appeared behind her and wrapped his arms around her waist. He nuzzled her neck with his nose and playfully nipped her ear, sending a shiver through her body. She closed her eyes and painted a mental portrait of that moment—that *perfect* moment she never wanted to end.

Danym released her. She opened her eyes, surprised by the way he squinted off into the distance. She followed his gaze down the steep slope of the cliff and spotted movement. Two brown-robed figures wound their way up the road on horseback.

"I guess thinking we lost them was too much to hope for." Danym sighed. "Let's get back on the road before they get any closer."

Jess couldn't think, just nodded and turned to mount Dittler. The fear that had retreated to the back of her mind now roared to the fore, driving her to move with purpose.

"We're about to start down the other side, and it'll be steep for a bit before leveling out. We can't let them scare us into moving faster than is safe for the horses. They'll have to slow when they get to this point, too." Danym patted his horse's neck as they resumed their trek.

Two hours later, they stopped for the first time since sighting their pursuers. Danym's lungs were burning, and the horses were struggling. Jess walked off the road in search of another hiding place, but returned with a shake of the head, "There's nothing on either side but steep declines."

"I'll be ok. Just give me a few minutes." Danym lowered himself to rest against a large tree.

Jess took the break to give each of the horses an apple. She poured water from one of their skins into a small bowl and held it up to let them drink. They finished the water quickly and looked at Jess in hopes of more. "We'll find a stream, and you can drink as much as you want. Just hang in there a little longer."

Dittler huffed his frustration.

The wind picked up, whistling an eerie tune through the trees. Jess rubbed her arms for warmth and returned the waterskin to Dittler's back. They mounted and continued downward for another hour before the sun began its rapid descent. They had to slow to round a sharp turn when Danym jumped at the sound of something whizzing by his head. He looked up sharply at the arrow lodged in the tree in front of him.

"Jess, go!" he yelled, dropping any pretense of secrecy.

They spurred their horses and moved as quickly as the road would allow. The sounds of hooves on gravel and men shouting were getting closer as another arrow flew past, barely missing Dittler's flank.

The road opened to a long, straight run where the trees cleared, revealing sheer cliffs on either side. They urged the horses for speed, but the sweaty animals were exhausted and thirsty after the last few days of climbing in the thin mountain air.

Jess searched ahead and could see another turn where trees filled the landscape again. Instead of the massive mountains they'd seen throughout the journey, only a few low hills rose to greet them, indicating their approach to the town of Spoke.

Three hundred yards to town.

Danym cried out, "Jess, push harder. If we can make it to town, we can get help."

Fear crept into their mounts, who whinnied loudly and pushed for even more speed. Danym looked back and saw a flash of brown growing larger over the hill.

Two hundred yards to town.

One of the robed men launched another arrow from an impossible distance that seemed a ridiculous attempt. But the arrow flew true and struck Danym in the shoulder. He cried out, then swayed wildly, desperate to stay upright.

One hundred yards to town.

A voice in front of them commanded, "Stop!"

Jess saw three men in green uniforms gathering just

beyond the edge of town, each nocking arrows in their longbows. They were aiming directly at them.

"Please! Help us!" she screamed.

The uniformed men looked over their shoulder and understood their plight. The one in front said something to the others, and all three fired over Jess and Danym into the ground in front of the robed men. They reined in their horses. After another volley that nearly hit one of the men, the robed figures disappeared back into the hills.

Jess tried to slow Dittler, but her spooked horse charged through the line of uniformed men. When he finally came to a halt, Jess looked back and realized Danym wasn't behind her. Panic gripped her, and she yanked Dittler's reins. What she saw made her heart plummet.

Danym was lying face down on the ground, an arrow poking out of his shoulder. He wasn't moving. Two of the uniformed men knelt beside him, assessing his wound. The third man clearly in charge, turned toward Jess. "Miss, care to tell me what this is all about?"

Jess ignored the man, hopped off Dittler, and ran to Danym's side. She couldn't lose him. She couldn't. He'd left everything to be with her, to keep her safe. This was *her* escape, and now Danym might die for taking part in it. The thought made her convulse with tears as she gripped his hand and pulled it to her chest.

"Miss, let us help him. Sergeant Kevon is a Healer, and the arrow doesn't appear to have hit anything important. Your friend should be ok if we can let our man work." The leader placed a hand on her shoulder from behind, urging her to rise and step back.

He turned to the third man. "Go get two more units. We need to chase those bandits down before they cause any trouble in town."

The man gave a crisp nod and disappeared.

Jess watched as Kevon took a thick handled knife from its scabbard on his belt. One edge of the knife looked razor sharp, while the other had a jagged edge like a saw. He turned the serrated edge to the arrow and quickly sawed through it, taking care to not disturb Danym any more than necessary. "Sir, come help me turn him over. I need to get this arrow out before doing any Healing."

As the leader knelt, Kevon handed him a palm-size cloth that had been folded several times and drenched in a sharp-scented liquid, "When I pull the arrow out, you'll need to press this against the wound on his back. Hold it there until I'm done. He might wake up or try to pull away when I remove the arrow, so we'll have to hold him down."

Jess took this cue and knelt with her hands on Danym's good shoulder, ready to assist. Kevon felt the flesh around the arrow with the tips of his fingers, then gripped it. "On the count of three. One … two …" He surprised Jess and yanked on two. The shaft slid free of Danym's body. The leader pressed the cloth as instructed, and Kevon quickly placed his palm above the wound. In seconds, his palm glowed a dim blue that traveled through his hand and into the whole of Danym's shoulder. Danym moaned in unconscious pain and tried to roll over, but Jess and the leader held his weakened frame in place.

The Healing took another hour. Kevon finally rose, the glow fading from his palm and a look of extreme fatigue creasing his eyes. Jess leapt to her feet and wrapped her arms around the Healer.

"Thank you. Thank you. Thank you."

He awkwardly patted her on the back, unsure how to respond. The leader chuckled.

Midway through the Healing, six new men in uniform arrived. The leader dispatched three of them to hunt for the robed men and instructed the others to remain with the group as guards.

While Kevon packed his Healer's bag and the other men prepared to carry Danym into town, the leader pulled Jess aside. "We'll take you and your friend to the local inn and get you settled, but I need to know what's going on. Who were those men chasing you?"

Jess's mind was spinning. She hadn't even thought about needing a cover story for the robed men. Of course they would be stopped by constables or asked basic questions by innkeepers or other locals. How stupid could they have been? The guardsman in front of her wasn't asking anything unusual, especially of someone he'd just rescued from bandits firing arrows at them. *C'mon Jess, think!*

"I don't know. We saw them about halfway from Fontaine, up in the Spires. They tried to steal one of our horses while we were looking over a cliff. Danym wrestled the reins away and knocked the man down, but they didn't give up and chased us all the way here."

The guard leader nodded but didn't say anything, just stood there staring at her, waiting for the rest of the tale. She had no idea what to say and decided to try something her mother once did to get out of a long, boring day at Court. Jess put the back of her hand to her forehead and feigned a dizzy spell, then toppled to the ground. Kevon was by her side in a flash, waving a small bag of something vile under her nose. She sneezed and gagged, nearly blowing her act. As she sat up on her elbows, the Healer checked her pulse and watched her breathing.

"She's exhausted and overcome by the trip, but otherwise fine. Nothing a good dinner and night's rest won't fix." Kevon stood, brushing off his uniform trousers.

"Alright, let's get them into town. Miss, we'll want to hear more about your trip tomorrow, but for now we'll settle for your names," the leader said.

Jess paused a beat too long, "I'm … I'm Petti, and he's my brother Gil."

Kevon and the leader exchanged a glance. "Alright, Miss Petti, let's get you somewhere safe. My men will bring Gil on a stretcher once the others arrive."

As she turned to mount Dittler, Kevon extended a hand to steady her climb. He took a hard look at her horse and whistled. "Only Cretian stallion I ever saw was carrying King Alfred through the countryside at the head of a column. Where'd you come by this handsome fella?"

*Spirits, this is going to be a lot harder than I thought!*

"He was a gift," was all Jess said as she mounted without assistance.

"That's a *royal* gift!" he said in amazement, hitting far closer to the mark than Jess would've liked.

She was relieved when the leader signaled to two of his men and Kevon to form up as her escort. A moment later, they were trotting toward the heart of Spoke, the town often referred to as the Gateway to the Spires.

The trek to the local inn only took a few minutes, but that was enough time for Jess to get a feel for the place. It was getting dark, and little lamps hanging from tall wooden poles were already lit, casting a cozy yellow glow. Most of the buildings and houses were made of rough logs. Sharply sloped roofs designed to allow seasonal snows to slide off to the back crowned each home and shop. The people walking about were even less colorful than the bland, rough-hewn wood of their homes, dressed in simple animal hides and furs. As rough as they looked, nearly everyone they passed made eye contact, smiled, and offered a warm greeting.

Jess was shocked when they stopped at a three-story gray stone building, the largest she had seen in town. A sign bolted into the wood above the large double doors was carved to resemble a large black bird with its wings outstretched. It read, "The Crow's Nest."

A young boy rushed out from around the side of the building and took Dittler. When Jess resisted handing over the reins, Kevon stepped forward. "This is my nephew, Ben. He'll take good care of your horse."

She reluctantly passed Dittler into the care of the youngster, who looked no more than ten.

They walked into a large open room littered with well-worn wooden tables and chairs. At the opposite end of the room, a grand bar sprawled, its rough wooden stools neatly tucked under its ledge. A massive mirror was mounted on the wall behind the bar, nearly spanning the whole width of the room. Rows of colorful bottles lined the shelves in front of the mirror.

The guard leader walked to the bar and greeted the innkeeper, a short round woman with enormous ears that reminded Jess of a strange mouse she'd once seen in a book. The innkeeper gave him a warm smile and giggled at whatever he said to her. Without warning, she reached chubby arms across the bar, took his face in both hands, and pulled him into a long slobbery kiss. The leader wiped his lips with his sleeve and gave the woman a wink and a smile. They spoke for a minute longer, the woman looking over his shoulder at Jess a couple of times, one eyebrow raised.

When they finished talking, the innkeeper disappeared through a half door behind the bar and returned through a side door at the edge of the room, a different young boy in tow. She waddled up to Jess. "Young miss, follow this lad to your room. There'll be a hot bath shortly, and you can come back down in an hour for supper. Your brother should be here soon. I'll make sure he's brought up."

Jess gave the woman a weak smile. "Thank you. A warm bath sounds wonderful."

Ten minutes later, Jess was submerged in steaming water when two guards knocked on the door. "Miss, we have your brother."

"One minute," she said, hopping out of the bath and wrapping a large fluffy towel around her body. *Bath, you stay warm. I'll be right back.*

The guards stared at her towel a bit too long as they carried Danym in on a stretcher, then placed him carefully on the large bed. "Healer says he'll be out another few hours, then'll be hungry as a bear."

One of the men snuck another peak before leaving.

*Men!*

Jess bolted the door and sank back under the soothing water.

## 20

## JESS

Jess emerged from her bath refreshed. She dressed and sat on the edge of the bed, watching the rise and fall of Danym's chest as he rested from the Healing. She carefully pried his shirt open, eyes wide. The angry hole left by the arrow was completely gone, replaced by fresh pink skin. There wasn't even a scar.

Comfortable Danym was safe, she left the room in search of dinner. She descended the narrow stairs and entered the common room on the first floor, greeted by the smell of savory roasted meats. Her stomach rumbled at the prospect of the first hot meal in days.

When they'd first arrived at The Crow's Nest, the common room had been empty and quiet, a stark contrast to the raucous, crowded affair unfolding before Jess. Most of the tables were filled, and the room roared with laughter and music and the clanking of utensils on plates. On the right wall, a fire crackled in its giant stone hearth, somehow making the huge crowded room feel warm and cozy. At the opposite end, a handsome young man dressed in dark-brown leggings and a bright-yellow vest sang and played happy, upbeat tunes on his mandolin. A small group of teenage girls packed around his little stage and squealed with delight as the music rose and fell.

The innkeeper looked up from flitting about the room and made straight for Jess.

"Young miss!" She grabbed Jess's arm and pulled her through the crowd toward an empty table near the fire. "Sit, sit. Looks like you cleaned up real nice; now let's get you something to eat."

The woman scurried away before Jess could speak, leaving her alone at a table for four. She leaned back in her chair and enjoyed the simple warmth of the fire, resting her head on the back of the tall chair. As she scanned the room, she realized there was more than a random scattering of patrons. Near the stage were the teenage girls who appeared to already know each other. Several tables were pressed together, barely containing twelve large men in rough-spun shirts and thick leather trousers. Large coats made of bearskin or some other woodland animal hung tentatively off the backs of their chairs. Most had sleeves rolled up, revealing crisscross patterns of scars both new and old. It made Jess think of a lumberjack she knew as a child, always scraped and cut from long days wrestling branches. The conjoined table was a constant blur of pitchers and mugs as the frazzled serving girl tried to keep up with the thirsty men.

In the far corner, three constables in deep green sat quietly around a table. They leaned forward and spoke softly, reminding Jess of the men of the Privy Council and how they would huddle and scheme in the Palace. *Thank the Spirits I'm out of that awful place!*

In the middle of the room, several tables were occupied by a large family—maybe a couple of families. The adults in the group laughed and ate at one table while seven youngsters entertained themselves at the two adjacent. One of the children appeared to be Jess's age, but the rest couldn't have been more than ten. Every few minutes, one of the parents would turn and half-heartedly address the chaos among their brood.

Those seated at tables near the fire were much older, reminding Jess of her Nan before she died. At one table, an ancient man, bent from seven or eight hard decades, sat peacefully holding the hand of his shrunken, silver-haired wife. They ate quietly and chatted even more so, happy and content, wrapped snuggly in the room's warmth. She watched transfixed as the man's face brightened every time he looked up and caught his wife's eye.

"They're here almost every night." Jess turned to find the innkeeper standing beside her, staring in the same direction. "Been coming here longer than I've owned the place —and that's a good thirty years. Makes your heart full just watching.

"Anyway, here ya go, miss. Beef stew, cornbread, some roots and greens. Oh … and a mug of ale to wash it down. Let me know if ya need anything else."

Jess couldn't believe how much food landed on her table. The innkeeper barked a deep laugh. "If that Healer knows anything, your brother should be down before long and will want to eat it all himself. You'd better get started before he shows up!"

Jess smiled at the mention of Danym and thanked the innkeeper before attacking her meal. The stew was flavorful and hot, perfect on a cool night. She didn't recognize what root she was eating, but savored the earthy beginning followed by a hint of spice. She took a sip of her ale expecting the infamous watery taste that seemed to plague innkeepers throughout the Kingdom, but she was pleasantly surprised at the rich, full balance of the fall brew.

The musician's tunes took a romantic turn, transforming his loyal following's squeals into dreamy stares. Jess was stuffed and happily enjoying her second mug of ale and the contentment that only comes with a full belly when Danym appeared in the doorway near the stage. He searched the room for a minute before settling on Jess and winding his way through the crowd. A pair of the teenage girls noticed him and started giggling and following him with their eyes. A wave of heat rushed through Jess, and she nearly jumped out of her chair before recognizing her own foolishness.

"Don't hate me for my fans. Fame is such a burden." Danym flopped into the chair beside her with a self-satisfied grin, flicking his hair dramatically.

Jess punched his arm before giving him a peck on the cheek. "Somebody sounds a lot better."

"Feels like I slept for a week. But yeah, I do feel a lot better. I'm starving, though." He grabbed a bowl and filled it with the now lukewarm stew, then filled a plate with the last of the vegetables and cornbread.

They chatted about little things, tired of weightier

topics involving robed men and monarchs. At one point, between bites of stew, Danym grinned up at Jess. "I've been meaning to ask about your horse."

"You want to ask about Dittler?"

"More about his name, really. Seems kinda … different. How'd you come up with it?"

She donned a serious, almost somber face. "It's actually a sad story. He's named for a pet I had as a little girl."

Danym felt a stab of guilt at his teasing, but prodded, "Go on."

"When I was little, my room was in the back of the royal quarters in the palace, close to the door leading to the stables. There was a large barn and huge fenced field out back, too. I could hear barks and snorts all day and night. The animals kept me company, became my best friends through my own private door to their magical world. There were horses, cows, sheep, pigs, chickens … ducks. I think we even had some geese in the garden pond. Oh, and there were always dogs and cats chasing each other. I had more fun behind the palace than I ever did in it. I loved that place." She lost herself in the memory and sighed.

"My father spoiled us with new pets, especially for our name day. It became something of a family tradition. One year, when I was probably four or five, he gave me the cutest little baby chick. He was so tiny, but he never seemed scared of me. His bright-white feathers were silky soft—and he had a streak of brown on his tiny forehead between his eyes. Papa called that streak his crown and teased that he would be my heir one day, so I'd better take good care of him. Every time he peeped, my brother Justin would point and squeal, 'Dit, dit, dit.' It was funny but seemed to fit. So, I named him Dittler." She took a long sip of her ale.

"I think it was the next day … It was so early, and all I wanted to do was sleep, but Dittler peeped and peeped and peeped. I reached down from my bed to get him out of his little box and accidentally got his leg stuck between my ring and finger. He squawked and peeped and squealed—jolted me right out of the bed. Without thinking, I yanked my hand away, pulling his tiny leg with me, snapping it right in half. It was terrible! The poor little guy was flopping all around, leg juice staining everything he touched."

Danym tried to stifle a laugh, his eyes twinkling as Jess finished her tale.

"Stop that! It was traumatic!" She feigned offense. "I didn't go see the chickens for weeks!"

Danym lost all composure and a good mouthful of ale. He doubled over laughing as tears burst from his eyes. Jess couldn't help herself and started laughing, too. Before they knew it, tables around them were staring and grinning.

"Leg juice? Really? Is that a thing?" Danym spat as he gasped for breath.

Jess tried to compose herself. "If you make me piddle right here in the middle of this room, I'll knock *your* Dittler off!"

Everyone sitting near the fire burst into laughter, and Danym thought he heard the whispering of "leg juice" several tables away. When the musician caught the fever and played *The Chicken Dance*, utter chaos ensued and the crowd leapt to their feet, arms flailing to the rhythm of the music. They laughed until their sides hurt.

*Poor little Dittler!* Jess thought between gasps.

It took a while for the room to settle, and by then, Jess felt sleep tugging at her lids. Out of the corner of her eye, she noticed the older couple from before, still holding hands, turn and stare with knowing smiles.

"Danym, look at that couple over there. They make me believe happiness really is possible." Jess's eyes fogged.

"Is that what you see for us? Sitting across a table, holding hands, wrinkles deepening with each passing minute?"

That earned him another punch.

"I'm serious. Other little girls dream of being a princess, wearing fancy dresses and living in a palace. I've done all of those things, lived them my whole life, and I'd trade it all for a lifetime like those two."

Danym reached across the table, took her hand and locked eyes. "You already did and here we are."

A huge "Awwwwww" was followed by cheering and clapping from the pack of girls who had quietly reposi-tioned themselves by the bar within earshot of Jess's table, where they hung on every word. Jess blushed brightly before covering her face with a napkin while clinging to Danym's arm. Tears of laughter clouded his vision again.

When Jess looked up again, the old couple had lost themselves in each other again, the man gently caressing his wife's weathered hand as she smiled.

THE NEXT MORNING, A KNOCK AT THEIR DOOR BROUGHT Danym and Jess to their feet.

"Sorry to wake you, miss, but the constables are back and asking for ya both." The innkeeper knocked two more times for good measure.

"We'll be right down. Give us a minute," Jess called out.

They wiped the sleep from their eyes and dressed. "We never talked about who we're supposed to be. What have you told them so far?"

"I told the leader of that city guard unit that you're my brother."

Danym laughed. "Well, we blew that last night. Our only hope is that he didn't talk to the innkeeper—or any of the other hundred people in the room last night."

"So, what now? What do we tell them?"

"My dad always says the toughest guys to crack are the ones who tell mostly truth but weave a lie inside it. Let's just tell them we ran away together. Your parents wanted to marry you off, and we couldn't live without each other. That's the truth, isn't it?" Danym finished lacing his boots and stood.

"I guess. What are our names? What if they ask who our parents are? Or where we live? Or—"

"Jess, breathe. We'll figure it out. If you act nervous, they'll know we're not telling them the whole truth." He placed a steadying hand on her shoulder.

"Nervous? Why would I be nervous? We just ran away from the King and Queen, are being pursued by mysteri-ously robed men who shot you, and are now being questioned by constables. I can't imagine what there is to be nervous about." She ran out of breath ... nervously.

"If you feel like the room is spinning, just let me talk. We'll be fine."

They reentered the common room to find it once again empty and quiet, except for the ever-present innkeeper who was buzzing about. Two uniformed men were seated at a table in the middle of the room, facing the door Danym and Jess walked through. Jess recognized the leader of the group that rescued them as he stood in greeting.

"Good to see you again." He looked Danym up and down. "And nice to see you on your feet, young man. You had us scared for a minute."

"I was too out of it to be scared, but thank you. I hear we owe you our lives."

"Just doing our job. Please, take a seat. We just have a few questions." He smiled warmly as they approached the table.

"Why don't we start with an introduction. I'm First Sergeant Betz and this is my partner, Constable Wilover. You are?"

Jess watched as Danym never broke eye contact with Betz. "Beryl. And this is my fiancée, Sylvia."

Pause.

"So ... You're not brother and sister?"

Jess shifted in her seat and stared at the table as she answered. "No, sir. I'm sorry about that. It's just ... everything moved so fast ... and Da—Beryl was shot. I couldn't think."

Betz's eyes never left Danym's. "Beryl, where are you two headed?"

"Probably east toward Huntcliff. We haven't thought that through all the way, but we had to get out of Fontaine." Danym reached down and grabbed Jess's hand under the table.

"Were those men chasing you in Fontaine? Is that why you're going east?"

Danym laughed. "Oh, no. We just want to get away from her parents."

"Is that right, Miss Sylvia?"

It took Jess a second to realize that Betz was addressing her. She nodded nervously, "Yes, sir."

Betz finally leaned toward Jess. "Sylvia, did your parents hurt you?"

"Oh, no! Never. Nothing like that." Genuine shock flooded Jess's face.

Pause.

Betz changed course. "So, what can you tell us about those men who were chasing you?"

Danym squeezed Jess's hand, hoping she'd take the hint and let him lead. "The first time we saw them, we were at the eastern edge of Fontaine, near the Temple of the One. We got a couple days into the Spires before we saw them again. That's when they started shooting, and we realized we'd better run. You know the rest."

Wilover scribbled notes in a journal. Betz just glared at Danym.

He just stared …

And thought …

And stared.

Danym felt the tickle of sweat bead forming on his temple. *Oh, this is bad!*

Abruptly, Wilover closed his journal and Betz stood. Danym nearly jumped out of his chair. "Well, I think that's all we need for now. Our Healer thinks you'll need a few days to fully recover, so I suggest you stay put for now."

"I'm not sure we can afford to stay too many more nights in this place. We really should get going," Danym said.

"Oh, don't worry about the cost. *The Crown* has you covered." Betz smirked on his way out the door, leaving Jess and Danym frozen.

## 21

---

## KEELAN

K eelan sat on the floor holding Sil. The next ten minutes seemed like hours as her body calmed and she stopped screaming. Everyone in the room was stunned by what they had just witnessed.

"That was unlike any scrying I've ever witnessed. What just happened?" Arch Mage Quin asked Daris.

The young mage ran his hand over his thinning scalp, straightening hair that hadn't been there in years. "Honestly, I'm not sure. I believe Sil connected to the Healer through her link with the horse. There was a close bond between the animal and its owner. Add the magic of a scrying that was focused on the Healer, and it makes a strange sort of sense. I don't know, though."

Keelan looked up. "I think it's safe to assume that Tiana is alive and being held captive. Daris, did you get any sense of her location, even a direction?"

"No. Nothing from the scrying. When Sil wakes, she

may be able to fill in some gaps. She was seeing and experiencing things we might not have seen in the bowl."

"Keelan, Atikus just arrived in Saltstone. He's headed our way and believes he has information that may help. I suggest we adjourn to my office where Sil can rest more comfortably until he gets here," Quin said.

Keelan nodded, rose, and lifted Sil, bracing himself for the long downward spiral of tower stairs.

An hour later, Atikus, Ridley, and Liv walked into the Arch Mage's office. Quin was seated behind his desk while the others claimed chairs around the table at the opposite end of the room. Keelan had placed Sil in one of the soft leather chairs beside the hearth where she remained asleep, wrapped in the warmth of a thick woolen blanket. Quin rose to greet his guests.

"Atikus, good to have you back." Quin gripped wrists with his old friend.

"It was only a couple of days, but I'm glad to be home," Atikus said. "Forgive my impertinence, Arch Mage, but we should talk. We have some idea which direction the Healer was taken, and I fear her time is running out."

Keelan rose to greet Atikus. "Should I send for the Captain-Commander? He will want a full report."

Quin intervened. "No. We can fill him in once we've spoken. Atikus doesn't have that urgency in his voice often. I've learned to listen quickly when he does." He looked over at Sil and thought for a moment. "Keelan, I hate to wake Sil, but we need to know what she saw before deciding our next steps."

Keelan nodded and knelt beside her, then placed a hand on her shoulder. When she didn't wake, he shook a little harder. "C'mon Sil, we need to talk."

Quin walked over and pressed his index finger into the middle of her forehead. A short pulse of blue-white traveled from his fingertip into her skin. Her eyes popped open, and she blinked her bleary eyes a few times. "Keelan, what happened?"

"You passed out while we were scrying with Tiana's horse," he said. "You looked terrified and kept saying 'Save me,' over and over."

Sil tried to sit up, but Quin placed his hand on her shoulder. "Don't get up. You'll be disoriented for some time and need to rest. Can you remember what you saw during the scrying?"

Everyone gathered around Sil's chair to listen as her weak voice walked them through the series of images that had shifted through her head. "It was so much more than just images, though. Emotions rushed through me with each new image. Warmth and love at Tiana's face. Sadness at images of her house. I think those were all the horse's memories and feelings.

"Then everything became really … intense. Fear, bordering on panic. Pain. A feeling of loss and loneliness. When the man appeared overhead, I felt a spike of hope and excitement, then confusion, then panic. I can't remember anything after that."

The office was still, save the crackle of the fire in the hearth. Sil leaned back in her chair, exhausted.

Ridley was the first to break the silence. "Lieutenant,

while searching the grounds behind the Freeport victim's last known location, we found her family's signet ring. The local Mages used this ring to scry for her location. They couldn't pinpoint more than a westerly direction involving mountains and the scent of pine, but this seems to match some of what Sil saw and experienced."

Keelan's mind was a jumble. It felt like the puzzle pieces were there, but someone kept shuffling them, preventing him from locking the full picture into place.

He looked at Ridley, "Let's go over what we know for certain, starting with Freeport. The victim was taken and moved west, likely beyond the mountains that border The Kingdom. She's now dead. Anything else material?"

Ridley shook his head. "No, that sums it up. Nothing else we found appears to connect to the Saltstone case."

"OK, let's turn to Saltstone. The healer was taken some time over the last four or five days. Her infirmary was ransacked, and her house was emptied, down to the pictures on the walls. We also know she ended up in the mountains, surrounded by the smell of pine, and was transported in a wooden container. What else?"

Sil's fragile voice interrupted. "Don't forget the man with the green eyes. I got the sense that he wasn't one of her kidnappers. A strong feeling of hope came over me when I saw his face."

"Can you describe him again?" Keelan asked.

"He was leaning over, looking down as if the Healer was lying down. He searched without looking like he saw anything of interest, then turned away," Sil said. "From that angle it was hard to tell, but he looked tall and had a strong jawline. His hair was wavy, almost curly, and one curl fell over his right eyebrow. His coat was the dark green of a uniform, maybe a Ranger's. I think there was a bow on his back, but the image wasn't clear. The one thing I saw more clearly than anything was his eyes. They were the brightest emerald-green eyes I've ever seen. They seemed kind, but there was also a sadness to them, too … I don't know. Maybe I was just feeling the Healer's sadness."

Keelan looked up at the Arch Mage and others in the room. "Is there anything else we can do using magic? We've narrowed our search down to west of the mountains, which leaves us a country the size of Melucia and all our border neighbors combined."

The Mages started talking all at once, and while Keelan had a hard time following their chatter, it was clear they understood each other well. The group spent another hour walking through possible next steps and questioning their theories before Keelan decided it was time to act.

"Thank you for your insight, everyone. We're heading west to Grove's Pass. Sil, I wish we could leave you here to rest and recover, but we may need your Gift before this is over. Atikus, I would like you and Ridley to join us. Guardsmen Buros and Wint, return to HQ and report to the Captain-Commander. Tell him everything, every detail, then ask for a new assignment. Thank you for your help." Keelan nodded to each of them.

He then turned to Atikus. "We need to restock for another trip. Let's meet at the Western Gate in one hour. There's enough daylight left that we should be able to knock out a third of the trip to Grove's Pass today. If we have decent weather, we'll make it there by nightfall tomorrow. Arch Mage, is there anything you can give Sil to help her? I need her on horseback for at least another three or four hours."

"I'm sure we can come up with something. Leave her with us while you pack," Quin said.

Keelan walked out as Quin and the other Mages worked on something for Sil. It was going to be a long night.

———————

THE GROUP MET AT THE WESTERN GATE A LITTLE MORE than an hour later. Keelan had visited the Officer's Mess and packed enough travel rations to see them to Grove's Pass. The Mages gave Sil some vile-tasting concoction that had her looking less glassy-eyed and somewhat rested. She said she felt like she'd been kicked by a horse but could ride. Ridley took the time to get fresh horses from the stables and a pair of small tents since there were no towns between Saltstone and Grove's Pass.

They made good time and camped in a clearing by the fork where the road splits between a journey to Grove's Pass and the tiny village of Crees. Atikus started a small fire and heated some stew. Sil stretched out to "rest her eyes" while Keelan cooked but was fast asleep when dinner was served. Atikus stopped Keelan from waking her, wagering rest was more important than food after her day filled with magical exhaustion.

The next day was spent mostly in silence, Keelan and Atikus occasionally talking through some lead or clue or image from the past few days. There was a slight chill as the sun dropped behind the mountains when they arrived at their destination that sat on the outskirts of Grove's Pass.

The Ranger's Headquarters was made of immense wooden logs and reminded Keelan of Tiana's infirmary but on a palatial scale. This massive building served as the governing center for Rangers throughout Melucia. It contained living quarters for over a hundred Rangers, a dining hall, administrative offices, classrooms, a small training arena, and even an indoor archery range.

Rangers had served Melucia as the first line of defense on the border for over a thousand years, claiming dominion over woods and mountains alike. Thanks to the peace that reigned throughout the past ten centuries, the Rangers' mission had morphed from border security to protecting wildlife and woodlands, attracting many whose Gifts touched the natural world. Rangers were often proud, solitary men and women more at home overlooking a waterfall or mountain cliff than on a crowded city street. And yet, there was a unity of purpose where protection of others was a core mission. Rangers valued life above all else, no matter what form it took.

Ridley and Sil had never visited Grove's Pass and were awed by the scale of the Rangers' Headquarters.

"When you said we were coming to see the Rangers, I had a tiny shack in the woods pictured in my mind. This place is huge!" Sil stared up with wide eyes.

The group walked through the main entrance and began looking around, hoping to get settled for the night and have a quick supper. An excited voice called out from across the large entry, "KEELAN!"

Sil and Ridley had to jump out of the way as a tall Ranger bounded across the room at a full gallop and slammed into Keelan, knocking him to the ground. Before Sil could blink, the two were wrestling and laughing like children. Sil didn't know what to make of the scene and turned to Ridley with a questioning glance. He shrugged and shook his head.

Atikus walked through the door and his face lit up with a bright, wide smile. The old man dropped his pack and shouted with mock indignation. "Declan Rea, what do you think you're doing down there on the ground? Did no one teach you manners, young man?"

Keelan and his assailant froze. Declan looked up and saw his adopted father for the first time in years. Tears of joy threatened to overwhelm them both as he leapt to his feet and into the old Mage's arms.

Atikus released Declan from the hug and stepped back to get a good look at him. "My boy, it's only been three years, and I think you've grown into a tree."

Declan couldn't wipe the goofy, boyish grin off his face. Atikus was the only father he'd ever known, and he couldn't believe the old Mage was standing in front of him now. So many times, he'd daydreamed about his years in the Mages' Guild as a little boy, wondering what the old mage was up to.

Keelan gathered himself and turned Declan around, facing Sil and Ridley. "I'm sorry guys, please let me introduce my little brother, Declan. Declan, meet Guardsmen Ridley Doa and Sil Wesser."

Ridley stepped forward and clasped forearms with Declan, but Sil stood transfixed, her eyes wide and mouth open in shock. Declan turned and gave her a little head bob and smile. "Nice to meet you, ma'am."

Keelan saw the look on Sil's face and stepped forward. "You alright, Sil?"

"It's him. The man in the vision." All color had drained from her face, and she wobbled. Ridley wrapped his arm around her shoulders to brace her and led her to a chair against the near wall.

Declan looked back at Keelan and asked, "What's she talking about? What vision?"

Atikus cleared his throat to get their attention. "Could we get settled, maybe have some supper first? Then we could talk somewhere more private."

"Of course," Declan said. He called out to a Ranger behind a desk at the far end of the entryway, asking him to get someone to retrieve the group's bags and find them rooms for the night. He then led them through a series of hallways to a small conference room with a simple wooden table and padded chairs.

As everyone took their seats, he closed the door, sat beside Atikus, and turned to Keelan. "The mess was already shutting down for the night, and it'll take them a bit to prep some dinner. Let's talk through things while we wait. My Ranger sense is going nuts, and it never lies. What's this all about?"

Atikus cocked his head at Declan with a curious look but said nothing.

Keelan and Sil told the story of the missing women again. The others interjected in places, filling in details from their parts of the tale. Sil was the last to speak as she recalled her experience with the scrying and the link to Tiana's horse.

"I still don't get why you think the man in your vision was me. I haven't seen anyone who matches your missing Healer's description, and I would've heard about it if another Ranger had run into her," Declan said.

Sil shook her head. "I believe you looked right at her but didn't see her. What about men in brown robes? Have you seen anything like that?"

"I remember a pair of men in brown robes. Gave me the creeps. I was returning to Grove's Pass after a day on patrol, and they were taking a cart through the mountains, looked like a return trip after selling whatever they had brought into the country. We've had some strange things going on and are searching every caravan that passes, even though travelers are a rarity these days. I didn't find anything when I looked in the back of the cart. There wasn't any reason to detain them, so they continued through the mountains."

After a moment of watching his brother think, Declan asked, "What was in that cart I missed?"

"We believe our kidnap victim. The Mages haven't figured out how, but we think a kidnapper used magic to disguise her presence from you."

"Hmm. Interesting trick."

Keelan leaned forward. "Dec, when was this? It's important."

"Yesterday, about an hour before dark."

"A two-day lead. Once they get through the mountains, the roads are good, and they can make quick time. How long would it take them to make it through with a cart this time of year?" Keelan asked.

"There wasn't anything wrong with the cart or its wheels that might slow them down; plus, it was empty, and that would help with speed going up and down. The pass crosses five different mountains, a couple are steep climbs and descents. I'd say an experienced team could make it in three or four days, no less. I stopped them at the base of the first mountain, which is the starting point, and they didn't seem in any hurry.

"Kee, I know what you're thinking. You can't go after them tonight. The road through the mountains is challenging enough in the daylight, but it's deadly at night, especially up top. We find dozens of travelers each year who try it, lose their footing, and die at the bottom. Besides, you won't be able to see enough to pick up their trail until it's light again," Declan said, a touch of urgency in his voice.

Atikus leaned in and placed a hand on Keelan's arm. "Keelan, listen to your brother. No one knows these mountains like a Ranger. We need a good meal, and Sil needs rest."

Declan nodded. "Let's get you settled into rooms, and we can meet back in the dining hall. You've got to be hungry."

Declan stepped out, returning a few minutes later with a lanky youngster to show them to their rooms. "Your packs are already waiting for you, so there's no need to go back up front."

A short time later, the group was huddled around a large wooden table in the dining hall. The table was piled high with slices of roasted boar, stewed greens, crusty browned potatoes, and several platters of various berries and fruits. Pitchers of ale and water were scattered throughout, reminding Keelan of the raucous inns he'd visited in his time with the Guard. Nobody drank like a man in blue—so they said. Based on this table, green looked pretty good, too.

Sil and Ridley realized they were attending a family reunion and focused on their plates and mugs. Atikus was usually the one lost in his plate, but he couldn't stop smiling and laughing as he listened to Keelan and Declan recounting the years they lived together with the Mages. At one point, Declan started telling a story but barely got a sentence out before Keelan took over. It was like watching a wrestling match as the two twisted and tossed their way through the tale. Atikus couldn't resist adding his own embellishment. The old mage's habit of making grand gestures as he spoke became a hazard when he forgot he was holding a very full mug and threw half of its contents all over Declan. The laughter of the table devolved into a bout of hyperventilating that seemed to last forever. Keelan sat back in his chair and watched the spectacle with tears streaming down his face. He hadn't experienced such simple pleasure in … well … he couldn't remember.

Another hour passed before Sil and Ridley stood, ready to end their long day. "Lieutenant, would you like to meet here in the morning?"

"Yes, that's good. We'll eat a bite and make our plan for the day. Declan, can you join us tomorrow? It would be helpful to have a guide who knows the mountains."

"I already cleared it with the Captain. We discussed a few ideas on where to start. I can go over it all with the group in the morning," Declan said.

Sil and Ridley offered their good nights and left Keelan, Declan, and Atikus to continue their reunion. Declan suggested they move their discussion to a more comfortable setting and guided them to a small reading room that shared a half-wall with the building's modest library. At the end opposite where they entered were four padded lounge chairs with small tables in between, forming a half-circle facing a cozy fireplace whose blaze crackled merrily. On the wall beside the door sat a small bar on wooden wheels, containing a few simple glass tumblers stacked beside several decanters filled with liquors of varying color. After Atikus sniffed and swirled and swilled, he mumbled his approval. The brothers rolled grinning eyes at each other and poured a glass, then fell into the comfortable chairs.

They talked late into the night, recounting childhood adventures, mostly involving Declan terrorizing some Mage or staff member. Declan peppered Keelan with questions about his Guard training and cases attributed to his now famous big brother. Atikus watched the two buzzing back and forth. It felt like he was in his office at the Mages' Guild watching 8-year-old Keelan for the first time, his tiny fuzzy-headed brother by his side. He leaned back, savoring the smooth liquor, and let the crackling fire warm his old bones.

"Kee, I still can't believe you're this big wig Guard in the capital," Declan said. "I mean, I can believe it. You were always gonna be in the Guard, and they all loved you for it. Everybody knew you were the rising star, while I couldn't even figure out which way to turn."

The sharp edge that crept into Declan's voice caught Keelan and Atikus off guard. Atikus leaned toward him. "That Ranger uniform seems to fit you pretty well, son. I'm proud you've found your way."

"Found my way? Huh … I guess." Declan stared into the fire. "Guess I like being a Ranger ok, but I spend a lot of time wandering around the mountains alone, trying to figure out what I'm doing up here. It's almost as lonely on a mountain as it was in the halls of the Mages' Guild."

"What are you talking about? You were the most popular kid in the Guild. They fell all over themselves loving everything about adorable little Declan," Keelan said, surprised by the bitterness flowing through his own voice.

"Yeah, right. I was right up there with the kitchen staff. The cute little Mute with the big hair that nobody thought would ever amount to anything."

"Declan, that's not true," Atikus said a bit defensively. "I've always believed in you, even if you never gave your-self much of a chance."

"How was I supposed to give myself a chance when

magic decided I wasn't good enough?" Declan snapped back.

A thick, smothering fog of silence blanketed the room.

Declan finally walked to the rolling table and refilled his glass.

"Why did you come out here? Join the Rangers?" Keelan's asked in a quiet voice.

Declan flopped back into the chair, set his glass down, and leaned over, elbows on his legs. When he spoke again, his voice was a whisper. "I don't really know, Kee. I had to do *something*. You were the one that was good at everything. All I ever did was make people smile a little, make 'em laugh at me. Guess I was just trying to fit into a world that didn't make any sense. Maybe I was running away. Or running to ... I don't know ... to a place without all those damn collars. Somewhere I could figure things out."

"Collars? You mean the Gifted collars?" Atikus asked bewildered.

"Yeah. Those." Declan sucked in a deep breath. "You won't get it. Nobody can. Well, at least none of *you* can."

Something in Declan was cracking open, and it tore at Atikus's heart. He leaned forward and put a hand on his shoulder. "Go on, son. I *want* to understand."

Declan took another deep breath. He sipped his drink and swirled his glass, eyeing the ice cubes as if they would hop out and run away. His gaze turned toward the fire. Anything to avoid eye contact with his brother and Atikus.

"Magic is everything, especially in a place like Salt-stone where your collar doesn't just represent your ability, but your social status, too. Keelan never even had to think about it. You handed him a gold collar the day you found us. But no matter how much I wanted it, how much I tried or begged or prayed, magic never came. Yes, I made people love me by acting out and making them laugh. But that's not the same. It's just not.

"Growing up, it wasn't that big of a deal because there was always hope. Hope magic would come. Hope I'd one day make you proud when you put the collar around my neck, too. But that day never came."

Declan took a long pull on his drink and stared into his glass. "People treat Mutes differently. Either they look down and say we're stupid, or they give us a look of pity, like we're crippled or somehow broken. Like *I'm* broken …"

Moisture reflected in Declan's eyes against the firelight. "When I got older, sixteen … maybe seventeen … I saw people's eyes change. They were afraid for me, for what I couldn't do, for what I might miss, for the life I wouldn't have. I could see it in their eyes. Spirits, Kee, I could see it in *your* eyes when I was a lot younger than that!" He snatched his glass of the table and downed the last of his drink in one large swallow.

The fire crackled for a long moment before Declan spoke again in a strained voice. "I had to get away from it all. I just couldn't take it anymore."

Atikus and Keelan leaned back in their chairs, speechless. Keelan ran a hand over his head, not believing what he was hearing. Sure, Declan was a little lost, never knowing what he wanted to be when he grew up. But what kid doesn't feel that? He was a happy boy. Always happy.

The Mages threw every subject they could think of at him to spark his interest, but studying just wasn't for Declan. He was a free spirit who thrived on making everyone around him smile and laugh. Keelan couldn't remember a time when Declan didn't seem upbeat. To hear what he'd carried inside for so long, what he still carried …

Declan set his glass down on one of the little side tables. "We need to get some rest before tomorrow. It'll be a long day."

Without another word, he turned and walked out of the room, leaving Atikus and Keelan staring at each other.

Keelan broke their stunned silence. "It's funny. I was always jealous of Declan. Sure, the Mages and Guardsmen focused a lot of energy on making me better, pushing me to be the best, but everybody loved Declan. No, they *worshiped* him. We would walk into a room together, and it was like I wasn't even there. He's six years younger, a life-time apart when you're a kid, and I looked up to *him*. I wanted to be that crazy and funny and … I don't know … free. Declan doesn't get how tight those collars fit. Around everything."

"Keelan, give your brother a little time. He started talking tonight. Maybe this trip will do you two some good, get things out in the open so you can help each other." Atikus offered a fatherly smile.

"You know, when I look at you two together again, I can't help but see those two scared boys who walked into my office just yesterday. Well, maybe a few yesterdays ago." He chuckled, smiling at the memory that felt far away.

Without another word, the two men rose and walked to their rooms for some much-needed rest. Atikus fell asleep with visions of a two-year-old monster topped with dandelion hair running through the hallways of the Guild. Keelan spent most of the night staring at the rough ceiling and wrestling with childhood demons, some of whom looked a bit like a dandelion, too.

## 22

## ISABEL

The Queen knelt cupping the small delicate flower with her hand. The heart-shaped petals carried a bright purple line down the center and were among Isabel's favorite in the lush royal garden. She sat on the ground and crossed her legs, facing the flower. The bloom's sweet fragrance hung in the crisp, near-winter air and heightened her awareness as she closed her eyes to meditate. The garden was the one place in the world where she, Queen of the largest nation on the planet, could be alone. No courtiers. No ladies. No peasants begging for this or that. No children. *Sweet Irina, no children! What a wonderful thought.*

She closed her eyes and her mind cleared, erasing the images of the garden, turning to dark, blessed emptiness. In this place of nothing, this darkness, she was most aware and could see beyond. Her mind's eye opened, and the darkness was filled with the scene of men marching along a road, the King's Road. Thousands upon thousands of archers in columns of three moved in unison toward the east. She shifted her Sight to the head of the columns to find the tail of another massive line of armed men. This line was comprised of mounted knights in tunics of dark green and gray, each wearing a sharply pointed silver helmet that glinted like the peaks of the Spires themselves. Dark green banners framed in gold fringe, embroidered with the artistic white outline of the Kingdom's famed mountains, were held aloft by men on either side of the columns. The pennants snapped furiously in the billowing wind. Ahead of the horsemen, she could see the towering eastern mountain range. They were close.

Her Sight shifted again, and a small town came into view. She focused intently on memories of her daughter and was rewarded with an image of Jess and Danym sitting at a small table by a large fire. They looked happy, content even. She watched for a long moment, trying to decipher the movement of their lips. Her Sight was a powerful Gift, but it only let her See, not hear or speak. Frustrating limitation. Perhaps one day—

"Issy, Council is assembling." The King's voice accompanied his hand on her shoulder.

Her Sight vanished, jolting her annoyed senses back to the garden … and the King.

She blinked a few times and rubbed her eyes. Reorienting herself after using her Clairvoyant Gift always took a few moments. "I'll be right there. Give me a minute or two."

Alfred patted her shoulder and left her alone in the garden.

She sighed. For one blissful moment, she'd had the world to herself. One day.

She unfolded her legs and stood in the fluid motion of an acrobat, never touching the ground with her hands. It was a point of pride for the Queen that, at forty-one, she was still athletic and limber. She reached down toward her toes, stretching her tight legs and back, and spotted the gold and purple bloom just inches from her face. A smile parted her lips as she reached toward the flower and held it between her fingers. Her Gift stirred at her calling, and the bloom burst into flame.

---

WHEN SHE ARRIVED IN THE THRONE ROOM, THE PRIVY Council was fully assembled, with the King seated on his throne and a heated discussion already in progress. She ascended the dais to her place beside the King, quickly judging the body language of the Councilors before her. All eyes were on Trade Minister Carver who appeared exasperated, with flushed cheeks and labored breathing. Chancellor Thorn sat at the head of the Council table, back straight, chin high, a stone unmoved by the storm. General Marks and Minister Bril whispered heatedly at the table's other end while the remaining ministers filled seats along the sides.

Carver waved his arms wildly as he spoke, lace ruffles flapping and snapping with each gesture. "Your Majesty, this is madness. Melucia is our largest trading partner. If the Chancellor's information is correct, they have four or five times the number of Gifted than exist in the Kingdom. Why would they need to steal what few we have? Why would they risk so much to gain so little?"

Isabel had never seen the pompous man so flushed. His powdered wig was disheveled and cocked to the side while his exquisite long-coat lay rumpled and tossed forgotten on the side of his chair.

Thorn didn't let the room breathe. "Because they know our military might would crush them without magic. They want to take the last of ours to ensure we can never attempt to master them again."

"Master them? Who wants to master anyone?" Minister Carver spit back, arms flailing over the polished table.

While the ministers argued, Isabel leaned toward Alfred and whispered, "What did I miss? You have them really worked up this morning."

The King didn't return her smile. Odd. "We have new reports from Sebastiano's network tying the missing Gifted to Melucia. The clues are nothing in themselves but paint a pretty clear picture when added together."

Alfred rose, silencing his advisors who turned to their sovereign. "Sebastiano, please walk us through your reports again. The Queen hasn't heard this information, and I need a moment to think."

"Of course, Your Majesty." The High Sheriff stood and gathered his notes scattered across the table. "As you know, the first reported kidnapping occurred in Marlon, a small fishing village that only has two constables. It took some time for a team from the capital to arrive, so most of the investigative trail was cold. There was only one item found where we believe the kidnapping occurred, a button embossed with the symbol of an owl, wings outstretched. This matches those worn by the Rangers, the border guards of Melucia.

"We disregarded the button as coincidence until our team in Cooper reported finding a few Melucian coins on the floor of the home where that kidnapping occurred. The coins are common, but Cooper is the farthest point on the map from Melucia. It's unusual to see them turn up so far west.

"In Ario, where the Natural was taken, we didn't find any relevant evidence. However, Crelt, where the most recent victim was taken, was a different matter. An old man selling clams at the docks noticed two men in brown robes helping a drunk friend onto a small boat. He watched as one of the men stepped off the boat, removed his cloak and bent to tie his boot laces. Our witness was only a few paces away. The old man served in the Royal Guard for twenty years, stationed in Huntcliff most of that time, and said he'd recognize a Rangers' boots anywhere because of the embossed owl on the ankle. He described the symbol perfectly. I've seen it many times myself."

This time, silence loomed uninterrupted, and all eyes turned to track the King as he paced thoughtfully in front of the throne.

The Sheriff spoke again, "Your Majesty, this is all still coincidental. As Minister Carver said, Melucia is our greatest trading partner, and the items found are common. That a man wore the boots of a Ranger may mean nothing more than he once served or bought them from another. No one has seen the missing Gifted cross the border, and there has been no aggression or incursion into our territory by the Rangers."

"Perhaps no aggression, but increased patrols and presence in the mountains." General Marks joined the fray. "Your Majesty, we must prepare for every possibility. The two units currently headed to the border will not be enough if the enemy attacks. We need enough force present to counter … or preempt it if necessary."

The Queen rose and walked to her husband with a raised brow. "Preempt?"

"Yes, Your Majesty. If we wait to defend, we allow Melucia's generals to choose the time and manner of the battle. With their advantage in magic, our border would be nearly impossible to defend. But if we attacked first, caught them unaware, we set the terms for engagement. With our advantage in numbers, that is a battle I'm confident we can win."

The table erupted, each Minister shouting to make his point above the other. Alfred couldn't make sense of the melee, so he whispered to Isabel, "What do you think?"

"We both want to reign in peace, but I fear others have already chosen the path of war."

The King bowed his head and rubbed his temples. When he spoke, his voice was low and quiet, but somehow calmed the chaos of the Council. "General Marks, how long would it take to get the army into position?"

"Winter is nearly here, Your Majesty. No one, not even the Melucians with their magic, could move an army over the mountains once the snows begin. That gives us four or five months to prepare."

The ministers shuffled uncomfortably as the King turned away and stared at the back of his throne for a long moment. He spoke in a near-whisper, his gaze never leaving the ornate crown carved into the top of his seat of power. "Get the army ready, General. No one crosses the border without my order, but I want the men in place before the spring thaw."

———

Isabel's mind raced as she hustled through the halls of the Palace toward her study. The pieces were falling into place. The Council supported preparations— well, everyone except that horse's ass Carver. The massive might of the military would move toward the border soon. The clues left at the kidnapping sites had worked perfectly, especially the Ranger's boots. Those little droppings had been Thorn's idea. His network of spies was buried so deep inside the Sheriff's organization that he knew about the kidnappings before the Sheriff. Adding a little seasoning to the crime scenes was simple.

But Isabel's well-rehearsed performance challenging preemptive action forced ministers to actively defend their suppositions and press for action. For thirty years, Alfred talked constantly about preserving the peace he was gifted by a thousand years of Kings before him. Yet today's act had won even the King to the side of battle.

The Kingdom was preparing for war.

Now all Isabel needed was to get Jess back under control. The thought of her spoiled, willful daughter made her neck turn red and hot. She was given everything—and would have everything as Queen. How dare she defy her mother when the family needed unity now more than ever? If her little adventure became widely known, it could shake confidence in the throne. Jess had to realize that some things were more important than her pitiful little heart.

Thanks to her Sight, Isabel knew exactly where Jess was hiding. Hiding—ha. She wasn't even doing that very well, sitting in the middle of a public tavern like some peasant. Between Thorn and the Queen, there wasn't an inn anywhere in the Kingdom that didn't have at least one agent as a permanent fixture. But now that she knew their location, how would she bring her home? She could simply have her taken by force and returned, but that would only heighten tensions between them. Somehow it would need to be Jess's idea to return.

Thorn was waiting for her when she entered her study. He offered a respectful bow.

"You did well this morning, Danai. I expected more of a fight, especially from Alfred."

"Thank you, Your Majesty. But I believe your deftness added the final bow." Thorn smiled and offered another deferential head bob.

Isabel walked to the tea cart in the corner and poured a cup, adding a small drop of honey. "So, where are we? Walk through it all again."

"Things are moving along nicely. Council broke three hours ago, and Minister Bril has already ordered units to prepare for travel to the border. He held back four units, one for protection of the capital and three to guard the port towns of Cooper, Kitchton, and Brighton. He also ordered our fleet to begin heavy patrols of the Fersh Bay and the waters off Freeport. This should get them out of colder waters before winter can immobilize them. Plus, they'll be in position to form a blockade when ordered. Unit commanders should receive their orders and begin preparations tomorrow. Bril even increased training quotas at the Academy and other military recruitment offices. I think he's actually excited to see some action for a change.

"As for our little escapee, thanks to Your Majesty, my agents note their every move. They stand ready for whatever action you command." Thorn waited for his queen to sit before following suit in a chair opposite hers.

"Good. Have them remain out of sight. I'm still thinking through how to handle her." Isabel took a sip. "What about on the Melucian side? You still haven't told me your plan there."

Something shifted in Thorn, and Isabel thought he suddenly looked uncomfortable. Interesting.

"The Melucians discovered one of my agents who was embedded in the Guard. He was captured a week ago and hasn't been heard from since. I immediately ordered all other agents into silence until further notice. Unfortunately, we are blind for the moment."

"They were bound to find one at some point. You have what, ten, twelve embedded throughout Saltstone?"

Thorn shifted in his seat, avoiding her eyes. "Roughly, Your Majesty."

Isabel gave him a stern look and shook her head. "After all this time, you guard your secrets, even from me."

"Forgive me, Your Majesty. It is for your own protection. You know that one effect of my Telepathic Gift is protection from mental intrusion. Without the Gift of Telepathy, your mind is vulnerable to those who might use their Gift to sift through secrets of your own. I merely act to protect our plans."

This was a painfully familiar conversation, but Isabel was still dubious. She'd never heard the magical theory from any other Mage. Then again, there were no other Telepaths in the Kingdom's Guild. Maybe he was being honest, but something made her pause every time he repeated this lesson.

"Fine. How long will you keep the network quiet?"

"That depends on the Melucians. They are searching for more agents—quite aggressively. We dare not move too quickly or we risk the entire network."

Isabel catalogued that conversation. Something didn't feel right, and she needed time to think. She switched directions. "What about the Conclave? The King will need to present the case for war to the Nobles. They feed and supply our armies, and we'll need unified support throughout the conflict."

Thorn spun the ruby ring he wore on his left pinky. Silly nervous tick. "Yes, he will need to be impressive on that day. But nothing today would force Conclave, so we have some time to build the case for war among the people. If they support the King, the Nobles will have no choice. They may be the only men ever born without spines."

Isabel nearly spit her tea as they both laughed. "You're probably right, but the whole plan hinges on their support. Think that through and come back to me by the end of this week."

She stood and set her cup down on a side table, then walked to a bookshelf and stared at its contents, not really seeing any of the books. "I need to think, Danai. Leave me."

Isabel heard the door close and smiled at the silence that filled the room. She scanned the ancient leather-bound volumes. This was her favorite room in the palace, and she realized she'd never even looked at the hundreds of books that filled the surrounding shelves. Histories of every nation, stories of great men—*Why always men?*—even fanciful fictions of magical lands and creatures and people. She noticed a few her mother had read to her when she was a child and smiled fondly at the memory.

As she turned, an old volume on the top shelf caught her eye. The leather had been dyed an odd deep crimson that time had worn down to near black. Faded gold script on the spine formed words she couldn't comprehend, but curiosity overcame her. She slid the rolling ladder into place and climbed a few rungs, now eye-level with the mysterious work. She could barely make out a date on the spine—nearly twelve hundred years ago! Her heartbeat quickened as she reached for the book, gently running her finger down the spine.

With a reverence Isabel rarely showed anything, she pried the book from its neighbors. Standing on the ladder, she opened the first few brittle pages and smiled at how well preserved they were. She couldn't puzzle out any of the strange symbols but found a map in the last section. It was stunning, both in its detail and artistry. She traced her finger over the familiar shape of her continent, surrounded by a smattering of islands. Gold filigree surrounded bright greens and blues, giving the map a richness rarely seen in works of art.

Two things leapt off the page. On a large island to the southeast of the Melucian end of the continent was a concentration of the shimmering gold, as if the artists accidentally dripped a large amount between indentations that represented mountains. But it couldn't be accidental. It was perfectly smooth, edges expertly rounded. Odd.

She grinned at the second revelation. There were *no borders*, no divisions, no national boundaries. The massive continent was wreathed in gold, but not separated by it. She scanned the page again and realized that there was only one name large enough to represent a nation and it hit her— there was only one nation, one Kingdom, and it included the entire continent and most of the surrounding isles. This had to be Irina's map, crafted when every lord bent the knee to her power and majesty. This book was a priceless relic of a time long past, a time when all people were unified under the rule of one woman.

This was the sign. The sign she'd been praying for. The Gods or Spirits or whatever was looming over humanity's shoulder had led her to this moment, to a new age—again, under one powerful woman. This would be *her* time.

## 23

## DECLAN

The next morning, the group met in the dining hall for a quick breakfast of fresh biscuits, eggs, and bacon. Declan was his friendly, gregarious self again, as if the conversation from the prior night had never taken place. He seemed at home making friends with Sil and Ridley, entertaining them with Ranger jokes and mountain tales, most of which sounded more like children's fables than actual events. He had them laughing through most of the meal. Atikus and Keelan gave each other the same questioning look before giving up and focusing on the meal.

As Atikus was reaching across the table to fill his third plate, Keelan cleared his throat to get everyone's attention. "Declan, before we make a plan for the day, something's been bothering me since we walked through the cases last night."

Declan almost looked through him, trying to decide which conversation was bothering his brother, and whether he should be angry about it being raised in front of the others.

"Has there been anything else strange going on up here? When we talked last night, you seemed a little guarded with how you described things around the border."

Based on the look on his face, Declan wasn't expecting that question. He looked at the table for a minute to gather his thoughts before speaking. "That's a question for my Captain. I'm sorry, but I really can't say more than that."

Keelan was dumbstruck. He was used to working on sensitive cases and understood the need to protect information, especially when there was a bit of rivalry between the Green and Blue, but he didn't expect Declan to play that card before they had even started their search together. He took a breath.

"Would I be able to speak with him today?"

"Of course. We don't get visitors from the capital that often, especially famous Guardsmen, so I'm sure he'll want to meet you anyway," Declan said, a slight edge returning to his voice.

He rose from his seat. "Why don't the rest of you get ready to leave and I'll take Keelan to see Captain Whitman."

Keelan took the hint and downed the last of his tea, offering Atikus another little shrug with his eyes. "Lead on, little brother."

Declan turned and walked two tables away from where they were sitting. Two men were finishing their own breakfast when he interrupted. "Sir. Sorry for the interruption, but I'd like to introduce you to my brother, Guard Lieutenant Keelan Rea."

Captain Whitman rose slowly from his chair, wiping a bit of egg from his chin. He stood just under six hands tall and had a lean, strong frame. His short-cropped black hair held more salt than pepper, but his hazel eyes were clear and unwavering. He turned and looked up at Keelan, assessing.

"I've heard a lot about you, Lieutenant. Good stuff, except what Declan here tells me, of course," he said with a bit of a chuckle before extending a hand. Keelan grasped his forearm while keeping his eyes locked on the Captain's.

"It's a pleasure, sir. Thank you for putting us up for a couple of days. Most of us have never seen Ranger HQ before. It's an impressive place." Keelan released his grip as the Captain sat. "Would you mind if I stole a couple of minutes before we head out? About something rather … sensitive?"

"Glad to have the company. Please, take a seat." Captain Whitman sipped his lukewarm coffee. "What's on your mind, Lieutenant?"

Keelan looked across the table at the Ranger who was eating with the Captain and gave Whitman a meaningful brow raise. The Captain's own brow lifted. "Please meet my second, Lieutenant Geros. You can speak freely at this table, just keep it low. We're well past the normal breakfast hour, so I doubt anyone will get close enough to overhear anything."

"Thank you, sir." Keelan paused, thinking through how he wanted to approach this with the Captain. "We're here investigating the disappearance of one woman, and the murder of another, two cases we now have reason to believe are linked. We have very few clues but are confident the kidnappers recently brought their victim through the pass to cross the border. Declan … er … Ranger Rea stopped a cart two days ago driven by two men in brown robes that matched the description we have of our suspects. The cart was empty, but we believe magic was used to conceal the woman from Ranger Rea's inspection.

"Sir, we're headed into the mountains today, following the trail we think they took. Before we do, I need to know if we're walking into more than just a kidnapping in those mountains. Has there been anything else strange reported recently?"

Captain Whitman never broke eye contact nor flinched. "What did Declan tell you? I assume you asked him before coming to me."

"Yes, sir. Just a few minutes ago, in fact. He said it was a question better left to his Captain, sir." Keelan returned the Captain's intense gaze.

Whitman nodded and looked at Declan. "Rea, Geros, give us a minute, please."

When it was just Keelan and the Captain at the table, Whitman's eyes found Keelan's again. "I understand your orders are from the Captain-Commander and Arch Mage directly."

Keelan's spine stiffened. No one was supposed to know that. "Yes, sir," was all he could think to say.

"Take a breath, Lieutenant. Your Commander sent word that you were on your way and asked that I give you whatever help you might need. He was vague in the details, but I'm used to that these days, especially when a courier is involved." He leaned forward. "Most people don't remember that the Rangers were originally founded to protect Melucia's borders. The war had just ended, and tensions with the Kingdom were still high. It took more than a hundred years for things to settle down enough for our mission to expand to forest patrols and wildlife conservation. Despite all that, our primary mission remains border security and ensuring the free flow of trade between the nations."

The Captain finished his coffee. "Six months ago, a trader and his family left Grove's Pass and headed over the mountains bound for Irina's Seat, a little town on a large lake a few days' ride from Huntcliff. The whole trip should've taken them eight to ten days, maybe a little more with the children in tow. Fifteen days after they left Grove's Pass, we received word they'd never arrived. In fact, the constables in Huntcliff report they never saw them come through. Not long after, another trader went missing, then a caravan of three. During that time, we haven't seen a single trader from the Kingdom headed into Melucia, when we would normally have one or two pass through each week. It's getting cold, and traders are usually racing to get into or out of the mountains before the snows make them impassible. In six months, we haven't seen one—*not one*—inbound from the Kingdom."

He waved a serving girl over and asked for more coffee.

"I sent a couple Rangers to the border to check things out. We've been on cordial terms with our counterparts, even have friendly competitions now and then. But not recently. The pair I sent reported that the border had been closed and large wooden barriers erected to prevent passage into the Kingdom. The border hasn't been closed since the Kingdom War ten generations past. I can't get any of our men through to see what's going on, and the commander of their forces in Huntcliff hasn't responded to messages in months. Our birds don't return.

"Honestly, I have no idea what to think, but I'm worried. Your team will need to be careful as you get close to the dividing line. If you learn anything, your Commander and I want to hear it immediately."

Keelan ran his hand over his head, scratching as if to spark some thought that eluded him. This was insane. Yesterday he was just a constable trying to bring a kidnapped woman home; now he faced missing traders, spies, and international border tension. A headache pulsed between his eyes.

"Sir, I barely know what to say. We need to head into the mountains to follow our missing girl's trail. Beyond that, we'll keep our eyes open and let you know what else we find. I assume this needs to stay between us?"

"Atikus is cleared for this information. The Arch Mage was specific on that point. No one else needs to know unless things change dramatically. Use your best judgement, but understand something; I've been doing this a long time and have never seen anything like this. Something serious is starting that the Rangers aren't prepared to face. Hell, Melucia isn't prepared for any of this. If you trust the wrong person, people will die. Be completely sure before you share any of this, alright?"

"Yes sir. Understood," Keelan said. "Thank you, again. If there's nothing else, I want to get started before we lose too much light. It gets dark fast in the mountains these days."

"You just said more than you know, son," Captain Whitman muttered to himself just loud enough that Keelan heard it as he walked back to the group.

An hour later, the group stood in the middle of the road on the edge of Grove's Pass. Declan explained that this was where he encountered the cart and robed men two days earlier. Sil, the most experienced tracker in the group, spent a long time looking at dirt and twigs and leaves. Keelan shook his head at her ability to see a handful of leaves and know what happened on that spot. She didn't use magic, but that's what it was—sheer magic.

Unfortunately, even her magic failed sometimes. There was enough traffic this close to town to muddle any tracks that might've helped. Declan said he never saw the cart veer off the road, so looking for tracks on either side was pointless. After an hour, Keelan decided they'd invested enough daylight in that spot and asked where Declan thought they should go next, desperate for anything at this point.

"We could just follow the road to the border and hope we see something, but that's more of a wish than a plan. There's a station about halfway to the border on the top of that mountain." He pointed at a spot no one else could follow. "The Ranger on duty up there might've seen or heard something."

"Anyone else? Other ideas?"

When no one said anything, Keelan nodded to his brother. "Lead the way. Sounds like the best we've got right now."

It took the better part of the afternoon to reach the Ranger station. The sun was setting over mountains that were already well shaded. They could barely make out the wooden fort on stilts when Declan held up an arm with his fist closed, indicating an immediate stop. His crisp, insistent motion put everyone on alert.

He stood frozen for a minute. "Something's not right. There should be a fire going, and those look like arrows in the ground over there." He pointed to spots on the ground about twenty yards from the base of the station.

"Keep everyone here until I come back," he said before making a wide arc around the station, careful to stay out of bow range should anyone still be up there. Nothing stirred. Finally satisfied he could move closer, Declan crept toward the base of the station and climbed the ladder. He looked back at where the group was hiding and gave a signal to stay in place, then continued his ascent.

Keelan watched as his brother disappeared into the wooden structure. A few minutes of tense silence passed before Declan emerged through the door and motioned for the group to join him. It was dark now, but Keelan thought he sensed something painful in Declan's expression.

They were greeted by a bloody scene. A ranger lay sprawled on the floor in a pool of nearly dried blood. One arrow had pierced through his neck, the head sticking completely out the other side. Another was lodged in his upper chest near his left shoulder. The glass of the one window was shattered and shards were scattered everywhere. The ranger's bow had fallen by the window and was now lodged behind a rickety desk. Every piece of furniture was broken or overturned, and the two lamps used to light the cabin had been smashed. The wood and coals in the fireplace were as cold as the forest outside.

"No sign of Tiana?" Keelan asked as he surveyed the scene with his inspector's eye.

"No. Looks like somebody put up a pretty good struggle, though," Declan said.

Declan started toward the door. "Keelan, investigations are your area. Why don't I go look for some firewood while you inspect, see if you can figure anything out? Atikus, would you send word to HQ that we lost Donny and ask that they send a team tomorrow to recover his body?"

Keelan nodded and turned to the others. "This is a small room, so let's take it one at a time and be careful where you step. Sil, you're our tracker, so you take the first look. Atikus, anything magical you can do to help us learn more here?"

Atikus rubbed his chin and looked around the room thoughtfully. "No, my Gift really isn't much help here."

SIL MENTALLY DIVIDED THE ROOM INTO A GRID OF THREE-hand squares, scrutinizing one box before moving to the next. She would occasionally poke something with her dagger, moving it so she could see its underside or what was behind it, then carefully return the item to its original location. Keelan admired her thorough, systematic approach and made a mental note to write something in her file to memorialize her solid investigative work.

Sil was about fifteen minutes into her search when Declan burst through the door. "Keelan, bring your tracker. I found their trail," he puffed from his run back to the station. He tossed the few pieces of wood he'd collected by the fireplace and turned to the door.

"Ridley, pick up where Sil left off. Sil, you're with us. Atikus, with your memory, can you take a snapshot of the room, all the details?"

"Of course. My Gift will pick up everything in sight. Anything under an item or covered up won't get captured, though," Atikus said.

"Do it, then please join us outside."

As Keelan and Sil walked out of the station, they spotted Declan kneeling about ten paces away from the northeastern side, staring at something on the ground. When the group approached, he held up a hand, indicating for them to stop.

"Sil, come look at this." He pointed up and down the area of ground he had been staring at. "Looks like they were in a hurry—or struggling with our Healer."

Sill knelt and studied the area for a moment, then slowly walked around the area, looking from different angles. Saying nothing, she walked into the woods, focusing intently on forest debris before taking each next step.

After about twenty minutes, Sil stopped and turned to the group who followed in her wake. "Their trail is pretty obvious. They were hurrying through the woods and took no care to hide it. There are three sets of footprints in places, sometimes only two with long stretches of bent and broken twigs, indicating they were dragging the third. About thirty paces ago, the group must've stopped and rested, because there's a few flattened places in the foliage. From that point, there are only two sets of prints and no more drag marks. They probably carried her the rest of the way."

She looked to Keelan. "Sir, they're headed for the border, I'd guess to Huntcliff. The main road is just over that rise in front of us where their trail is leading. It's weird, though. They'll have to take a kidnapped girl through a border checkpoint without raising suspicion."

Declan stepped up. "Actually, it makes sense. Their magic completely masked the Healer's presence from me. I couldn't see or hear her at all, and she was literally right in front of me. That same magic might be what they're counting on to get them into the Kingdom without trouble. Any search will turn up empty, confirming whatever the Kingdom soldiers are led to believe.

"Our biggest problem is beyond the border. Once they get through Huntcliff, they could go anywhere, and we'd never be able to find them again. The Kingdom is huge."

"Alright. Well, we have to try. Dec, can I speak with you a moment?" Keelan placed a hand on Declan's shoulder and steered him away from Sil to a spot where they could speak more freely. "Is there a way into The

Kingdom other than through the pass at Huntcliff?" Keelan asked.

"There are several, but getting to those entry points is the problem. Other than the road on the pass, the mountains are pretty steep. Getting over them and through to the other side is dangerous, even for the best climbers. If the Kingdom really is up to something with this border closing, I bet they'll have patrols all over the base of the mountains. All of our reports from their side went dark months ago, and we have no real intelligence to help with a plan. But we do have one thing in our favor—it's a long rough border, so we might slip past them if we're careful."

They continued talking through ideas for another ten minutes, not finding any great options among them. Just when the conversation was hitting a lull, Keelan spotted movement in the distant forest, past the road. After a couple of seconds, he recognized what was causing the trees to rustle and whispered urgently, "Everyone down."

They all dropped, except Atikus, who just cocked his head at Keelan, not comprehending the sudden change. "Atikus, get down. NOW!"

Keelan then whispered to his brother. "Man in a Kingdom military uniform moving through the woods. He's scanning back and forth, bow in hand, nocked."

Declan motioned for the group to lie flat and not move as he edged carefully to the top of the rise. What he saw made his heart catch in his throat. He crawled back to the group and signaled for them to follow in silence.

When they were back in the clearing of the Rangers' Station, he turned to the group. "Keelan, you saw a scout off in the woods, one of several I could see from the ridge all walking in a line about a hundred yards apart from each other heading southwest toward Grove's Pass. I couldn't see anyone on the road, but the Kingdom isn't scouting the area for the fun of it. We need to warn the Captain."

"What are they up to?" Keelan asked no one in particular.

Declan whispered, "We've had troubling intelligence of movement on their side of the border. Traders, back when they could actually get through, described formations of tents popping up in the fields around Huntcliff. We initially thought they were just reinforcing their border or running some sort of exercise, but those scout movements look offensive. I'd wager they're testing our defenses, at least trying to identify what we have out here."

"Atikus, can you send word to the Captain-Commander, Arch Mage, and Declan's Captain right now?" Keelan asked the Mage.

"Of course. It shouldn't take more than ten or fifteen minutes." Atikus climbed into the Rangers' station, the quiet of the building helpful for concentration required to communicate via his Gift.

Declan turned to the others. "We need to learn as much as we can if this really is the start of a military operation. After so many years of peace, we barely have a standing army."

Sil spoke up for the first time since they spotted the incoming army. "Lieutenant, if we can get anywhere near a bird or some other animal, I may be able to help without putting any of us in direct danger."

Keelan deferred to Declan, who nodded. "Good thought. But I suggest we abandon this station as quickly as possible. The scouts will fan out and find this place before too long. Our best advantage right now is that they don't know we're here.

"Kee, they won't be looking on the mountain tops once they've cleared the lower areas around the road, and the height would help with finding the birds Sil needs. We'll still need to be careful to stay out of sight. They may not be looking up, but movement is easy to spot up there where the trees thin out."

The group waited another ten minutes before Atikus emerged from the station. He assured Keelan that the reports were received, reciting exactly what he had said to each leader. Once satisfied, Keelan asked Declan to take the lead in shepherding the group to the upper part of a neighboring mountain to the northwest. The initial hour of the trek passed easily but grew intense as they started their steep ascent to the top. Atikus's breathing became labored, forcing the group to stop and rest frequently.

Four hours later, they stood about two hundred yards from the top of the neighboring mountain. It was one of the shorter peaks in the range, but the view was breathtaking. As far as they could see, emerald green intermingled with flashes of yellow and orange and gold. Keelan smiled as he breathed deeply the crisp air steeped in pine's sweet scent.

Peaks of the taller surrounding mountains sported snowy white caps and were shrouded in a light mist that shimmered with shades of dusky purple and gray. The place held a majesty and mystery unlike anything Keelan had ever seen. He stared open-mouthed.

Declan started laughing, and everyone turned. "I remember my first time up here. It took me a few minutes to stop staring, too. Now it feels almost like they're family, those peaks. Living, breathing family. I know, I know, they're just mountains. It's hard to explain." A hint of pride crept into his voice.

Atikus put a hand on his shoulder and squeezed affectionately. "Declan, I believe you're growing into that uniform of yours after all."

As the group snapped out of the mountain peaks' trance, Sil took a few steps away and sat on the ground, legs crossed. A short time later, two large black birds landed in front of her and cocked their heads, looking between Sil and the rest of the group. She reached out and gently stroked one of the birds under its neck. It cooed and stretched out its neck to help her get a better angle. After a minute or two, the birds looked at each other, cocked their heads again, and took flight. Sil stood and walked back to the group, which was watching her with interest.

"You're not going to like this," she said. "All I get when I commune are images. The smarter the animal, the better the image. Birds aren't on the higher-intelligence end of the scale, so what I saw was quick and fuzzy."

"Whatever you saw is more than what we have now. Go on."

"First, they showed me a brief glimpse of their nest. It appears to overlook the fields to the west of Huntcliff. I could see the town to the northeast and got my bearings from there. The next few flashes were in flight looking down at the ground, I think of those same fields around Huntcliff, but it's hard to be sure. There wasn't any actual point of reference to help fix a location other than the mountain range to the right, and it was hard to adjust to the dizzying view.

"Lieutenant, we were pretty high up, but there was no mistaking the orderly rows of white tents covering the land-scape. The image came and went too quickly to count, but I would estimate tens of thousands of soldiers camped there. The birds grew bored and severed the connection before I could see anything else."

Everyone stood in silence, trying to absorb what Sil had seen. For over a thousand years, the Kingdom and Melucia lived in peace and were each other's primary trading part-ners. The two nations were never overly friendly thanks to the historical resentment that followed the destructive Kingdom War that no one living had experienced. But they were cordial, respectful, and generally good neighbors. Declan couldn't fathom what would have provoked the Kingdom to consider invading Melucia and disrupting everything they'd worked so hard to build together. But he knew they needed to find out if there was any hope of avoiding another disastrous war that could destroy every-thing he cared about.

"Can we start by getting a little further down this moun-tain? I can't feel my toes, and we can't help anybody if we freeze to death," Atikus grumbled while rubbing his hands together.

Declan led the group down the northern face of the

mountain, the Kingdom side, but well under cover of the thick forest that surrounded them. The descent wasn't nearly as arduous as the climb, but everyone was still careful and moved slowly. After an hour of cautious progress, the group stopped to rest and refill their skins with crisp, clear water from a trickling stream they found winding its way down the mountain.

Declan renewed their conversation as they sat on a pair of fallen trees near the water's edge. "We don't have time to go back to our side of the border for orders. We need to gather as much information as possible on the Kingdom's forces and get it back to command. Now's the time for ideas, no matter how crazy. Talk to me."

Keelan and Atikus gave each other a meaningful look as they heard the confident, commanding tone in Declan's voice. Keelan heard Atikus in his mind. *"Your brother really is coming into his own. I don't think he's nearly as lost as he thinks."*

As useful as Telepathy was, Keelan couldn't stop the shiver at having someone speak into his mind. He looked up at Atikus and arched an eyebrow, earning a small smile and a wink.

For the next thirty minutes, the group threw out every idea they could think of. Sil suggested focusing on using more animals to view things from a distance. Ridley wanted to take out a scout or two and find a way into Hunt-cliff wearing their uniforms. He reasoned that counting troops was helpful, but they wouldn't be able to learn *why* the Kingdom was acting without hearing people on the streets and in the pubs, where alcohol would loosen lips.

Declan spoke more in favor of finding an alternate route through the mountains a little farther south to avoid conflict as much as possible. He was concerned that any information they gathered would be wasted if they were caught by enemy scouts. Atikus remained uncharacteristically quiet during the discussion.

As the group stared at the ground, struggling to come to a consensus on the best path forward, a snapping sound in the distance below turned all their heads. Declan stood quickly, holding up his fist, the signal for everyone to freeze in place. Several snaps followed the first, along with a crackling of dry leaves. Someone was out there, and they weren't worried about staying quiet.

"Stay here. I'll go look," Declan whispered.

He returned a moment later, sweat beading his brow, bow in hand, nocked and ready. "There's a team of four scouts in Kingdom colors headed this way. I spotted another team about a half mile down the other side, also coming toward us. We have to move. Now."

They scrambled as quietly as possible, but Declan was the only one of the group trained to move quietly in the woods. A shout from behind spurred them forward, abandoning any thoughts of silence.

Sil and Declan led the way down while Keelan and Ridley helped Atikus. The old Mage's knees struggled in the cool mountain air and rocky terrain, slowing them to a crawl.

"Dec, we're never going to make it. I can hear their voices now," Keelan whispered as Declan ran back to help.

"He's right, son. I can't keep up," Atikus said.

Declan didn't hesitate. "Listen to me, both of you. We're *all* getting off this mountain. Keelan, Ridley, get Sil and meet me down the southern side of this mountain, about a hundred yards. We'll hide Atikus and deal with that team. Tell Sil to have her bow drawn and ready in case they spot you before we're back together."

Declan tucked his shoulder under Atikus's arm and practically lifted the Mage off the ground. "This may hurt a little, but we'll be fine. Just stay quiet, alright?"

Atikus grunted but didn't protest.

A few minutes later, Declan stopped and pointed to a crack in the mountainside. "You'll have to squat to get in, but it'll keep you hidden. Don't come out until we come back."

As Atikus bent to wedge himself into the mountain, Keelan, Ridley, and Sil trotted up. "We nearly missed you down here," Sil whispered.

Declan ignored her. "There's four of them, all armed with bows. We need to lead them west to a clearing where two mountains meet. Sil, you and I will set up on opposite sides. That'll give us a bit of high ground. Keelan, you and Ridley stay back and close around behind them. You're our last defense if one of them bolts. We can't let any of them escape or we might be dealing with the whole Kingdom army up here."

The sounds of pursuit grew closer as they raced down the mountainside. Keelan heard one of the Kingdom scouts call out, "I see them. Down here."

They barely made it to the clearing in time to hide.

The scouts formed a diamond compass formation, the

first three men looking in different directions while the trailing man scanned back and forth. Sil's arrow struck the lead man through the neck, dropping him before he could cry out. Declan's bold hit the north compass point in the chest. The other two men stepped back into the trees, stunned by their fallen comrades. Declan could see their bows, arrows scanning back and forth for a target.

He nocked another arrow and slowed his breathing.

They heard the scouts split up, one circling the clearing toward Declan, the other toward Sil's position. Sil's stalker cried out before getting within twenty paces of her, Keelan's sword lodged in his back. The last scout heard his fellow cry out and turned to run. It was his last mistake. Declan took two paces, aimed, and dropped him with a shot between the shoulder blades.

A few tense minutes later, the four stood together in front of Atikus's cave. Declan maintained his command of the situation.

"Keelan, Sil, you need to lead the way north, be our forward eyes. I'll help Atikus again and watch our rear. Try not to get more than a couple hundred yards ahead. It's too easy to lose each other in these woods, and we obviously can't go calling out anymore."

Kelan and Sil nodded and headed north. As Declan braced Atikus again, the Mage whispered urgently, "Declan, wait."

The almost desperate tone in Atikus's voice made Declan freeze. "Are you alright? What's wrong?"

Atikus returned Declan's gaze but not his smile. His voice was serious and quiet, carrying a slight tremor. "Son,

I'm sorry for what I'm about to ask of you. This was supposed to be my mission, but with the scouts in the mountains, I won't make it. And *everything* hangs in the balance."

"Atikus? What are you talking about?"

"You know our border security better than most. It's thin. The Rangers are capable but have turned more into Royal Guards of wildlife than border guards. The state of Melucia's army is closely held, but even a small challenge would pose a grave threat. Our neighbors to the east are so weak and fractured that I don't think we could even unify them before an invasion succeeded. Without serious help, Melucia won't last more than a few months."

"Are you saying …?"

"War is coming. The Guild is preparing, but we're not enough. We need help."

Declan leaned against a tree for support and stared off into the distant forest. Atikus was careful not to interrupt his thoughts, understanding the weight of what he'd just said. When Declan finally spoke, his voice was quiet and serious, the steel tone of command returning as an undercurrent.

"I don't have any experience with the eastern border, but Rangers I know who served on that side of the country talk about the border states like they're backwards, stubborn children, always squabbling. You're right about them being useless in a fight. Who else is there? The islands barely have towns and roads, much less standing armies."

"The islands may not hold great cities or armies, but they contain something far more powerful." Atikus looked away as he tried to order his thoughts. "The help only magic can give."

Declan's head snapped up at the mention of magic. His brow creased and eyes narrowed. Spirits, he didn't even *have* a Gift. Why wasn't the old Mage talking to Keelan about this … or Sil … or Ridley … or anyone else who wore that stupid gold collar? The more he thought about it, the more frustrated, even angry, he became. It was like Atikus was dangling the one thing he'd wanted his whole life, and he knew it would get yanked away before he could grasp it. It always did. He turned away, not realizing how tightly he was clinching both fists.

Atikus seemed to read his mind.

He snapped at Declan with a stern, scolding tone. "Declan, look at me. This is too important to let your personal grievance with the life you were given cloud your judgement."

Declan slowly turned to face the old Mage, matching his scowl.

Atikus continued with more measured control. "What I'm about to tell you has been passed from Arch Mage to Arch Mage for thousands of years. I may be the only person in our lifetime to know this secret beyond our own Arch Mage, which is why he asked me to join this party. You must guard this with your life and reveal it to no one, not even your brother. Do you understand?"

Declan nodded cautiously. "Go on."

"Rea Utu, the largest of the two Utu Isles, southeast of the coast of Drea, is more than the capital of a small island nation. It is the very heart of magic, some say the birthplace of magic. A tiny village is nestled close to the island's eastern shore. Deep in one of the mountains that shelters the village lies a wellspring that the Arch Mage believes is the source of magic—and the heart of the natural world.

"There are many legends about the place, most ridiculously false and designed to scare children into their beds at night, but one kernel of truth makes its way through all these stories. Living in the mountain, as the protector of magic's cradle, is a man known as the Keeper. That simple title was crafted thousands of years ago to mask the old man's true identity and further protect magic's source. The Keeper has served as the protector of magic and a sort of chief among the Arch Mages of the world. He is said to be the wisest among us, possessing an understanding of magic unlike any other. We found two ancient texts that reference the Heir of Magic, one who would rise or step forward in a time of great need. The translation is weak, but that's the basic idea. We don't know if the Heir is the Keeper by another title, someone meant to follow him, or someone completely different."

"Or if this Heir is a myth written on scrolls you can't even translate." Declan said impatiently. "Besides, there's hundreds of leagues and an ocean between us and Rea Utu. The Kingdom army is at our back. How can this Keeper help us?"

"I'm getting there," Atikus snapped. "The Keeper is a powerful magician. He doesn't simply have a Gift; he actually communes with magic at its source, and it often grants him knowledge or responds to his pleas for help in miraculous ways. The way it was explained to me, he doesn't actually wield magic so much as he speaks to it, and it flows through him, through his thoughts. I'm sorry. What we know was passed down through the centuries, and it's vague—intentionally so."

Declan's head swiveled, impatiently listening for approaching enemies.

"Declan, the point is this. We decided that appealing to the Keeper for aid would be our ultimate safeguard when all else failed. We're out of cards to play, and we need help if we're going to survive. We know he can do incredible things, but we honestly have no idea whether he can help in *this* situation."

"Again, I don't see what this has to do with me, a magical reject," Declan said with acid in his voice.

Atikus let out an exasperated sigh, then sucked in a deep breath. "Declan, I don't know how to explain this. You just have to trust me. Trust the Arch Mage if you can't trust me. Keelan and his team have a different mission. We don't understand what's going on with these missing women, but I believe it has something to do with the King-dom's recent military buildup and potential aggression. There are too many coincidences tying things together, and Keelan is the best investigator we've got. You know I won't make it to the gate on my own. And I think Keelan may need my Telepathy before his search is over. You're all we have left. We need you to do this in my place. You need to appeal to the Keeper."

"Atikus, we don't even know for sure that war is coming," Declan argued stubbornly.

"Yes. We do. In your heart, you know it, even if you

don't want to admit it. *Spirits*, none of us wants to admit it, but it's still coming.

"Declan, I've known you since you were barely old enough to walk. I've seen you struggle with your identity, your value, where you fit in. I know you are still searching for where you belong and what you should become. But right now, I also know that this is your journey, your duty —*yours alone*. It's time for you to believe that you are here for something larger than yourself and accept the calling before you."

Declan stared at him with caution and disbelief—and more than a little curiosity. A moment later, he nodded. "Alright, I'll go."

Atikus smiled up at his adopted son. Declan started to brace Atikus again, to take him to Keelan and Sil. The Mage stopped him with a raised palm and stern glare.

"What I'm about to tell you has security implications you'll appreciate more than any of us. All of what I've said —but especially this—must go with you to your grave." Atikus waited for Declan to hold eye contact before continuing. "There's a cave in these mountains that contains an ancient magical gate. It is one of a pair, the only pair known to exist. When a person passes through this gate, he is transported directly to its twin in the mountains of Rea Utu. Here is a map I drew of both sides and the location of both gates."

Atikus removed a folded parchment from inside his coat and handed it to Declan. The Ranger's eyes widened when he opened it.

"You can map the mountains both here and on the island from memory?"

"Oh, son, you forget my Gift. I could draw every hair on your two-year-old head even today." Atikus said wistfully before continuing.

"The gate is not on the same mountain as the Keeper. You'll likely need to go down into the village for supplies, maybe even rest for the night, then head to the Keeper's domain. No one knows what he looks like, and some fables spin the tale he appears to each person differently, in a way that he or she will best receive his teaching. You'll have to use your best judgement once you find his home.

"Inhabitants of the island are short and have the most beautiful, deep brown skin. For a tall, pasty mountain man like you, blending in will be impossible. You should expect to be watched from the minute you set foot on the island. Oh, remember this, don't tell any of the locals where you're headed. The Keeper is sacred on the island, and you're likely to earn more enemies than friends if they find out you're looking for him."

"Alright. Is there anything else I should know? We need to get back to the others before more scouts show up."

"Only to be careful. And try to learn something while you're over there. Visiting Rea Utu has been a dream of mine from the day I learned of the place." He was quiet for a moment before adding, "And Declan, just know that I'm sorry. Please don't ask why. Just forgive me when you have the chance."

Declan stared in confusion, expecting more to that comment. All he got was silence.

A half hour later, they rejoined Keelan and Sil. Atikus took the initiative, speaking before anyone else could start. "Declan has new orders from his Captain. He gave them to me before we left, and I was to show them to Declan as we neared the border. The scouts changed the timing, but not the orders. They were sealed, and Declan was instructed to keep their contents to himself. What I can say is that his mission is extremely sensitive, and he won't be continuing with us from this point. He needs to leave immediately, so say your goodbyes now."

Atikus patted Declan on the shoulder. Sil and Ridley gave him a respectful nod and offered their thanks for his guidance in the mountains.

Keelan walked over and grabbed Declan in a tight, awkward hug. "Be careful, little brother. You're all the family I've got," he whispered in his brother's ear.

As they pulled apart, Keelan was surprised to see a tear forming in Declan's eye. He shoved him away playfully before turning to the others.

"Alright. Ranger boy is on his own. Let's get moving toward the border while there's some light left. If we're going to cross near the coast southeast of Huntcliff, we have a long hike ahead."

As the sun began its descent beyond the mountains, Keelan looked back and watched as his little brother was wrapped in the dark cloak of the forest and faded from view.

## 24

## JESS

"What do you think he meant by that?" Jess stared at Danym across the table.

"Well, I'm guessing the … I mean, your mother and father … probably know where we are. That explains why we haven't seen those robed men anywhere. Constables are probably posted all around the inn to keep you safe."

"I guess that's a good thing." She leaned forward on her elbows then put her face in her hands, mumbling, "Danym, she's going to make me go back. Please don't let her take me back."

Before he could respond, the innkeeper appeared at their side. She leaned toward Jess and placed a hand on her back. "Is everything alright, dear?"

Jess started sobbing and found herself wrapped in the innkeeper's arms, head buried in her shoulder. A small voice pleaded, "Please help me. I can't go back."

The innkeeper rubbed her back. "Of course, I'll help you, Your Highness."

Jess jerked back. "What did you call me?"

"It's alright. I've known since you walked in." The woman's warm, toothy smile made Jess's shock turn into a grin of her own. "I've dreamed of a life in the Palace since I was a little girl. Following the lives of the royal family has always been a pastime for my sisters and me."

Jess gave Danym a questioning look, receiving a confounded shrug in return.

"Why don't we go back into the kitchen to talk in case someone else walks in?" The innkeeper motioned toward the door behind the bar, then released Jess and turned.

They walked into a spacious kitchen. Tables covered in pots and pans ran the full length of the room. On the far wall were two large fireplaces with suspended pots already boiling, preparing the day's lunch. The innkeeper sat on a stool and motioned for Jess and Danym to do the same.

"Why don't you tell me what's going on?"

"Danym and I just want to be together. My parents want me to marry someone else, so running away was our only option. Now it looks like they know where we are, and it's only a matter of time before they make us go home." Jess started to sob again.

"If we could just get to Huntcliff, I think we could be free," Danym said. "That's where we were headed."

The innkeeper knelt in front of Jess and took both of her hands. "The constables are watching the inn. There were a few inside and more surrounded the building last night. But our stables are across the street, and I doubt they're watching them since you're trapped in here. If I can get you into the stables, you should be able to take your horses out the back. It's the best I can think of at this point."

Danym stood and paced the length of the table. "How would you get us to the stables?"

"The inn shares a storage basement with the building next door where we keep meats and barrels of ale. It opens into the neighboring building but also into the stables. I can come get you around midnight and lead you to the cellar."

"Do you think it could actually work?" Jess's eyes pleaded.

"I don't know," answered Danym. "The worst thing they can do is send us back, and they'll do that if we just sit here. It's worth a try."

Jess sat immobile for a minute before nodding once.

Danym put his hand on Jess's shoulder. "We need to pretend we never heard the constable today. Show up for lunch and dinner. Act like we don't know anything. If they get a hint we're up to something, they'll drag us back."

Jess wiped the tears from her eyes. "Alright."

She then raised the innkeeper's hands to her lips and kissed them. "I don't know how we can ever thank you for your kindness."

The woman beamed. "Your Highness, you're letting me play royal for a day. What more could a poor girl like me want? Now, you two go back up to your room before one of those men comes looking for you."

DANYM AND JESS HELD HANDS AS THEY STRODE BACK upstairs to their room. Once the door was locked, Danym pulled back the curtain covering their window and peeked out at the street. The innkeeper was right. He spotted four constables across the road, opposite the main door to the inn. There was nothing to do about them at the moment, so the pair decided to get some rest. They had a long night ahead.

The day passed without incident. Lunch in the common room was a simple meal of pork stew, greens, and corn-bread—remarkably similar to dinner the previous night. Dinner was *exactly* the same as the night before. Jess chuckled at the lazy pattern shown in the kitchen's offerings.

Danym and Jess were sitting on the bed, bags packed, when the knock came at midnight. The innkeeper might offer a limited menu, but she was pleasantly prompt. She bustled them downstairs and into the kitchen before speaking.

"There's no one stirring right now, but that could change any moment in a place like this. We'd best get you on your way."

They walked to the back of the kitchen, to the wall beyond the second hearth. On the floor, Jess saw a large metal ring on a door she hadn't noticed earlier in the day. The innkeeper grabbed a candle in a tin holder and lit it. She then pried the door open and led them down into a large musty room. The floors of the room were mostly packed dirt, with a few wooden platforms built to hold casks and other foodstuffs. Everything was maintained in neat rows, far more organized that Jess expected. There was a clear demarcation between the inn's items and those of their neighbor, even hand-drawn signage to remind employees who owned what. They walked twenty yards before coming to a wall with a ladder bolted into its boards. The innkeeper stepped aside and motioned up the stairs.

"That's your exit, Your Highness. It will open into the middle of the stables. I gave the stableboy the night off, so there shouldn't be anyone up there. The hinges on the stalls squeal something awful, so be careful. Those constables are probably standing just outside on the street."

Jess surprised the innkeeper with a tight hug. "Thank you so much. One day I will find a way to repay you."

"Dear child, go and be happy. What more repayment could an old woman want?" She cupped Jess's cheek and smiled.

"Oh, I almost forgot," the innkeeper reached behind a cask and handed Danym a sack packed with bread, apples, and dried meat. "You're a week and a half to the next town. I can't let you starve on the way to freedom!"

Jess gave the woman one last thankful hug as Danym opened the hatch, climbed the ladder and began saddling their horses. Dittler nuzzled Jess affectionately as soon as she opened his stall.

"Alright, alright. I missed you, too," she said, stroking him between the ears.

Once the packs and saddles were in place, Danym gave Jess's arm a quick squeeze. "We'll walk them out to the street and make sure nobody's out there, probably go three or four blocks to be sure. Then we can mount up and get out of this town."

He opened the back door and they walked onto a gravel road that ran behind several businesses situated across from the inn. The skies were clear, but the night was dark and cool, exactly what they'd hoped for. They passed several blocks in silence. The town was shuttered tight for the night. Danym finally stopped and motioned to mount their horses, leading them further east toward the town's edge.

It took another hour of slow, careful trotting before the last of Spoke's houses faded from view. Jess let out a breath she didn't know she'd been holding and smiled at Danym. "We actually did it."

———

ISABEL LET HER SIGHT FADE. HER MIND RACED AS SHE processed what she'd just seen. Jess was convinced she would escape her marriage—*her duty*. How could she live her entire life in the Palace, watching a King and Queen rule, and think to outrun the Crown? Stubborn, stupid girl! This ridiculous charade had to end, no matter what Alfred said. He had a blind spot where Jess was concerned, but she was putting the entire succession in jeopardy. If confidence in the royal line failed, the nobles could take matters into their own hands. Who knew what those petty, squabbling little men would do if they smelled fresh blood?

There were also larger plans in play. Plans Jess knew nothing about and would never understand. Plans that would give the Kingdom more power and wealth than they had ever enjoyed. Isabel had spent decades preparing for the coming spring and *nothing* would stand in her way.

She gave the garden one last glance before marching back into her study where Chancellor Thorn waited.

"Your Majesty," he bowed. "Were you able to See anything useful?"

"My Sight is *always* useful, Danai. Never forget that," she snapped. Thorn flinched.

"They left Spoke on the King's Road, headed east."

"So, my innkeeper played her part well?" Thorn asked.

"It appears. See that she's well rewarded in case we need her … services … again one day," she reached for her wine glass.

"Yes, Your Majesty. What about the loving couple?"

"It's time we end this before they go beyond the limits of my Sight. Send your men to follow them. There's nothing but farmland and wilderness between Spoke and Cradle. Bring them in when they're halfway between the two towns. But Danai, whatever you do, there can be no witnesses. We don't need the press babbling about the cruel queen in her tower tearing apart two young lovebirds. And you know that's exactly how they'd write that story."

"Yes, Your Majesty," Thorn bowed, then backed out of the room.

Isabel savored a sip of wine and stared into the fire for a long moment. Why did everything have to be so difficult? Maybe it would be easier to let Justin ascend the throne next. He was a sweet, obedient boy, and he'd always been her favorite. Alfred wouldn't like it, but if Jess didn't straighten up, he might not have much choice.

————

DANYM AND JESS RODE UNTIL THE SUN CRESTED THE mountains, offering a hint of light to come. They found a small wooded area a few hundred yards off the road where they could get some rest. Given their pursuers, Danym was adamant that they only travel at night. It would add days to their trip, but he argued safety was more important than speed. She couldn't fight that point, especially after their close call heading into Spoke.

During the second night, Jess realized how vast and empty much of the Kingdom was. She'd lost track of how many leagues they'd traveled and still hadn't seen a farm or house … or *anything* other than empty fields and trees. Her tutors drilled her in the history and geography of the land, but it was completely different when seen from horseback. A book might give knowledge, but the mind needs experience to truly understand vastness. She looked up at the unending ocean of stars and laughed to herself, thinking back only a few days to a time when she saw the Palace as a huge world unto itself. Everything seemed so small now. Her focus shifted to a forest coming up over a ridge that nestled a small pond. A family of deer was grazing and darted away at their approach. Places on the map seemed so distant, so irrelevant, when part of a lecture or exam. Jess looked around in wonder at the majesty of the land she was meeting for the first time.

Then her mind wandered back to the innkeeper who risked so much for them, all in the name of love. She was kind and caring, ultimately aiding them in their flight to freedom. It felt strange that a common old woman would be so enamored with the royal family. Then again, she supposed that was part of the point of having royals, to give the commoners something to look up to, an ideal to which they could aspire. As much as she enjoyed their time in the inn, Jess couldn't imagine spending thirty minutes *working* in one—certainly not thirty years! Still, the woman had treated her more as a daughter than one of her betters.

Her father would tell her to look for the lesson, to find the kernel in every experience that teaches how to be a better ruler. Spirits, she'd heard that a thousand times growing up. So, what was the kernel with the innkeeper? Or with the constables who saved them and healed Danym? She hadn't really thought about them, and they didn't even know who she was when they risked their lives on her behalf. Would she have been kind in the innkeeper's place, sheltering strangers running from powerful parents? Would she risk herself to save another? Her mind's immediate reaction sent a chill of shame down her spine.

She shook her head free of those jumbled thoughts. She'd spent the last ten years fighting her parents every time they tried to teach her, and now, when she'd won her freedom, she couldn't stop trying to find the lesson. They really had to get out of her head!

Danym's horse snorted, and she watched as he bent to stroke its neck and mutter calming words. She smiled again, thinking back to the day they'd first met. She had been riding Dittler through the capital after one of her many vicious battles with her mother. Heavy rains had recently filled pockets in the city's old streets, making the jaunt both hazardous and filthy. As she'd rounded a turn, Dittler had stepped squarely in a puddle, splashing murky water all around, coating the young man walking toward her. She remembered every clump of mud and how it had clung to his long dusty-brown hair. *Muddy brown was more like it.*

She laughed out loud at her own inner dialogue, causing Danym to turn with a questioning glance. "Did I miss something funny?"

"Oh … no. Just remembering … something."

He turned back to peer at the road ahead as she watched him. He sat so tall, so proud. Yet he was warm and gentle and, well, beautiful. She couldn't miss that. Her heart quickened at the thought of his caress on her cheek, his eyes meeting hers. And he'd shown himself capable of making quick, smart decisions in the face of challenging situations. He was a natural leader and could be a great one someday. She'd definitely made the right decision, leaving for a new life with him. Leaving … Something inside tugged at her conscience—some annoying, tiny prickle in her chest that made her uncomfortable.

A high-pitched shrieking sound brought her back to the present. Danym's head whirled around, and he traced the whistler arrow as it crossed the now full moon.

"That's a patrol signal. They've spotted us. Come on, we can lose them if we move fast enough." Danym spurred his horse into a gallop, and Jess followed suit.

The King's Road was long and straight in its path from Spoke to Cradle once travelers made it past a major bend that occurred roughly halfway through the journey. As the couple again raced for their freedom, the bend loomed in the distance.

After a minute of hard riding, Danym had an idea and turned and yelled to Jess, "THEY'RE GAINING, AND WE'RE NOT GOING TO LOSE THEM! KEEP GOING STRAIGHT! I'LL SPLIT OFF AND LEAD THEM AWAY. MEET ME IN CRADLE."

"DANYM, NO! DON'T LEAVE ME ALONE!" Jess screamed, as he turned away from her and headed off the road into a large grassy field.

She saw a thick forest lining the end of the field and understood his plan. As badly as she wanted to follow, she turned back to the road and begged Dittler for speed. The magnificent beast relished the chance to run after so many days of slow trotting and flew over the road in a blur of fur and teeth and hooves. If she hadn't been so terrified, she would've loved the wind in her face and the sensation of flying through the countryside. Dittler was incredible.

The gap between Jess and her pursuers widened, and she lost sight of them as the bend came into clear view ahead. The road rose gently as she approached, but Dittler matched the slope with untiring effort. After ten minutes of an extraordinary pace, they finally reached the crest of the hill as the road began its turn, forcing Dittler to slow.

Jess's heart stilled as they rounded the corner and robed men came into view. Eight of them. Four on horseback and two on either side of the road waited eagerly for their prey. The men on horseback held bows, nocked and ready. Those standing by the road lifted small tubes to their lips.

One of the men called out in a voice muffled by his

mask, "STOP! Come with us quietly and you won't be harmed, *Your Highness.*"

Tears streaked down Jess's face as Dittler slowed to a canter. Her mind raced. How could this be happening? Where were those damn constables? She looked closer at one of the men, at his terrifying mask shaped like a snarling bear with wings where there should've been ears.

*"This isn't happening!"* her mind screamed.

She gave Dittler a sharp kick in his flanks. The horse whinnied, but before he could launch into another desperate run, two small darts struck, one in his shoulder and the other his neck. He reared once, then began to stagger. Two of the robed men were at their side before Jess could think. A sharp pain pierced her shoulder, and she looked down to see a dart poking through her tunic. The world spun and blurred.

The two men, one wearing the face of a lion, the other an angry, masked raccoon, pulled at her numbing limbs and lowered her to the ground. She stared up at the night sky. Terror faded to emptiness, and the face of a distorted raccoon appeared overhead. She gazed at the mask through her haze, puzzled. It reminded her of something that she couldn't quite grasp—then it hit her. The eyes staring out of the mask's little holes.

She knew those eyes.

She'd know them anywhere.

They were so deep and green.

"Danym? No…"

## WHAT'S NEXT?

I sincerely hope you enjoyed Heir of Magic. If you did, please leave a review filled with stars. Reviews are incredibly important to the success of independent authors, and I appreciate your support.

Visit my webpage at www.jdruffin.com where you can subscribe to my newsletter to receive free updates on upcoming releases and new projects. You can also join the J.D. Ruffin community on Facebook or Instagram.

# BOOK 2: DAUGHTER OF MAGIC

ENJOY A FREE SAMPLE OF THE NEXT CHAPTER IN THE
KINGDOM WAR SERIES!

High Chancellor Danai Thorn walked through the massive, golden-bronze doors of the Temple of the One. At midnight, the Temple should have been deserted, but one lone supplicant rested on her knees, forehead reverently touching the cold, dusty stone floor.

He loomed over the praying woman and barked, "Out, now! The Cathedral is closed."

The woman flinched back. "This holy place is never closed, and I am in prayer."

Anger flared in Thorn's eyes. He thrust out his palm and called to his Gift. A ball of brilliant blue flame blazed to life. The woman fell back and scurried away before gaining her feet and hurrying out of the building, casting a frightened glance over her shoulder as she crossed the threshold.

*Silly, pious fool. If she only knew The One she actually worshiped...*

Thorn dismissed the flame and stalked the length of the cathedral's nave, taking in every corner of the grand hall. As the Kingdom's principal basilica for followers of the One, the Temple served as a religious focal point, a place of peace and unity. Normally brightly lit, only a few candles still flickered, casting eerie globes that hid nearly as much as they revealed. Enormous colorful tapestries hung on the walls, depicting The One, generally as an ambiguous ball of light, comforting some commoner or healing the lame. Thorn's favorite was viewed by many, even some priests, as a garish misrepresentation of their benevolent, loving god. It depicted troops locked in a bloody battle, the field littered with the dead and dying, and the familiar bright light of the One guiding *their* side to victory. Few knew that tapestry was older than the Cathedral, even older than the people's false god.

But Thorn knew.

He climbed the few steps that led to the massive white marble altar, then walked around it toward the small chapel in the building's eastern end. He knelt, lifted the ancient rug, and found the ring to the trap door. After a final check for witnesses, he descended into the catacombs where a millennium of the Kingdom's monarchs lay interred. He summoned the blue flame again, giving the hallowed ground an otherworldly hue.

The walls of the narrow hall were adorned with large,

golden plaques, engraved with the names and honorifics of long-dead Kings and Queens. The marble walls, with their golden monikers, were smooth and well maintained, somehow humble in their simplicity. What an odd way to honor the most powerful rulers to ever live. No elaborate statue. No grand public display. Just cold, smooth stone. Thorn shook his head.

The end of the corridor held a set of golden double doors, each etched with the flowing phoenix symbol of magic, the majestic bird rising out of four pillars of flame. The fist-sized rubies that were the eyes of the phoenix glowed, gaining brightness with each step Thorn took in their direction. He was startled when the rubies flared to brilliance. Thorn stood before the door and extinguished the blue flame hovering above his palm.

"E vesh Irina," he whispered, placing his palm to the breast of the phoenix on the right door. *Irina, take my life.*

The ruby eyes pulsed once, and Thorn heard a small click. He gripped the handles and pulled, the doors swinging easily on their ancient hinges. That always amazed him. Those things had to be over a thousand years old, yet they opened with no effort, no squeal of protest.

What opened before him took his breath. The large, perfectly square room was brightly lit by dozens of braziers that never failed, blue flame dancing above their silvery bowls. A semicircular three-hand-tall wall stretched nearly the width of the room, connecting on either side to taller sections that curved like waves across their rim. Ten water-filled paces spanned the area between the apex of the short wall and two steps of the next section, giving the impression of a quiet sea leading to its shore. The steps led to a dais containing a large block of polished blue-black marble that swirled and churned as Thorn watched. A sarcophagus of pure, unmarred gold rested atop the marble. The wealth of that golden coffin could purchase a kingdom, but no price could replace its value within.

The carved artwork on the wall behind the golden coffin reminded Thorn of a massive headboard towering over its slumbering guest. It was divided into three distinct pieces, the left and right pieces of perfectly white marble arched inward, mimicking a profile view of two praying supplicants facing each other. In contrast, the center piece rose as a massive black marble tombstone, rising nearly to the ceiling. The color black barely described its surface. Thorn thought it was more like looking into some abyss, a void where no light *could* exist, calling out and luring onlookers to join in its eternal nothingness. Golden script etched in the inky black stone shimmered, as if freshly hewn, just as it had for a thousand years.

Thorn crossed the lake, ascended its shore, and stood before the monolith. He was transfixed. He tried to shake his head free of the paralyzing lure as his skin crawled and he sensed the stone assessing his presence.

Nothing moved.

Nothing breathed.

Nothing mattered but the stone.

After an eternal moment of disquiet, tension evaporated from the room as quickly as it had captured him, and Thorn again stood before a simple monument. He reverently traced its glittering script with his fingers. The Prophecy had lived in his memory for most of his eleven centuries of life, but seemed to gain power each time he stood in awe before its golden text.

*Seven Scattered as lands shattered.*
*Bind the Heir. Make diamonds bleed.*
*Speak the Words.*
*E vesh Irina.*